Donato Carrisi was born in 1973 in Martina Franca and now lives in Rome. After studying Law, he specialised in Criminology and Behavioural Science. He is a director as well as a screenwriter, for both television and cinema. He writes for the newspaper *Il Corriere della Sera* and he is the author of several bestselling international novels (all published by Longanesi): *The Whisperer, The Lost Girls of Rome, The Woman with the Paper Flowers, The Vanished Ones, The Hunter of the Dark, The Master of the Shadows, The Man in the Labyrinth, The Whisperer's Game* and *The Girl in the Fog* (which was made into a film of the same name and won the David di Donatello award for Best New Director).

Also by Donato Carrisi

The Whisperer
The Vanished Ones

The Lost Girls of Rome
The Hunter of the Dark
The Girl in the Fog
Into the Labyrinth

DONATO CARRISI

THE WHISPERER'S GAME

Translated by Katherine Gregor

abacus
books

ABACUS

First published in Italy in 2018 by Longanesi
First published in Great Britain in 2022 by Little, Brown
This paperback edition published in 2023 by Abacus

1 3 5 7 9 10 8 6 4 2

Copyright © Donato Carrisi 2018
Translation © Katherine Gregor 2022

A CIP catalogue record for this book
is available from the British Library.

ISBN: 978-0-3491-4488-7

Typeset in Horley by M Rules
Printed and bound in Great Britain by
Clays Ltd, Elcograf S.p.A.

Papers used by Little, Brown are from well-managed forests
and other responsible sources.

Abacus
An imprint of
Little, Brown Book Group
Carmelite House
50 Victoria Embankment
London EC4Y 0DZ

An Hachette UK Company
www.hachette.co.uk

www.littlebrown.co.uk

To Antonio, my son,
my continuity

To Luigi Bernabò,
my friend

The call to the police was recorded on 23 February at 7.47 p.m. A woman's distressed voice, from a mobile phone, asking that a patrol car be sent to an isolated farm some fifteen kilometres from the city.

A violent thunderstorm was raging over the area.

When the operator asked the nature of the emergency, the woman replied that a man had trespassed into the farm and was standing outside, in the rain and the dark. Her husband had gone out to persuade him to leave but the intruder was refusing. He was just standing there, silent, staring at the house.

The woman was unable to describe the stranger because her position and the torrential rain meant that she could only see him clearly during flashes of lightning. She said he'd arrived in an old green station wagon and that her two little girls were scared.

The operator took the address, assured the woman that someone would be sent to check it out but also told her that, owing to the adverse weather conditions, they were currently swamped with calls for help because of road accidents and flooding. She would therefore have to be patient.

The first available patrol car wasn't free until five the following morning, over nine hours later. The police officers took a long time to reach the farm, partly because a stream had burst its banks, flooding the road in several places.

Shortly after dawn, the scene that awaited the two officers was one of calm. A traditional timber farmhouse, painted white, with a silo for storing apples alongside. A giant sycamore cast its shadow over the farmyard. A rocking chair stood on the porch and there were two identical pink bicycles next to the tool shed. The letter box, painted scarlet, bore the inscription ANDERSON FAMILY. Nothing to suggest anything untoward. Except perhaps the silence, disturbed only by the constant barking of a mongrel tied with a long lead to a kennel.

The officers called out to the residents but there was no response. They assumed that as there was no one at home, perhaps they were no longer needed. Just to be sure, before turning back, one of the officers climbed the two steps to the porch, knocked on the door and noticed that it was only partly closed. He peeked inside and saw chaos.

After radioing headquarters for authorisation, the police officers went into the house to investigate.

They found tables and chairs knocked over, torn furnishings and shards of glass on the floor. The situation upstairs was even worse.

There was blood everywhere. In the bedrooms, pillows and sheets had been drenched in it, now dried. The family's belongings – a slipper, a hairbrush and the faces of the dolls in the girls' bedroom – were covered in blood spatter. There were trails on the floor and handprints smeared on the walls, signs of a desperate attempt to escape. The officers were looking at the scene of a bloodbath. But what troubled them most was what they could not find. The bodies were missing.

All that was left of the family members – a father, a mother and eight-year-old twins – were their photos, either standing in frames or hanging on the walls. From these smiling pictures, the Andersons had witnessed their own slaughter.

By eight o'clock, the police were swarming over this remote location in full force. While teams of investigators, aided by cadaver dogs, combed the surrounding countryside for any trace of human remains, a forensics team were analysing the crime scene in an attempt to reconstruct what had occurred. At the same time, an full-scale manhunt was launched, focusing on the stranger Mrs Anderson had described so vaguely. All that was known about him was his sex. There wasn't even a broad description or any detail that could lead to an identification. The only useful piece of information was the green station wagon the woman had mentioned, but without a licence plate or a model, this couldn't be considered a proper lead.

By midday, rumours of what had happened and what was about to happen had reached the media. It immediately hit the headlines. By dinner time, Karl, Frida and young Eugenia and Carla had gone from being an anonymous little family to the protagonists of a sensational crime that was keeping millions of people in suspense.

The mystery of the vanished family.

What made the story even more compelling was the fact that the Andersons had moved to the country and renounced technology. They had no electricity, no internet and not even a phone. The one exception was a mobile phone, strictly for emergencies, which had been used only once to call for help. The macabre details of the case – in addition to the certainty that there was a monster still at large – led to widespread panic. Everyone was terrified the killer would strike again. Pressure was mounting for a rapid conclusion to the investigation and the arrest of the person responsible.

However, the police had little to go on. Despite the resources and manpower deployed, the only thing the investigators could be certain of was that the murderer had taken the bodies away in his station wagon, though they hadn't a clue what he had done with them. There wasn't much hope of a swift resolution.

Although the investigators thought it probable that by now the intruder would have disposed of the vehicle, they combed through all available security footage recorded during the hours just before and after Mrs Anderson's call. Given that it was an old-fashioned model, it ought to stand out. Moreover, a special helpline was set up so that people could report sightings of old green estate cars. Predictably, this resulted in countless – and for the most part baseless – calls from local residents.

With one exception.

In the late afternoon, an anonymous caller reported seeing a 1997 green Volkswagen Passat parked in a disused warehouse near the old abattoir. When a team of officers, along with the dog squad, showed up to check the vehicle, they saw through the windows that the upholstery was saturated in blood. Expecting a gruesome discovery, they opened the spacious boot but, once again, there was no sign of the bodies.

As officers set about cordoning off the area to allow Forensics to work on this new crime scene, the dogs suddenly started to bark. They had sensed a presence in the abattoir.

Within thirty minutes, the entire area was off limits and, shortly afterwards, Special Forces raided the complex. It was a no-expense-spared operation with dozens of men equipped with state-of-the-art gear. The teams separated and combed through every room and every possible hiding place. The abandoned building echoed with the tramp of boots, the barking of dogs and the shouts of the raiders, until one of the officers radioed that there was 'something on the third floor'.

The units assembled at the indicated spot. In a dark room, amid the carcasses of old computers and other obsolete electronic equipment, there was a man.

He was standing, strangely motionless, facing a wall of blank monitors. He wasn't wearing any clothes. He raised his arms in surrender and slowly turned towards the officers, who were aiming their assault weapons at him and blinding him with their flashlights. Besides the peculiarity of his hideout, the police were immediately struck by two things. It was difficult to make out how old he was and his entire body, including his face and bald head, was covered in tattoos.

Numbers.

The man put up no resistance and let himself be handcuffed without a word. There was a small, bloodstained sickle next to him. The murder weapon, presumably.

The capture of the principal suspect took place just over forty-eight hours after Mrs Anderson's call for help. Though initially confounded, investigators had achieved a rapid and unexpected solution to the case – albeit brought about by a tip-off.

The chief of police publicly thanked the nameless informer for aiding the law and stood before a forest of microphones to declare that another victory in the fight against evil had been claimed. The Andersons' gruesome deaths were by now taken for granted, despite the absence of bodies. With the tattooed man in custody, law and order had been restored, and the public could breathe a sigh of relief. Their focus shifted from the perpetrator to the victims, with an outpouring of compassion and prayers for the Anderson family, wherever they might be.

Little did they know that the time for fear had only just begun.

ENIGMA

1

The letter arrived punctually, as it did every February.

Its contents were more or less the same every time. She was informed that the clinical situation was unaltered and that for the time being there were no significant signs to indicate how it would evolve. Whoever it was who wrote the letter always concluded with the same words:

'The patient's general condition remains incurable.'

A sentence that was a subtle request to decide whether or not to prolong assisted breathing and artificial feeding for another year or else put an end to this vegetating life once and for all.

Mila put the letter in the drawer and looked up at the view outside the kitchen window. The setting sun had strange grey tones in its reflection on the lake and, in the wooded field a few metres from the pier, Alice was chasing after leaves in the wind. Winter had stripped the two lime trees dominating the house some time ago and she wondered where those dried leaves came from – perhaps from the dense forest that surrounded the clear mirror of green water.

Alice was wearing a thick jumper and a scarf that fluttered along with her red hair. Her breath condensed in the cold air but she looked happy. Meanwhile, Mila was enjoying the warmth inside the house. She was preparing vegetable stew for dinner and there was an apple cake in the oven, which filled the room with a sweet aroma of sugar and cinnamon. She had discovered an unexpected habit over the past few months. She, who had considered meals as energy fuel for the body, was now actually deriving taste from food. No doubt it had come as even more of a surprise to Alice, since cooking was something the other mothers did – not hers.

There had been many changes over the past year. It hadn't just been a matter of taking up new habits but starting a new life.

Mila had been in great danger during her last investigation. Until then, the prospect of dying on the job had never fazed her. It was a risk every police officer had to factor in. But after a brush with death she had reconsidered the issue and suddenly been forced to ask herself a simple question that had never occurred to her before.

If she died, what would become of Alice? It was hard enough for her daughter as it was, growing up without a father. So Mila Vasquez had decided to quit the force and abandon the mission she had devoted herself to for what felt like a century: finding missing people.

She had never thought of herself as an ordinary police officer. Moreover, she had never been an ordinary person, else she would never have chosen to hunt shadows. Mila had been sixteen when she realised that she was different. Unlike everyone she knew, she was incapable of empathy. It was something she was ashamed of for a long time, something that prevented her from having normal relationships and made her feel like an outsider. When, at twenty-five, she finally mustered the courage to tell a psychiatrist about it, he had given her condition a name: alexithymia – a kind of emotional illiteracy. Mila was unable to relate to others in an emotional way, and wasn't capable of identifying or describing her own feelings either. It was as if she was emotionally bereft. Some called it 'a frigid soul'.

In time, Mila understood the reason for this obscure gift and realised she was a portal, endowed with access to a dimension of shadows and evil. Once opened, though, this door could never again be shut.

I come from the darkness. And to the darkness I must sometimes return . . .

As a policewoman, she'd considered her condition a precious ally because it allowed her to handle her cases with clear-headed detachment. And this was useful particularly when dealing with the disappearance of minors, where a high degree of emotional involvement was liable to impair the objectivity of an investigator. Her colleagues were often tempted to give up rather than face the terrible reality almost always lurking at the tail end of an investigation.

Mila knew it: searching for a missing child was like chasing a black rainbow. It wasn't a crock of gold that awaited you at the end, but just a silent monster, greedy for blood and innocence.

Alexithymia was both her curse and her armour. But there was a price to pay.

The lack of empathy gave her a dangerous affinity to the monsters who fed on the suffering of their victims, unable to feel sorry for them. In order to be different from them, Mila had often resorted to the secret help of a razor blade. Small acts of self-harm she used in order to trigger inside her a sense of someone else's pain. The scars marking her body were a testimony of her constant effort to identify with the missing people she was investigating and create an empathic contact with them. The physical pain stood in for that of the soul and made her feel less guilty about her indifference.

Aside from those acts of self-harm, the only time she had felt something – something human – was when she was pregnant with Alice. An emotional experience which, sadly for them both, had ended with the birth. After that, Mila had never been able to be either a good mother or a bad one. She simply didn't possess the right tools for that. Her care for Alice had been no different to what one could give a plant. And yet she had looked after her daughter as well as possible – possible for her, naturally.

All that was now in the past, however. A year earlier, Mila had decided that the moment had come to break the deadlock of her heart and soul. So she had rented this house by the lake and escaped from the world with Alice.

It hadn't been easy. They still had to get used to each other. But, little by little, they discovered that they weren't total strangers, even though Mila often had to fight the temptation to hide in the bathroom, unwrap one of the razor blades concealed in a packet in the cabinet behind the mirror, and inflict a wound on a part of her body that was already marked. A way of letting not only blood gush out but also a jolt of pain to make her feel she was human after all – because sometimes she had doubts about it.

Now, on a cold late-February evening, Mila was watching her daughter having fun on her own in the field, and couldn't help wondering how much there was of her in Alice. The girl was ten years old. Soon, hormones would be turning her life upside down. Her innocent games would be cast aside without regrets, with deliberate ruthlessness. She, like everyone else, would suddenly forget what it means to be a child. However, as adults know well, she would nevertheless miss these days for the rest of her life.

But that wasn't what worried Mila. What she feared was that, along with adolescence, frigidity of the soul might also arrive. There was no scientific evidence that alexithymia was hereditary, but case studies seemed to suggest it. The alternative was that Alice should take after her father, but Mila could not accept that either.

Not that man. Not him, she thought, remembering the letter from the hospital.

She never uttered his name. That name didn't even deserve to be thought. Alice never said it either.

As though summoned by her mother's gaze, the girl turned towards her. From behind the windowpane, Mila gestured at her to come indoors.

'There's a squirrel's den in the tree,' Alice announced as she stepped in, chilled.

Mila put a blanket over her shoulders because the dampness in the wintry air had clung to her. Another mother would have welcomed her daughter into a warm hug, but Alice didn't have another mother; she had her.

'Any sign of Finz?' she asked.

Alice shrugged her shoulders.

Mila worried about her indifference to the recent disappearance of their cat. Was it a sign of alexithymia?

'What's for dinner?' the girl asked, changing the subject.

'Vegetable stew and apple cake.'

Alice looked at her, puzzled. 'If I eat the stew, may I take the cake into the shelter?'

It was what she called the hut made of blankets she'd built herself at the top of the stairs. She spent a lot of time there, reading by torchlight or listening to music on an old iPod – recently, she'd become obsessed with Elvis Presley.

'We'll see,' Mila replied. She never wavered when it came to granting exceptions to house rules.

'Do you think he'll come this weekend?'

She was taken aback. In the past, Alice would seldom ask but it was already the third time she'd done it this month. She wondered why the girl had got it into her head that her father would come and visit them. Mila had explained that this wouldn't happen, that he'd been in a coma for years and would never wake up again. At least not in this life. Perhaps only in hell. Yet Alice had created this fantasy that sooner or later he would appear and they'd spend time together, like a real family.

'It won't happen,' Mila said for the umpteenth time, and saw the light go out of her daughter's eyes.

Alice huddled in the blanket and sat in an old armchair by the fireplace. She never insisted. Mila knew things she wished she didn't, things nobody should know. Unspeakable things about human beings. Things about the harm some people do to their fellow creatures. And Alice must not discover that her father was one of those sadists – it was too soon. She'd made up her mind that her daughter would discover the crime behind her birth – and the evil in the world – as late as possible. She had to protect her.

Since she couldn't close the portal to the dark dimension,

she had severed all links with the past. Even though she always kept her pistol in the drawer by her bed, she was no longer a hunter of evildoers. She'd convinced herself that if she no longer sought the dark, the dark would no longer come after her.

Just as she was formulating these thoughts, however, she noticed a slight change in the landscape outside the window. The sun had almost set but Mila saw its faint reflection in the windscreen of an anonymous dark saloon driving along the lakeside road.

She felt a familiar tickling at the base of her neck – as well as an inkling that this unexpected visit would bring something unpleasant.

The saloon car with tinted windows pulled up in front of the house, next to her Hyundai, and stayed there with the engine running.

Mila watched through the French window but nothing happened for a few seconds. Then she saw the back door open and Joanna Shutton got out, motioned the driver to stay in the car and rearranged the long blonde hair that cascaded softly on the shoulders of her camel-coloured coat. Then she headed to the front door, wobbling as her stilettos sank into the damp soil of the lawn.

If the Judge had taken the trouble to come here personally, Mila thought, it must be a really important matter. She was carrying a small folder.

The wind carried a waft of perfume towards Mila as she opened the door. For a moment, she felt uneasy, greeting the Judge in a tracksuit and slipper socks.

Shutton gave her a reproachful look and a forced smile. 'I

didn't wish to intrude,' she said, the attempt at justification unconvincing. 'I would have warned you I was coming but we couldn't find your new phone number.'

'We don't have a phone.'

The Judge looked at her as if Mila had just uttered a blasphemy but refrained from commenting. For her part, Mila maintained her position in the doorway. She wanted to make it immediately clear that there was a boundary between her old life and this one, and she wasn't about to step aside and allow that line to be crossed.

Shutton held her stony gaze. The Chief of the Federal Police Department was a determined woman who did not allow anyone to get the better of her, but she was clever enough to know when she needed to negotiate. After all, that was one of the reasons they'd nicknamed her 'the Judge'.

'I've come a long way, Vasquez. So before you send me away, could I at least ask you for a cup of tea?'

Mila stared at her, decided to hear what Shutton had to say but solemnly promised herself that she wouldn't let herself get involved. After tea, she would send her back where she'd come from.

She turned off the gas ring under the vegetable stew and, since dinner was to be delayed, covered the pan with a lid. Then she took the apple cake out of the oven and put it to cool on the windowsill. She also sent Alice upstairs.

'Why can't I stay?' the girl protested. They never had visitors, so the presence of a stranger was a tempting novelty.

'Because I want you to run yourself a hot bath,' Mila replied. 'You have to go to school tomorrow.'

'May I listen to some Elvis in the shelter first?'

'All right,' she conceded, chiefly because she wanted to

make sure Alice wouldn't hear whatever Shutton had come to tell her.

Mila then set about making the tea, poured a single cup and carried it through to the living room where the Judge was sitting. Shutton took a small sip of the scalding tea and immediately put it down on the coffee table in front of the sofa. The mysterious folder was lying next to her, closed.

'It's lovely here,' she said, looking around. The fire was crackling and gave the rustic room a cosy, amber hue. 'My father loved fishing. He had a hut by the lake and when we were children, he'd make my sister and me spend endless weekends in the woods.'

Mila couldn't picture Shutton in trousers and walking boots. Maybe her overt femininity was the Judge's response to a father who'd wanted a son.

'We don't go fishing. My daughter and I are vegetarians.'

The Judge offered no response to this, maintaining her stoic expression as Mila stared at her in silence, wishing she would stop stalling and ask the favour she'd come all this way for.

'You know, I was very surprised when you decided to quit,' the Judge said. 'I didn't think cops like you could just walk away from the job.'

'Did you miss me?' Mila replied provokingly. Now she was a civilian, she was free to be impudent.

'Many people were sorry to see you go.'

'But not you.'

'True,' Shutton freely admitted.

Still no mention of the folder, Mila observed. This continued stalling suggested the Judge couldn't afford to leave with a refusal. She was curious to find out what her guest was after.

'I don't see a television,' the Judge said, indicating the furniture.

Mila shook her head.

'No internet connection either?' Shutton asked, astounded.

'We have books. And a radio.'

'In that case you will have heard the news over the past couple of days.' And before Mila could reply, she jumped in with a name: 'Anderson . . . does that ring any bells?'

'You've got the tattooed man; I thought it was over.'

The Judge gave a faint smile, uncrossed her legs and recrossed them the other way. 'There's enough blood at the crime scene and in the car to assume it was a massacre,' she said, trying to appear confident. 'The fact that the subject was in possession of the murder weapon made the prosecutor's job much easier, so he charged him with multiple homicide without hesitation.'

'At this stage, I don't think any lawyer could get your guy out of the mess he's got himself into,' Mila said to settle the matter. 'So what are you worried about?'

'It's not that simple,' Shutton replied. 'The place where we arrested him had a camping bed, a few clothes, a camping stove and tinned food. He lived like a tramp surrounded by the carcasses of old computers. It's because of that and the numbers that the media started calling him "Enigma".'

'Where did he get them?'

Shutton frowned. 'What?'

'The computers.'

'Who cares? He must have picked them up somewhere, either from rubbish bins or the abandoned offices near the old abattoir: the place looks like an electrical appliances dump.' Shutton sipped her tea again but only to steady her nerves.

'The media want to build a story around him, but I won't allow them to make a celebrity out of some madman who probably goes around in a tinfoil hat to prevent extraterrestrials from reading his thoughts.'

Mila immediately realised that Shutton was evading the real issue. Something else was worrying her. 'You still don't know who he is, do you?'

The Judge confirmed it: 'There's no match in the database, no record of his fingerprints or DNA. But the real mystery is, despite media reports describing his tattoos, nobody has come forward to identify him. Actually – would you believe it? – it appears no one has ever set eyes on him.' Shutton shook her head in disbelief. 'How can someone covered in numbers from head to toe – including the soles of his feet and the palms of his hands – go unnoticed?' She started a list, counting each item off on her fingers. 'No one has ever seen him or taken a picture of him, even unintentionally. There are security cameras in every corner of the city, but not one of them has ever captured him. There's no trace of him anywhere except in the warehouse where we arrested him after the anonymous tip-off. Where did he suddenly appear from? Why was he sheltering there? Where did he get the things he needed? How the hell did he get his food? And how did he make himself invisible all this time?'

'And, naturally, he's not saying anything,' Mila concluded.

'Not a word since we discovered him.'

'And so there's a chance that the Andersons' bodies may never be found . . .'

Shutton fell silent for a few seconds. A silence intended to convey that Mila had hit the nail on the head.

'The numbers are the only lead we have,' she admitted.

19

And with that, she finally picked up the folder, opened it and began setting out on the coffee table in front of Mila a series of detailed photos of the man's body.

'We know that he tattooed himself. From the condition of the ink, we also know that he did it over an extended period ... At the moment, we're trying to work out if there's some meaning concealed in these sequences or if it's just the fruit of some absurd obsession.'

Mila sensed that although Shutton was trying to cast him as a madman, she was afraid of what the man might really be.

'Is someone trying to put together a psychological profile?' Mila was surprised at hearing her own voice uttering the question. She had sworn to herself that she wouldn't get involved, but for a moment her hunting instinct had got the better of her.

Shutton took this small concession as a point in her favour and rushed to answer. 'The number of traces he left behind – which incriminate him without the shadow of a doubt – suggest a disorganised perpetrator who acted impulsively ... And yet he's so cold, impassive and self-controlled. He's so docile and calm, you'd almost think he'd planned it this way from the beginning and is laughing at us while we're getting all worked up trying to understand.'

Mila began to study the pictures on the coffee table without picking them up. The numbers, all of one or two digits at most, covered practically every millimetre of the man's skin. They were different sizes. Some were smaller, others larger or bolder. There was method in this process carried out over the years, a meticulousness that troubled her deeply. A shudder went up her back.

'Why have you come to me?' she asked, looking away from

the photos on the table as though trying to rid herself of the images. 'I don't see how I can help you.'

'Vasquez, listen—'

'No, I won't listen,' Mila said abruptly, nipping the negotiation in the bud. 'I know what you're after: you need someone to help you find the Andersons' bodies. Perhaps a missing-persons seeker who left the police some time ago, so in the event she fails it won't reflect badly on the force.' And who better to divert the attention of the media than a policewoman who miraculously survived the last investigation of her career. Mila was disgusted. 'In case you haven't yet realised, Mrs Shutton, I'm not going to help you. Because I'm done with this kind of shit for ever.'

'I'm not here to ask you to find the Andersons,' the Judge stated calmly.

Mila was lost for words.

'Vasquez, I've come here because you're probably the only one who can find out who Enigma is.'

While Mila stood gaping at her, Shutton began rummaging through the photographs.

'Among the tattooed numbers we found a single word. On the left arm, mixed up with the sequences of digits and well hidden in the crook of the elbow, *this* was tattooed . . .'

As soon as the Judge unearthed the picture, she handed it to her. After a brief hesitation, Mila took it and felt the blood drain from her face.

Four letters. One name. Hers.

2

Knowing she wouldn't be able to sleep, Mila spent the night curled up on the sofa on which, a few hours earlier, Joanna Shutton had thrust in her face a truth she wished she didn't know.

'You're probably the only one who can find out who Enigma is.' The Judge's words still echoed in the room. 'You won't have to meet him,' she'd hurriedly assured her. 'Just listen to the account of everything we know about him and tell us if it reminds you of anything, then you're free to forget all about it.'

'How can you be sure that it's my name?' she'd protested. '"Mila" can stand for a thousand other things, just like the numbers – you still don't know what they symbolise.'

'We may well be wrong, but we have an obligation to try.' By appealing to her sense of duty, Shutton had played her biggest bargaining chip.

Mila watched the fire slowly burn out then go out completely, leaving her alone in an all too familiar cold. The muffled sounds of the forest filtered into the silent house: the wind pushing its way through the tree branches and, in the distance, the lazy sound of the waves lapping the shore.

Alice had sensed that something was wrong and had seemed agitated. Mila felt guilty, so had allowed her to sleep in the shelter, with her torch, her favourite books, and the iPod loaded with Elvis, surrounded by the comforting smiles of her soft toys.

The darkness had come to find Mila, and she had to make a decision that would also involve her daughter. A decision from which she could not potentially turn back. Everything had been going so well until now; why had she opened the door to the Judge? By allowing her in she had also let in a nameless presence that fed on the anger and screams of innocent victims and that, predictably, now refused to leave. Mila could see it lurking there, like a shadow amid the shadows in the room. And she didn't know how to drive it away.

The stranger who had slaughtered the Andersons had tattooed her name on himself. The thought of this tormented her. It wasn't so much the meaning of this act that troubled her as the actual practice of marking one's skin with a sign. How many times had Mila gouged her own flesh in an attempt to release a human response, a pain that could imitate the pity and compassion she was unable to feel? She was terrified by the resemblance, or worse, the affinity between her and the murderer. It couldn't be a coincidence.

He knows. Is that why he's trying to involve me?

Questions and doubts crowded her mind. A voice within her told her to leave it alone, to forget Shutton's words and this case, to re-immerse herself in the total isolation she had chosen for her and her daughter and carry on with her new life. After all, nobody could force her to go and see what was hiding behind the Enigma riddle. And the tattoo was an invitation: of that Mila was certain.

I won't allow myself to be sucked in, she told herself. The prospect of dealing with that man, even if she didn't have to meet him, troubled her. There was a part of her, however, deep down and irrational, that was pushing her in the opposite direction and yearned to expose the deception.

I want to see what's behind the screen, look into the magician's eyes and expose the trick.

It was a dark call, she could clearly sense it, but no matter how hard she tried, she could not ignore it, because even though Mila was able to keep her second nature at bay, she hadn't yet succeeded in taming it.

When dawn came it dissolved both the shadows and what was left of her resistance. Despite the long night, Mila was alert and aware that, if she tried to ignore Enigma's message, this business would still find a way of flushing her out of the safe haven she had so painstakingly built by the lake, a refuge as shielded and comfortable as Alice's blanket shelter. Therefore, she might as well face the problem.

She told herself that she was also doing it for the sake of the Andersons, to help find their bodies so they might be given a decent burial. But, deep down, she knew that wasn't true. It was the thought of solving the mystery that attracted her. Not a desire for glory, but the absurd certainty that if she were to win the challenge against the darkness it would make the world a safer place for her daughter.

She went to wake Alice up with the aroma of freshly made pancakes.

The blanket shelter was a hut built with ropes and clothes

pegs on the small landing at the top of the stairs, right outside the door to the loft. Mila moved aside the green-and-red tartan that served as an entrance and a beam of light penetrated the small, warm cave. The little girl raised her dishevelled head from the carpet of cushions laid out on the oak floor. Once again, she'd slept with the iPod earphones in her ears. She rubbed her eyes and stared, puzzled, at the tray her mother was holding. 'It's not Saturday,' she said, sensing that a change to their routine implied something.

Mila immediately changed the subject. 'You're going to Jane's house after school today. I'll tell her mother.'

'Why?'

'I'm going into the city, but I'll be back by evening. Is that all right with you?'

Alice looked at the pancakes again and said nothing. Mila realised that her daughter suspected she'd made her favourite breakfast by way of an apology. And she was right, because Mila was about to go back on her decision to leave her past life behind.

'Are you going to see him?'

Mila sighed. 'No, I'm not going to see your father.'

'Okay.' As usual, Alice was quite happy with the answer but, Mila thought, if this obsession didn't stop she'd have to take her daughter to a psychologist.

'In any case, I'll be back home in time for dinner.'

'All right, Mummy.'

The word caught her off guard. Alice almost never called her that and, whenever she did, Mila felt a shudder because she was sure that her daughter was trying to communicate something important, and she didn't know whether she was able to grasp the meaning of her message.

She left her the tray with the pancakes, maple syrup and a glass of milk. 'Finz didn't come back last night either,' she said. 'Maybe we should go and look for her in the forest.'

Alice bit into a pancake and simply registered the information.

'After you've finished eating,' Mila said, 'get ready. The school bus will be here in half an hour.'

Mila then went to get herself ready, too.

She had put a large box in a corner of the wall cupboard. She dragged it out and opened it. It contained combat boots, black jeans, a roll-neck jumper and a leather jacket: clothes she had once worn to be invisible. A dark patch that blended in with a thousand other patches, immersed in the incessant teeming of colours on the planet.

At the bottom of the box there was also an item she hadn't used for a while. She took out her mobile – an antiquated model and certainly not a smartphone – and plugged it into a socket since the battery had been out of charge for a long time. She had to make a few calls. Her first was to Shutton. 'Twelve hours,' Mila said as soon as she'd answered. 'After that, this business will no longer concern me.'

She drove her old Hyundai to the station, boarded the seven-thirty train and arrived in the city half an hour later. No sooner did she step down on the platform than the metropolis greeted her with its usual din, except that Mila had grown unused to it. The lake had made her forget what it meant to live without silence. She suddenly felt under attack.

In the outer square, she recognised an old friend who was waiting for her next to the newsagent's kiosk, as arranged. Simon Berish hadn't changed: he still dressed like the perfect gentleman. He caught her eye from afar and raised his arm.

'I didn't think I'd be seeing you again,' he said, sounding disappointed.

'Neither did I,' Mila admitted, although she wasn't sorry.

They'd said goodbye when she'd decided to leave the police. She could still remember their last conversation, when she'd told him about her plans. Even though Mila hadn't said it in so many words, her intention to draw a line through the past included him, and Berish had accepted that. In the end, they'd parted believing they would never see each other again.

'Have you got time for a coffee?' he asked.

'I don't think so: the Judge has called a meeting in my honour twenty minutes from now.'

Simon nodded and showed her the way. They walked towards the parking area.

Grey clouds were gathering in the sky above the city. It had already rained and the asphalt was studded with small muddy puddles. He walked a couple of steps ahead of her, deliberately avoiding her gaze. Mila knew him well enough to wonder how long he'd hold out before the inevitable outburst came. She didn't have to wait long.

'I still can't believe Shutton managed to persuade you to return,' Berish muttered.

'I haven't returned,' Mila replied. 'I'm only staying a few hours.'

'I'd even deleted your number from my contacts. When the phone rang this morning, I had no idea it was you, otherwise I wouldn't have answered.'

He was trying to be surly, but Mila knew that, deep down,

he was doing it for her own good. A year earlier, to make things easier for her, Berish had taken her place in Limbo – the nickname the Bureau of Missing Persons was known by. It certainly wasn't the most sought-after position in the department, but he'd wanted to send her a reassuring signal: that the work they'd done up till then wouldn't be wasted and that the people in the photos on the walls of the Waiting Room would not be forgotten.

They reached an economy car with its windows slightly lowered to let the air circulate. Berish searched the pockets of his jacket for the keys. Hitch's muzzle popped out through the gap in the rear window.

'Hey, boy,' Mila said.

The Hovawart had grown old but recognised her immediately. He, at least, was happy to see her again.

'How's life by the lake?' Simon asked shortly afterwards, while driving through the Friday-morning traffic on their way to the Federal Police Department.

'Different – and that's all I need.'

A sickly-sweet perfume – jasmine and lily-of-the-valley – lingered in the car. It didn't smell like the typical air freshener. Perhaps there had been changes in Berish's life, too.

'And how's Alice? Don't you two feel lonely?'

'Alice is growing and we're not alone: we have a cat called Finz.'

Hitch grumbled at the word 'cat'.

'You're right to keep well away,' Berish said. 'This place has got worse. Don't believe the stories you'll hear about how there's been a drastic reduction in crime, a new peace between gangs and all that rubbish.'

They called it the 'Shutton Method' and it had yielded

unhoped-for results ever since the Judge had been in charge. Mila knew that life in the city had been much better in recent years, but that hadn't made her change her mind about moving away.

Berish didn't have much faith in this sudden improvement either. 'You can now go out in the city centre in the evening, whereas until a couple of years ago it was like a desert. But is it real?'

Mila could recall a time when, if you poked your nose outside your home after dark, you risked being robbed, at best.

'Where are the criminals, the thieves, the rapists and the dealers? Sure, now we can go to the cinema or have an ice-cream without worrying about not getting back to our loved ones safe and sound. But nobody wonders what happened to all the hatred that was around before . . . '

'Do you have any idea?' Mila asked while looking through the windscreen at the tall buildings that seemed to be competing to see which would touch the sky first.

'Everything seems normal on the surface,' Berish replied. 'All spick and span . . . But a quick surf of the internet will show you it's anything but normal. They're all full of anger, even if it's not clear why. And every now and then this crap finds a way to emerge from the depths, but we downplay it as a random event . . . The day before yesterday, a guy beat an eleven-year-old boy until he bled, just because he'd accidentally walked in front of his smartphone camera while he was taking a picture to put on social media.'

Berish wasn't just some disillusioned copper, Mila thought. He knew what he was talking about. For years, he'd been the best interrogation expert in the department. 'Everybody wants to talk to Simon Berish,' his colleagues claimed. 'Even

29

the most diehard criminals.' Simon knew the city's residents better than anyone else.

'This Enigma business is all we needed,' he said, glancing at her. 'I know you're here because of him.'

Mila hadn't told him the reason for her visit to the city. She'd just mentioned that the department wanted her advice on a case, but hadn't gone into detail. 'What do you think?' she asked, keeping her tone neutral.

'I don't like it at all,' he replied, worried. 'There's too much agitation in the department; I get the feeling they haven't told us everything, that they're hiding something . . . '

Mila didn't respond.

'After the fake astonishment at the Andersons' deaths, all hell broke loose on the internet. The more civilised ones are indignant at the police for not sending the patrol car to the farmhouse until many hours later. But there are those who've already started picking on the Andersons for having shunned technological civilisation, for living in the country with two small children and no electricity . . . The worst ones, however, are those who are singing the praises of the tattooed psychopath.' Berish's tone grew darker. 'They celebrate his actions as if they're possessed. Hearing that kind of talk, you realise the violence didn't stop the other night, in that remote house – it's still echoing like a seismic wave that's going to lead to more destruction. You tell yourself that these fanatics are only a small minority, but then you notice that among them there's an office worker, a student, a father . . . And what's worse, they post their comments openly, with their own faces and names displayed.'

'What's your explanation?'

Simon Berish scratched his white-haired temple. 'I've

questioned dozens of murderers and got them to confess. There would always come a moment when even the toughest would be ashamed of what they'd done. That would usually happen when I said the name of the victim. It was only an instant, but you could clearly see it in their eyes . . . Maybe the police have got better, and crime may well have diminished, as Shutton says, but ordinary people no longer have a sense of decency.'

As she listened to Berish, Mila couldn't help thinking that she'd made the right decision in severing all links with him. Friendship can't work between two police officers if one of them leaves the force: it's the rule. After all, the only thing her former colleague could talk about was crime, murder victims and all sorts of suffering. He could do it because he knew she was here on department business. But if she'd invited him to the lake for the weekend, they wouldn't have known what to say to each other.

Berish pulled up twenty metres or so outside the main entrance of police headquarters. Mila gave old Hitch a pat and got out.

'What time's your train this evening?' Berish asked.

'Seven.'

'Good. I'll come and pick you up at six thirty and drive you back to the station.'

3

The briefing room was a small auditorium on the fourth floor of the department, furnished with blue plastic chairs, a speaker platform and a screen. The windows overlooked the inner yard and the vertical blinds were always drawn for the sake of privacy. There was a lingering smell of dust and nicotine even though smoking in public buildings had been forbidden for over thirty years.

Mila recognised the stale odour as soon as she came in. She'd forgotten it, but one breath was enough to transport her back in time to her old life.

The eyes of all those present immediately shifted towards her. Besides Shutton, who was wearing a perfect pin-striped suit, there were Bauer and Delacroix, the officers appointed to the case. The former was blonde and stout, with a thick moustache and a permanently pissed-off expression. The latter was black and looked like the brighter of the two. There was also a middle-aged man in a spotless white coat – Mila gathered he was the pathologist assigned to the case – and

32

a young woman in a forensics uniform who had the sharp, stern face of those who think that the police are superior to the rest of the human race. Finally, there was Corradini, the Judge's adviser as well as spokesman, complete with his dark suit that made him look more like a manager than a cop. Mila had never met him but had seen him on television whenever the department claimed the credit for solving a case. He was the strategist behind the 'Shutton Method'.

None of those present said hello to her; only the Judge offered a greeting. 'Welcome, Officer Vasquez,' she said, smiling.

Mila felt embarrassed, since she was no longer an officer and was wearing a visitor's badge around her neck. Looking around the room, she could easily imagine what was going through her former colleagues' minds. In their eyes, the tattoo of her name on his body made her Enigma's accomplice. It mattered little whether or not it was true; what mattered was that she was involved in some way. Moreover, the fact that she'd abandoned the uniform made their judgement of her even worse, because coppers usually don't leave: they either retire or die on the job.

Shutton was aware of the tension in the room but chose to pretend that everything was under control. 'Let's start,' she said, sitting in the middle of the front row and insisting that Mila sit next to her. Mila didn't like to be in full view like this but couldn't avoid it this time.

While the others were taking their seats, Corradini dimmed the lights and stepped onto the platform. He then addressed Mila. 'We've had you sign a non-disclosure form whereby you pledge not to divulge the contents of this meeting, on pain of being charged with aiding and abetting and obstruction of justice.'

This bothered her. There was no need to reiterate the warning, but now she was a 'civilian' she had to put up with it.

'Let me explain how we're going to proceed, Miss Vasquez. Officers Bauer and Delacroix will first summarise the Anderson case and then you'll give us your impressions.'

Mila wasn't sure she could help and realised she risked disappointing them.

'During the presentation of the facts you're free to ask questions you think relevant,' Shutton went on. 'The aim is to understand the reason the tattooed man decided to involve you.'

The Judge had forbidden her men to refer to the murderer by the name chosen by the media, but Mila was no longer in the police, so she would continue to call him Enigma.

Bauer began: 'So, let's go over everything that happened at the Anderson farm the other night.'

Even though the summary was only for Mila's benefit, he was addressing the entire room. This made his hostility towards a former colleague obvious to all present. He took a small remote control and activated the ceiling projector. Photographs taken at the scene of the crime began to fill the screen.

'Based on Mrs Anderson's phone call, we can state that the murderer arrived at the farm at around eight p.m.'

They noticed him in the lightning storm, Mila thought. The nightmare had appeared like a mirage. Who had seen him first? Frida, Karl or one of the girls?

'He had all night to carry out the massacre but we think he needed only a few hours.' Bauer clicked on the remote. 'Exhibit one: the sickle.'

There was a detailed image of the murder weapon.

'We don't think the murderer brought it with him. He

34

probably took it from the farm's tool shed: perhaps his initial intention wasn't to kill but simply to steal something.'

The sickle blade and handle were stained with dark red patches.

'It's been impossible for us to find fingerprints on the weapon,' the officer from Forensics said emphatically. 'Too much blood.'

'Exhibit two: the mobile phone.'

Another picture: the mobile that had been used to make the emergency call, lying on a kitchen cabinet. Through the window next to this cabinet you could see the farmhouse porch and the yard outside it.

'This is where Mrs Anderson was standing when she called the police. Although she wasn't able to describe the intruder because of the rain, she said her husband was talking to the man while standing outside the house.'

Mila pictured the head of the family plucking up courage to go and assess the stranger's intentions. Surely, Karl Anderson must have sensed in his heart what could happen. But he had to protect his wife and daughters, that's why he hadn't cowered indoors.

'We assume that, after noticing the stranger on his property, Karl Anderson went to tell him to leave.'

Mila imagined him walking the few metres that separated him from the intruder, trying to think of what to say to persuade him. Maybe he considered offering him money, as threatening him might have been far too risky for his family. But, she thought, his heart must have stopped at the first glimpse of the tattooed face. All his fears, no matter how irrational, must have suddenly acquired shape and substance before him.

'When Karl Anderson saw that he was holding a weapon,' Bauer said, 'maybe he thought it was all over. No matter what he might say or do, it wouldn't change anything.'

Even so, Mila thought with certainty, he was polite and tried anyway. Because when a victim knows there's no way out, they can't help but try to bargain with their killer. First, they appear absurdly accommodating. Then, once they realise it's no use, they beg for mercy.

Many sadistic psychopaths stall until that fateful moment, not because they have any scruples but because they relish hearing their victim pleading.

Meanwhile, on the screen, there was a bird's-eye view of the farm.

'Exhibit three: the blood,' Bauer said. 'It's the only evidence we have that the murders took place there. Although the night's thunderstorms washed away all traces of blood outside, according to our reconstruction the murderer stabbed Karl Anderson to death in the yard.' He indicated the exact spot in the photograph. 'Then he headed to the house.'

There was another image, this time of the inside of the house in total disarray. Mila visualised the wife by the window, seeing her husband suddenly collapsing on the ground. Without a second thought, she grabbed the girls and quickly dragged them to the only place she thought was safe: upstairs.

'At first, the murderer vented his anger on furniture and furnishings. Maybe he was looking for the victims, or perhaps he simply enjoyed terrorising them.'

Then he went up, Mila thought. In her mind she could hear his slow, heavy footsteps on the stairs.

Bauer ran through the pictures of the smashed bedroom

doors, the bloody handprints on the walls, the red trails with the murderer's footprints on the floor.

'All the blood in the house belonged to the woman and the twins,' the young forensics officer piped up. 'This supports the theory that Karl Anderson was killed first, outside.'

'Arterial blood,' the pathologist, who hadn't said anything yet, added. 'This leads us to believe that the victims had no means of escape.'

Bauer looked into Mila's eyes. 'Frida Anderson fought till the very end to protect Eugenia and Carla; we know this from the signs of struggle we found everywhere. But the murderer didn't stop, even when faced with two eight-year-olds crying in despair.'

He paused, letting silence hang over the room. 'The rest of the story is easy to imagine,' he concluded. 'The murderer takes the bodies, loads them into the green station wagon and drives them heaven knows where before returning to his lair.'

Now the analysis of the crime's dynamics was over, it was time to focus on Enigma's profile.

Bauer and Delacroix traded places on the platform like a well-rehearsed relay, handing over the remote control in lieu of the baton.

Unlike his colleague, Delacroix addressed Mila directly. 'The first element of the killer's profile is, once again, the blood,' he said, picking up from the last point. 'Blood is crucial to this case. First and foremost, at the secondary crime scene – the abattoir where the tattooed man was living – there was a car with the Andersons' blood in it, as well as the murder weapon. Secondly, our man's blood is also a mystery: we analysed it and found the presence of a chemical component.'

'LHFD,' the pathologist said. 'A hallucinogenic blend known as "Angel Tear".'

A synthetic drug, Mila thought. Could it have triggered the killing spree? Had the murderer acted under its influence?

'I know what you're wondering, Miss Vasquez,' Delacroix said, reading her thoughts. 'But we won't allow that bastard to get away with it by blaming drugs.'

'In any case, this isn't a problem for the moment,' Shutton intervened. 'Our man is not only refusing to talk to us but also to the court-appointed lawyer.'

'Second element: his identity,' Delacroix continued. 'Since we still don't have a name for the murderer, we've tried to draw up a psychological profile ... The camping stove, the food, the clothes and the other items we found where he lived tell us that he's capable of looking after himself. We don't yet know the meaning of his habit of surrounding himself with old, broken-down computers. Perhaps he sold parts in order to support himself, or maybe this can all be filed under plain obsessive-compulsive disorder.'

Mila knew that psychopaths sometimes collected objects to placate their need for possession. The same process applied to their victims: once dehumanised, they ceased to be regarded as 'people' and became 'things'. This made it easier to annihilate them.

Delacroix showed a few shots of Enigma's den. A room with walls covered in black mould, the floor raised in several places, stacked high with the vestiges of outdated digital eras. Phosphorous and cathode-ray tube monitors were piled up on top of one another, forming a wall down which moisture ran from the ceiling. The main units, complete with floppy disks and CD burners, were accumulated in a corner, gutted, their exposed circuit boards corroded by rust, some of them reduced to the mere casing.

It was like travelling back in time, Mila thought. It seemed like centuries ago, and yet that technology had gone out of everyday use only a little over a decade earlier.

'A team of experts is checking if anything still works,' Delacroix said. 'Or if there's anything in the memory of one of these computers that could lead to our man's identity.'

That was the point. Enigma seemed not to have a past.

'All this makes us wonder how he could move around undisturbed without being noticed.'

He'd learned to evade the eyes of passers-by and the electronic eyes of security cameras, Mila thought. He probably travelled only by night. He exploited our indifference to the poor and the marginalised, became invisible and cheated us. Such behaviour requires significant discipline and long-term self-denial. She hated to admit it, but she secretly admired his willpower.

'What about the anonymous phone call that led to him?' Mila asked.

Delacroix seemed taken aback. 'It's the usual: a tip-off from a private citizen who chose not to leave his details. What's strange about that?'

'What I find strange is that after being invisible for such a long time our man was suddenly tracked down so easily, that's all.'

'They reported the green car, not him,' Shutton reminded Mila briskly. 'Now, let's get on with it, please.'

Mila let it go for now.

'The third element is the body, tattooed with numbers.' Delacroix brought up on the screen the close-ups the Judge had already shown Mila the previous evening. 'They go from zero to ninety-nine and are sometimes repeated. Starting with these repetitions, we were able to make out four groups: left side, right side, hip and lower limbs, chest and head.'

Mila had thought about it all night: an obsession with numbers is typical in some categories of psychopath. The worst. For example, some serial killers relied on complex calculations and patterns of their own invention. Naturally, not having any mathematical basis, the logic that drove them was understandable only to them and so unfathomable to investigators. That's why most profilers considered numbers an obstacle to enquiries and felt it was preferable to discard them as a useful tool for understanding a killer's modus operandi.

'Is it clear so far, Miss Vasquez?' Delacroix asked.

'Yes,' Mila replied. Nothing she'd heard thus far was likely to help her identify the tattooed man.

Delacroix aimed the remote control at the projector again. Enigma's face appeared, impassive in the identification photo taken after his arrest.

When she saw it, Mila moved back on her plastic chair without realising it. The man's dark eyes, set in a web of numbers, were so penetrating that they seemed to emerge from the screen and bore into her head. The power of those eyes was frightening.

'Have a good look at him, Miss Vasquez: does he look familiar to you?'

Mila obeyed and studied the photo carefully. A few seconds later, she shook her head.

Delacroix did not give up. 'We've doctored the killer's face on the computer and deleted his tattoos.'

The result appeared on the screen: the face of a normal man. Clean shaven, with very ordinary features. He could have been anybody. Only his eyes still had the dark energy that had just troubled Mila. Nevertheless, once again she had to give a negative answer. 'I don't know him. I've never seen him before.'

There was a frustrated grumble in the room. Shutton, too, was disappointed. 'Are you absolutely sure?' she asked.

'Yes, I'm certain,' she replied. 'And nothing I've heard so far rings any bells.'

More disappointed mumbling. Shutton was thinking while toying with the heavy gold bangle on her wrist.

'Why haven't you released the doctored picture to the public?' Mila asked. 'Somebody might recognise Enigma without the tattoos.'

'The last thing we need is to fuel the myth of the monster,' the Judge said. 'There are enough lunatics cheering for him online as it is.'

Berish had mentioned the fanatical supporters earlier, but Mila thought that not releasing the photograph of Enigma before his tattooed transformation was an error: showing him as a banal human being would have weakened his aura of mystery.

'I need to talk to you,' Shutton said, standing up and gathering the officers and the pathologist around her.

Mila was excluded. Her presence was probably no longer required, so they were acting as though she wasn't there. She tried mentally to isolate herself from their conversation and, instead, focused on what she'd heard so far.

The police theory was that Enigma was a vagrant addicted to hallucinogenic drugs, who probably supported himself by selling old computer parts, a psychopath obsessed with numbers, who one evening had chanced upon the Andersons' farm and wreaked this carnage while high on Angel Tear.

Everything made perfect sense.

So why am I here? Mila wondered again. I'm here because Enigma tattooed my name on his arm, she remembered. The reason was plain: he wanted me to be here. And there can be only one explanation for that. I am the answer to the Enigma riddle.

She'd listened to the reconstruction of the slaughter and the murderer's profile, but there was still an element missing. The victims.

'Removing the bodies was important to him,' she said, without realising she'd spoken out loud, catching the attention of the group gathered around Shutton. 'What do we know about the Andersons?' she added, heedless of having interrupted them.

They looked at her uncomprehendingly. 'What's that got to do with anything?' Bauer snarled.

'I think the tattooed man is very shrewd,' Mila said. 'Maybe he knew there would be a meeting like this,' she added, motioning at them. 'He imagined that the officers in charge of the case would be present, but equally a pathologist and a forensics expert. What if he wanted me here just so that I could give you my point of view?'

'I wouldn't be so sure, Vasquez,' Bauer replied with contempt.

Mila felt obliged to explain. 'When I was at Limbo, whenever someone went missing, I never knew if it was because they'd decided to escape, they'd had an accident, or some third party had made it happen. Unlike in murder cases, where you have a body, a weapon and possibly a motive, my only resource was the missing person . . . As a result, I learned that it was crucial to analyse the behaviour of the subject before they vanished into thin air . . . So I'd ask myself a series of questions: is the person I'm looking for at low or high risk? Have they said or done something that has put them in danger or turned them into a potential victim?'

Shifting the focus from possible culprits to the victims was a method she'd used many times.

'A long time ago, a criminologist told me that you can't get inside the mind of a serial killer, because his actions are the result of urges, instincts and fantasies that have taken root over the years, ever since he was a child. But he also told me that you could get inside the minds of the victims.'

She avoided mentioning that this criminologist was also her daughter's father, but she saw from their expressions that she had almost succeeded in convincing them.

'Hard as it is to accept, sometimes victims and perpetrators are drawn to one another because they have things in common: they're alike without knowing it.'

A murderer is destined for each and every one of us. Like with a soulmate, we sometimes meet them, sometimes not.

'Carry on,' Shutton replied.

'As I was saying, removing the bodies was important to the tattooed man. He makes no attempt to clean up the blood but takes the bodies; why? After all, we know from the amount of the blood found at the scene that the Andersons are dead. He doesn't want to erase the traces of what he did – on the contrary, he displays them. But he also tells us

43

that we mustn't stop at appearances, that we must continue to investigate . . . Maybe we mustn't just look for the bodies. Maybe, in order to find them, we must discover something else, something about them . . . Instead of asking "where are they?" we should be asking "why the Andersons, of all people?"'

Delacroix exchanged a glance with Shutton before reaching to take some papers out of a folder lying on an empty chair. He flicked through them. 'We know the Andersons were living in the countryside and had shunned technology.'

Mila remembered that their decision had been much criticised. If they hadn't been in such a remote location, the police would probably have arrived in time to save them. Or perhaps Enigma wouldn't have shown up in the first place.

'Some media reports have compared them to the Amish, but they weren't like that,' Delacroix continued. 'They used medicines and dressed in normal clothes. They just didn't have electricity. No electrical appliances, no TV, computer or internet. The only exception was a mobile phone in case of emergency.'

Mila knew there were various movements of people who rejected technological civilisation, like 'Luddites' and laggards. Some for ethical or religious reasons, others political.

Meanwhile a picture of the family was projected on the screen: father, mother and the twins were smiling happily at the camera, wearing the same red jumpers, in an old Christmas snapshot. Mila felt surprise: the Andersons in a previous life.

'Before he became a farmer, Karl Anderson worked as a broker for SPL&T, a bank that dealt with businesses. He was a very high earner.'

At first, Mila had imagined that the Andersons had always lived on the farm, so she'd been wrong about that. But were they really that well-off? And had they really given up on comfort to go and live in the open air with their daughters?

'A flat in a prestigious block in the city centre. A life insurance policy with a very high premium, investments in stocks and bonds. A sailboat. A luxury car in the garage. Private school for the twins, holidays in exotic, expensive locations.'

How could you go from that kind of life to one that was diametrically opposite? Victims and perpetrators are sometimes alike, she repeated to herself. Perhaps, before becoming a vagrant, Enigma had also been a model citizen, with a family, a job and property.

'According to our information, the Andersons bought the farm about a year ago.'

Mila looked at the Christmas photo again and felt an odd sensation: the tickling at the base of her neck, which was almost always a premonition.

'They paid for it in cash. The rest of their belongings were set aside in a trust for the girls, but they would have been entitled to it only once they were of age.' Delacroix paused to take a closer look at what he was reading, as though he couldn't believe it. 'Close relatives say that it was the husband who decided to drag his wife and daughters to that godforsaken place. Apparently, Karl Anderson quit his job overnight, closed his bank accounts and cancelled all the contracts in his name – from cable TV to the internet, even water and electricity.'

So Karl had made the decision on everybody's behalf; Mila couldn't believe it. *Why had he done it?* Suddenly, the Judge's words when she'd come to see her by the lake echoed in her head. 'I don't see a television,' she'd said. 'No internet connection either?' she'd added, astounded.

'We have books. And a radio,' had been her reply.

Like the Andersons, she thought, deeply troubled. *The similarity isn't with Enigma but with me.* Like Karl Anderson, Mila had abandoned everything and chosen to isolate herself, taking her daughter along without asking her opinion. Although her own decision had not been as drastic, the reason was blatantly obvious: she was afraid for Alice, afraid the darkness would find her.

They hadn't moved to the countryside to be surrounded by nature; the Andersons had fled. Karl was afraid for his family, and that was why they'd gone to live in that remote location.

At that very moment, she saw something, bounced to her feet and walked up to the screen.

'What's the matter?' Shutton asked.

Mila remained silent for a long time. 'Enigma and Karl Anderson knew each other,' she stated without hesitation.

The others stared at her, dumbfounded.

'And how the fuck do you know that?' Bauer asked.

Mila raised an arm and pointed at the image before them. 'Look at his watch,' she said.

They all looked, and understood.

On Karl Anderson's wrist, between the red jumper and the sports watch, you could make out a tattoo.

A number.

4

She'd been wrong about Karl Anderson.

When Enigma had arrived at the farm, Karl had gone out to speak to him. But about what? Was he perhaps already aware of his intentions and hoping to stop him? What about Karl's wife? Did Frida know who he was? You couldn't tell from her phone call to the police. It was evening, however, there was no electricity, it was pouring down with rain and the tattooed man was some distance from the house. Even so, Mila suspected that the woman didn't know anything.

Karl, on the other hand, was afraid of Enigma. That was why he'd taken his family away from the city, giving up a well-paid job and a comfortable lifestyle. Where others saw an unfathomable choice, Mila clearly detected evidence of flight. The Anderson family story was a sinister echo of her own choices, and this bothered her.

Naturally, she didn't expect her former colleagues at the department to agree with her. As she stood mulling it all over in the corridor, she could hear snatches of the heated discussion going on behind the closed door of Shutton's office.

So far, they'd taken the easy route and attributed this brutal act to the diseased psyche of a killer, but the tattoo on Karl Anderson's wrist had complicated matters. Now the Judge, Corradini, Bauer and Delacroix were discussing the merits of her theory that there was a motive behind the slaughter.

Eventually the office door opened and Corradini motioned Mila in with his head.

Shutton was first to speak: 'Moving fifteen kilometres out of the city doesn't sound like running away to me. If that were the case, surely the Andersons would have dropped everything and left the country.'

'I don't think it was a matter of distance but of shunning technology,' Mila replied, convinced, even though the connection was still somewhat tenuous. 'Enigma surrounds himself with broken computers while the Andersons reject progress: don't you think there might be a link?'

'These are just assumptions, Miss Vasquez,' Corradini said. 'Dangerous assumptions.'

Delacroix chipped in. 'We need tangible evidence to support these theories.'

'What about the tattoo on Karl's wrist?'

'The picture isn't very clear,' Bauer said. 'Personally, all I see is a faint mark. We can't be sure it's a number.'

Mila couldn't believe it. 'I was brought here for a reason,' she reminded them. 'And it wasn't you people who summoned me but the man in jail.' How could they fail to understand something so simple? 'Maybe I'm the key to the mystery, don't you think?'

Nobody replied, which she took as a good sign.

'I don't know the tattooed man, and that's a fact. But maybe I know something without being aware of it. Enigma's certainly proved he knows me well.'

Shutton looked baffled by this, and Mila wondered whether there was anyone in that room willing to believe her.

'There's a train in half an hour. If I hurry, I could get home early. It's up to you, Judge.'

Shutton thought for a moment then turned to Corradini. 'What do you suggest?'

The adviser shrugged his shoulders.

'All right,' Shutton said, her mind made up. 'Let's take her to meet the prisoner.'

Nobody had mentioned a meeting. On the contrary, the Judge had ruled out that possibility when she'd showed up last night to persuade her to lend a hand with the case.

Mila had no intention of being face to face with Enigma. She was already regretting attending the briefing on the investigation thus far. What she'd heard had engendered a series of doubts. And the only way to dispel them was to meet the man who had involved her in this business; she could not back out now.

The maximum-security prison was just three blocks from department headquarters. It was a reinforced concrete skyscraper. Even though it towered over the surrounding buildings it was known as the Grave, because no one who entered ever came out again. The place was like a hollow tower; the outside walls had no openings whatsoever and the windows of the cells looked into a central well. What made the prisoners' sense of being buried alive even worse was the fact that sunlight penetrated that narrow gap only for a few minutes, exactly at midday.

And it was approaching that time as Bauer and Delacroix drove Mila through the entrance, past the waiting crowd of media correspondents. They too were there in honour of the latest addition, she thought, looking at them through the window. The party had just begun and it was all because of Enigma.

As they passed through the first of three gates to the super-max prison, Mila looked up at the sky one final time and studied the imposing grey monolith that seemed to be swallowing the almost perpendicular sun. She wondered what the convicts felt as they crossed this threshold for the first and last time, knowing they would never return.

They parked the car, which was immediately subjected to a series of checks by prison staff, despite being a police vehicle. Standard procedure based on the fear that, unbeknown to its occupants, somebody might have planted a device in it. There were prominent members of the Mafia and terrorists among the inmates, and somebody out there might be hell-bent on eliminating them before the harsh detention regime could lead them to repent and confess.

'Welcome to the Grave, Miss Vasquez,' said one of the guards. He was seated behind the desk of an ultra-modern reception room with monitors and sophisticated electronic equipment. 'I'm Lieutenant Rajabian and I'll be your guide.' He handed her a badge with a barcode. 'Put it on and don't take it off for any reason or the infrared cameras will think you're an intruder and our officers will be authorised to shoot you on sight.'

Mila put the badge around her neck.

'Now I'm afraid you need to undress for the body search.'

Mila, Bauer and Delacroix were taken to separate rooms where they were subjected to a thorough search by the guards before being issued with navy-blue uniforms, like those the prisoners wore, although the colour differed depending on which block they were housed in.

Mila felt she was in a world apart, where everything was measured according to its own rules and time had no meaning.

Rajabian led them down an endless series of identical corridors illuminated by cold LED lights. The air circulated artificially. At the prospect of being enclosed within walls that were over three metres thick, Mila felt an attack of claustrophobia coming on. She took a few deep breaths and thought about the light by the lake, about the wind blowing through the two lime trees outside her house and managed to keep her malaise momentarily at bay.

They reached a lift. 'Have you been here before, Ms Vasquez?' their guide asked after pushing the call button. 'I know that until recently you were a police officer.'

'I don't think so,' Bauer cut in with a snigger before she could answer. 'She used to work at Limbo.'

'Then let me explain a few things,' the guard continued. 'The Grave has twenty-three floors. The first five house offices, storerooms and the equipment room. The actual prison blocks start from the sixth floor: each is identified with a colour. The prisoners are divided according to the crime committed. On the lower floors, we keep white-collar workers, people found guilty of political misdemeanours and the odd murderer. The higher you go, the greater the danger and so the degree of security increases.'

Like in Dante's Hell, Mila thought, except that this one expanded upwards.

The lift finally arrived and Rajabian ushered the visitors in. Stepping in after them, the lieutenant used a magnetic key to unblock the keypad, then pushed the button for the required floor. When Mila saw the number, she remembered what the guard had just said and felt a pang in her stomach. They were heading to the top, to the twenty-third floor.

It took them less than thirty seconds to reach their destination but it felt like an eternity to Mila. The automatic doors opened to reveal a pink corridor. Everything was painted pink, from the floor to the ceiling lights.

'Some psychologists believe that pink appeases anger,' Rajabian explained, observing Mila's astonishment. But it wasn't the colour that surprised her; she was remembering that a similar experiment had been carried out in the 1980s in another prison. The inmates had eaten the plaster and then attacked the guards.

The lieutenant led them to the cell block. 'This is where we keep the psychopaths,' he said. 'Serial killers, pyromaniacs, paedophiliac murderers – those who've committed the worst crimes imaginable. We even have a cannibal.'

As they walked, Delacroix turned to Mila. 'You'll meet the tattooed man in his cell. Moving him could make him agitated and this way we can evaluate his reactions better.' Before she could reply, he added, 'You'll have no contact, because there'll be ten-centimetre-thick glass between you.'

'But he'll be able to see me, right?'

'Yes, of course,' he replied. 'I've just told you it's a glass wall.'

Mila was sorry she'd asked that silly question, but she was nervous.

They reached an armoured door. 'You'll be alone in the room adjacent to the cell,' Delacroix said. 'Our presence might inhibit or irritate him, but maybe he'll open up with you.'

Mila nodded. 'All right.'

'We'll be constantly watching you through the camera,' he added.

'You don't have to reassure me, I've known worse.' It was true, but she also realised that she was out of practice at this kind of thing.

'I know,' Delacroix replied, but his attitude suggested that the past was the past and that she shouldn't rely too much on her experience. 'If you want to put an end to the meeting, all you have to do is touch your hair.'

Lieutenant Rajabian punched in a code on a keypad next to the armoured door. A brief, five-second countdown with an electronic beeping began, and the lock clicked open.

Delacroix looked at Mila. 'Ready?'

She took a deep breath and exhaled. 'Ready.'

'One more thing,' Bauer said. 'He doesn't know you're here.'

You're wrong, Mila thought. He knows.

Every psychopath is a prison per se, she reminded herself. There's a demon living inside him, who spends his restless life trying to get out any way he can. The fiercest killers always looked docile and kind in the eyes of observers, but violence could rear its head at any moment. The demon wants to show the outside world that he exists and is totally in control of his host.

The armoured door closed behind her and Mila found herself in a tiny, dimly lit room. While her eyes were getting accustomed to the new surroundings, a partition began to rise before her.

A bright, blinding white light burst from the other side. The barrier gradually revealed a form standing in the middle of the cell beyond the glass.

53

Enigma stood motionless in the pink uniform, like a parody of good and evil. He was bathed in the midday sunlight that filtered through a narrow slit. In that glow, he looked like a wicked angel. He was holding his hands together in front of him, fingers interlaced, and was looking at her.

He knows, Mila thought, remembering Bauer's last words. He was waiting for me. She took a step forward towards the glass partition, to allow him to recognise her and also to have a better look at him. It was as though the tattoos on the portions of skin visible under the uniform weren't ordinary patterns. The numbers moved, as though slithering over him – alive.

Naturally, this was just her imagination and she had to be careful not to let it take the upper hand. He's only a man, she told herself. He's not a monster. He's made of flesh and blood. He's not invulnerable. He can be killed. And he can suffer.

'I imagine you know who I am,' Mila said. The man did not reply. 'Here I am. Isn't that what you wanted?'

The silence was unnerving her. While she tried to come up with something to open a dialogue with the prisoner, she studied his cell. Apart from a bed nailed to the floor and a metal toilet, the room was bare. No marks on the walls, no personal items. Four cameras were constantly focused on him and nothing could evade their electronic eyes.

Mila let a few more seconds lapse before speaking again. 'If you've changed your mind and don't want me here, I can go.'

The man unclasped his hands and raised his right one to scratch his neck then his temple. His movements were jerky, as though he had a kind of nervous tic.

'Tell me about Karl Anderson,' she said. 'I saw the number tattooed on his wrist, so I assume you knew each other.' Except for those two initial movements, there was no reaction.

'I may be wrong but I have a feeling you didn't just happen at the farm by chance, I think you went there on purpose. What were you looking for?'

Enigma moved again. This time he smoothed a crease in his uniform at the level of his sternum, then brushed imaginary dust off his left shoulder. His gestures were quick but gauged and hypnotic, elegant almost.

'I think you made me come here because you have a story to tell me. Am I wrong? Maybe you want to tell me what really happened the other night. I'm curious to hear your version of events.'

The prisoner showed no sign of being interested in what she was saying. He just kept staring at her with his very dark eyes. Mila had the unpleasant feeling those eyes were looking for a chink to penetrate her.

'I'm not sure this interview is constructive,' she said dismissively. The truth was, she was trying to conceal her unease. 'You know that if you won't speak to me they won't let me come back, don't you?'

Enigma seemed indifferent to her every word. As if he knew that Mila had no intention of setting foot in this place again. Just a couple more hours and I'll be taking the train home, she told herself. But she knew that nothing would ever be the same again. Even if this man had no possibility of getting out of there, the mere thought that a being like this existed troubled her.

Who are you? What are the numbers you wrote over yourself? Why did you want me here?

Determined to put an end to her hesitation, she searched in her pocket and took out the only thing she'd been allowed to bring. A copy of the computer-doctored photo of Enigma shown to her during the morning briefing, in which his face looked like it would have been originally, before the tattoos.

The face of a normal man.

Mila pressed it against the glass partition so that he could see it clearly. 'Is this what you're running away from?' she asked, casting caution aside, hoping to provoke him. 'Maybe you think your current appearance will inspire fear in others. I have no doubt you managed to terrify Frida Anderson and her little girls as you chased after them with your sickle – well done, you made their fairy-tale monsters come to life . . . But here's a newsflash: you're no less banal than the next man. You're just a little man who did something cruel, stupid and obscene. History is full of people like you, so you're nothing special. Your feats are good for the sponsors who buy advertising space during the TV news: you'll help them sell a few more detergents, but that won't make you immortal. Everybody's talking about you now, but they'll soon find another scoop, another horror to entertain them, and you'll be forgotten . . . You're already dead even if you don't realise it. You'll notice in a few years, once you've lost the habit of keeping time and suddenly see that in here you're not even allowed to take your own life.'

After Mila had bluntly told him these home truths, the tattooed man reacted with a new tic: he put his hand on his left elbow then slid it down his forearm as far as his wrist. Then he leaned towards Mila as she stepped back.

'*Fishhhboone . . .*'

A shudder of pure terror went through her. Mila would never forget that sound. It would accompany her past the boundary of these walls, follow her to the lake and creep into the bedtime stories she told Alice to make her fall asleep.

While she stood paralysed, Enigma resumed his earlier position, his hands in front of him, fingers interlaced. The midday sun vanished in a fraction of a second and a heavy semi-darkness took its place.

The prisoner turned his back to her. She understood that this marked the end of the meeting. She waited a little while longer, hoping for something to change. Then she raised her hand and stroked her hair. The men watching her from outside picked up the signal, the partition began to lower in front of the glass and, five seconds later, the electronic lock of the armoured door clicked open.

'Fuck, Vasquez,' Bauer said aggressively as soon as she'd stepped out. 'You should have stayed there and insisted.'

Mila walked past him and asked Lieutenant Rajabian, 'Is there a toilet here?' She wasn't feeling well and was afraid she was about to vomit.

'There's a staff toilet in the guards' room,' he replied.

Angry at being ignored, Bauer stepped in front of her. 'We have a word that's totally useless. "Fishbone"? What does "fishbone" mean? I knew we shouldn't have involved you, that we didn't need some has-been from Limbo.'

Delacroix tried to hold him back. 'Stop it, it's not her fault, we'll find another lead.'

Mila forgot her nausea and turned to face him squarely. 'I think he told me everything.'

'What the fuck are you on about, Vasquez?'

'That nervous tic of his . . . He scratched his neck, then his temple. Then he smoothed a crease on his uniform at the level of his sternum and brushed dust off his left shoulder. Finally, before turning away, he touched his elbow and wrist, again on his left side.'

Bauer wasn't following but Delacroix understood.

'Let's watch the recording again and find out which numbers correspond to the parts of the body he indicated ... Maybe that bastard has sent us a message.'

5

They went back to the department to analyse the footage. It wasn't hard to locate the numbers indicated by the prisoner's gestures in his mute dialogue with Mila. There were six in total, without any apparent connection. A single sequence of random figures. 'Fishbone', however, the only word uttered by the tattooed man, still had no plausible interpretation and Shutton had asked the best cryptographer on the force to solve the riddle.

They called him Surf, because he enjoyed surfing in life and on the internet. He was a man with a large body and a disproportionately small head, as if he hadn't been assembled correctly. He wore cargo Bermuda shorts and Hawaiian shirts, even in the winter. He was unequalled in his field.

Surf's lab was in the basement, the only room in the department without heating, and didn't look like a government office. There were computers with sophisticated decryption programs, books piled everywhere, but also surfboards, bottles of bodybuilding supplements and a lot of dust. The walls were covered in posters of exotic, faraway beaches, and there were four desks heaped with papers. This mess, however, seemed to make sense to Surf.

His speciality was decrypting complex codes devised to conceal the financial transactions of organised crime. Even so, Mila had seen him in action a few years earlier during the 'crossword case'. The police had been hunting a serial killer who left a different crossword at the crime scene every time he struck. From the information in the clues, Surf had succeeded in anticipating his moves, which allowed the police to arrest him before he could kill again.

'The Book of Genesis: "The seven years of abundance in Egypt came to an end",' Surf read aloud, then looked at those present. 'Does that ring any bells?'

Nobody responded, then:

'The Gospel according to Matthew: "Because of the increase of wickedness, the love of most will grow cold",' Delacroix recited.

Mila and Bauer shook their heads. Apparently, these words meant nothing to Shutton either. Corradini had stepped away from the group to smoke his e-cigarette but continued to follow the discussion that had been going on for an hour and a half.

They had tried dozens of combinations but reached no satisfactory outcome. Still, the possibility that those numbers could refer to verses from the Bible wasn't completely unfounded. The main categories into which sadistic killers were divided included one designated 'missionaries': those who killed in the belief that they'd been invested with the task of purging humanity of its sins by eliminating those who, in their eyes, appeared impure. Their victims tended to be prostitutes, or LGBTQ+, but some also preyed on fraudsters and lawyers. And they would use the Holy Scriptures as their signature.

'Maybe we should change our approach,' Mila suggested. 'Our man doesn't seem like an evangelist.'

'And how do you know?' Bauer answered. 'Perhaps he surrounded himself with broken computers because he's a technology fanatic and wanted to punish the Andersons for relinquishing progress.'

Mila was amazed that there was still somebody in that room who considered Enigma fit the profile of a killer driven by mental illness. For all his quirks, she thought the Andersons' killer had a high intelligence quotient and, above all, that he didn't act on mere impulse.

He had a specific aim in mind.

'I still think the key to everything is in "Fishbone",' the Judge said. 'If we discover the meaning of this word in relation to the numbers, we'll have a solution.'

'We've already tried,' Surf replied. 'And the computer didn't pick up a connection between them.'

'Computers can sometimes be wrong,' Bauer said.

'Not mine.' Surf strode to the board where he'd made some notes and stared at it, stupefied, his shoulders hunched from the muscular mass and his strong arms hanging down his sides. 'Fair enough. After all, we're only at the beginning and we've still got a long way to go.' Having said that, he began frantically erasing the notes with the palm of his hand.

Mila wondered if he was doing this to avoid an afterthought.

'Forget about the Bible and let's assume our man is more subtle than that,' Surf said, taking from the pocket of his cargos the materials he needed to roll himself a joint.

Shutton shook her head and looked at the others to share her incredulity. But no one intervened.

'Maybe he's using a secret numerical language of some sort,' Surf said, arranging the grass on the cigarette paper. 'Perhaps our friend used to be in the army or the secret service.'

Delacroix disagreed. 'If that were the case, his fingerprints and DNA would be in the system.'

'What if he's just a mathematician?' Surf replied, forgetting his joint and crossing the room to rummage through the manuals stuffed in a cardboard box, tossing out those he didn't need. 'I remember once stumbling over some complex number systems . . .'

'Stumbled over what?' Corradini asked sceptically.

'A complex number is made up of a real and an imaginary part,' Surf explained, as though it were the most evident thing in the world. 'So it can be represented by a combination of both.'

'Fascinating,' Bauer replied sarcastically.

Surf looked at him sternly. 'You know when you write a long sequence of figures on a calculator and when you look at it backwards you come up with an obscenity? For all we know, our tattooed man just wants you to go fuck yourself, Bauer.'

Bauer turned scarlet and was about to retaliate when Mila intervened. 'He feels contempt for us, he doesn't think we're up to the task, but he would never use a code that was too complicated. He wants to humiliate us but at the same time he wants to be understood. Otherwise, what he did – his "work", his "masterpiece" – would have been in vain.'

'She's right,' Delacroix said. 'It has to be something simple.'

Surf considered this. 'Okay then – let's watch the recording again.'

He went to the trolley with the television on which they'd watched over and over again the footage of Enigma at the Grave and dragged it to the middle of the room. He also took the photographs of the tattoos. Clearly he hoped that, by analysing everything they had again, they would be able to grasp something that had previously eluded them or else have some sort of epiphany.

Surf switched on the DVD player and the recording ran on the screen again, without the sound.

Even though it was the umpteenth time she was seeing it, Mila experienced the same feelings she'd had when she was there. She wished she could look away but didn't. It's too important, she thought, forcing herself to endure it again.

Enigma was in the middle of the cell, bathed in the midday light as though surrounded by a mystical halo. Filmed from a high angle, he appeared even more eerie.

'The numbers on his body go from zero to ninety-nine and are then repeated,' Surf said more to himself than to those present. 'On the basis of these repetitions, we are able to distinguish four ensembles or groups.'

He was reiterating what Mila had already heard from Delacroix at that morning's briefing and at least ten times since they'd been shut in that basement room.

'Left side, right side, hip and lower limbs,' Surf said, looking again at the tattoo pictures he was holding, 'chest and head.'

Mila sensed that the others had little confidence that the riddle would be solved quickly. Meanwhile, Surf was summarising Enigma's gestures. 'He scratched his neck then his temple. Then his sternum and his left shoulder. Finally, his left elbow and wrist.'

Corradini was the first to lose hope. 'Maybe we should seek advice outside. We could try the intelligence services.'

Shutton said nothing, considering this suggestion.

'I don't think we should leave any stone unturned,' Corradini added.

Surf suddenly aimed the remote control at the DVD player and reversed the footage to the beginning. As the images rushed on the screen, Mila saw a change in the cryptographer's expression. He'd spotted something.

'Look,' he said, eyes sparkling.

They all leaned towards the television.

'What?' Shutton protested. 'I can't see anything.'

'Wait, I'll show it to you from the beginning . . .'

Surf replayed the images, again at full speed. In the scene, which had always seemed rather motionless to Mila, there was actually a change. Enigma's shadow was moving on the side wall of the cell owing to the sunlight from the slit shifting. A phenomenon you couldn't really detect at normal speed.

Nobody had yet understood why this was so important but Surf seemed to have an inkling, because he bounced to his feet and went to look for something on one of the paper-heaped desks. Once he'd found it, he returned.

He was holding before him a map of the city and his eyes were darting up and down it, searching for something. 'The Grave is in the north-west. The cell windows look out into the building and sunlight only reaches them at midday, is that correct?'

'Surf, tell us what's going on,' Delacroix demanded, on tenterhooks, like everybody else.

Only Mila had worked it out. 'Enigma knows the position of the sun at that moment, so he indicated the numbers by touching first his chest and head, then the left-hand side of his body: North and East. Like a compass . . . A human compass.'

'Jesus! Those numbers are geographical coordinates,' Shutton said.

'Latitude and longitude,' Surf confirmed, excited, going to one of the terminals and searching for a geolocation program.

Everybody gathered around him in trepidation.

'I'll try and follow the sexagesimal method,' he said. 'Degrees, minutes and seconds.'

Shortly afterwards, he typed the numbers into an appropriate grid on the computer screen, and subdivided them into two groups of three: North and East.

The calculator took less than a second to supply the result.

'Got it,' Surf announced, looking at the map. 'It's the old refinery in the bay.'

6

They were certain that Enigma had indicated the place where he'd hidden the bodies of the Andersons but in actual fact, nobody could know for sure what they'd find. What if it were another deception? After all, they didn't know why the killer had decided to take his victims' remains away after the slaughter. What if he was luring them into a trap?

Shutton didn't want to take risks, so she arranged for special teams to carry out a sweep on the site of the former refinery first, to enable her colleagues to operate in a safe environment. Bauer and Delacroix would join the intervention squad to coordinate the procedure.

The department was in turmoil. Between field agents and support groups, over two hundred officers would be deployed. As a civilian, Mila wasn't involved but was watching the preparation ritual.

The police were equipped with bullet-proof vests, helmets and assault weapons. Since there wasn't enough room for everyone in the changing rooms, people were getting dressed all over the place: in the toilets but also in the offices and corridors. A feverish silence fell as the men helped one another tighten the belts of their Kevlar gilets. Mila savoured the electricity that always filled the air in the moments of calm before a mission. She felt unexpectedly nostalgic for the days when she was still a part of that body of men and women in uniform. That sense of being united by a badge helped them push away the fear of death.

The Judge came up to her. 'I must ask you a favour,' she said. 'For the time being, let's keep to ourselves the fact that Enigma and Karl Anderson probably knew each other.'

Mila was surprised to hear Shutton use the name after banning it, but not that she was trying to bury the most insidious detail of the case. She'd somehow expected this move. If that piece of information reached the media, they could turn against the Judge.

'The coincidence of the number tattooed on that man's wrist would only cast a shadow on the tragedy of a wretched family and needlessly sully their memory – don't you agree?'

Mila hated to admit it but her former superior was right. The reasons of the dead had to remain with the dead. They'll never discover who Enigma is, anyway, she thought. Besides, in less than two hours I'll be on the train home and can forget about all this for ever.

'All right,' she said.

'Do I have your word?'

'Yes.'

Shutton seemed satisfied. 'Would you like to come into the operations room? The twelve hours you granted me aren't quite over yet,' she added sarcastically. 'Besides, I think you've earned it.'

Mila would have liked to reply that she didn't want to in the least, but it wouldn't have been the truth. So she accepted.

As soon as she came into the room, she looked around. All the heads of divisions were there, as well as their deputies and assistants, but also a sizeable delegation of civil servants. They would follow the raid live on a wall of screens, through images transmitted by cameras fixed on the helmets of officers in the field.

Joanna Shutton was the only woman of a high rank, Mila noted. So it was understandable that she'd want to show off the efficiency of the police and, above all, the effectiveness of the method named after her.

Mila sat on one of the chairs at the back as the Judge launched into a brief introduction.

'This year, we've had many success stories in the fight against crime,' she began, addressing the guests, who were still standing. 'Murders are down by eighty-seven per cent and rapes by ninety-three per cent. Gangs have been defeated and there are fewer and fewer drug addicts and dealers on the streets. Most importantly, the public now feel a lot safer. For that reason I want to say that what happened over the past few hours should be seen as an exception, and I'm proud of the fact that my men and I managed the situation successfully: the culprit was promptly apprehended and all that remains is to tie up the last few loose ends. If, as we all hope, we're about to find the Andersons, we can consider the case closed . . . Sadly, there's nothing else we can do for those poor people. But our prayers over their graves will carry the promise that we won't forget them.'

There followed a solemn silence so fake that Mila feared it might end in applause. Instead, it was broken by Corradini, who said, 'Judge, we're almost there.'

Everybody took a seat. Armoured vehicles and police cars took less than fifteen minutes to cross the city and reach the abandoned refinery that Enigma had indicated in his most recent riddle. The resulting military-style parade brought the entire city to a halt. People watched, speechless, from their apartments or through shop windows as the army of police officers drove by. And the whole thing was being televised, naturally.

A deployment of power on this scale could only be justified one way, Mila thought. Whatever happened at the old refinery, no matter what they found there, this would draw a line under the whole business. Shutton would not allow any further discussion that might overshadow all the good the department had done under her management. Enigma was in jail and people would soon forget about him. The pomp and circumstance were for the grand finale.

That was why the Judge didn't want anyone to mention the tattoo on Karl Anderson's wrist, Mila thought. And though she'd agreed to keep quiet, she was no longer sure it would be right to do so.

Meanwhile, the officers from the special teams gathered in formation around the refinery and waited.

It was a vast area, the size of at least six football pitches, with a central building and warehouses branching out of it, the industrial equipment they'd once contained now obsolete. On the pier outside there were large cisterns connected to the oil pipeline, rusty giants sleeping on the shore of the bay. Of the twelve tall chimneys – towers that had once belched out fumes generated during the refinery process – only seven were still standing, making the place look like a phantom cathedral. This was usually a no man's land, inhabited only by drug addicts and the homeless. The special forces' rules of engagement involved shooting on sight so, before the raid, loudspeakers transmitted a warning to anybody in the area that they should surrender themselves to the authorities immediately.

A radio communication arrived in the operations room, saying that eighty-six people had been arrested and that they were being subjected to rigorous checks. There was no reason to delay further, so at five p.m. sharp, Shutton gave the order for the operation to begin.

Watching the images on the screen, Mila felt as though she was in the field. The thud of boots on uneven ground and metal stairs, the jingling of assault rifles and flashbang grenades attached to the vests, the puffing of dogs and the trained breathing of officers charged with adrenaline.

Every now and then, there was a signal failure and the voices of Bauer and Delacroix, who provided constant updates on the raid, would fall silent.

'We've combed through about seventy per cent of the complex,' Bauer announced after the first twenty minutes. 'The bomb disposal equipment hasn't picked up on any C4 or other explosives.'

These were sophisticated electronic devices capable of identifying suspicious chemical substances. Good news, Mila thought. She had feared they would come upon a dirty bomb, put together with stuff you could easily buy on the internet or even at the supermarket. After all, Enigma had nothing to lose: he'd already earned himself a life sentence in the Grave, so taking the souls of a dozen police officers wouldn't change anything for him.

Shutton wasn't sitting with the rest of the audience. As a

good commander-in-chief, she had removed her suit jacket, which was now hanging over the back of a chair, rolled up the sleeves of her silk blouse, and was standing, hands on hips, watching attentively as the raid progressed. Mila noticed that she was biting her lower lip from tension. After all, her credibility was at stake.

'The dogs haven't sniffed any corpses in the area and the men haven't detected anything so far,' Delacroix said. 'So we'll continue to the next phase.'

There was obvious disappointment in his voice, and it spread across the room.

Mila saw Corradini approach the Judge and whisper something in her ear. Maybe they were already wondering how to handle a defeat.

'Just a minute . . . what the fuck is this?' Bauer blurted out on the radio.

Eyes lit up in the room as everybody searched the screens for a clue. Stirred with new hope, Shutton pushed Corradini aside. But when one of the cameras finally framed the scene, a chill fell on the operations room.

'What does this mean?' a high-ranking official asked, getting up from his seat.

In the frame, the men from the special teams had assembled in a vast deserted hangar. They'd lowered their weapons and were looking at one another, puzzling over the meaning of what they had found.

In front of them on a ten-square-metre wall, an inscription had been sprayed, the work of a graffiti artist, now faded as if it had been there for many years.

One word.

Fishbone.

7

'What would you like for dinner?'

'I don't know,' Alice replied.

'Since I'm in town, I could pick up something special we can't get at the lake.'

'Like what?'

'I was thinking of Indian.'

'I like Indian food,' the girl said.

It was almost six and Mila wanted to make sure that Jane's mother had picked Alice up from school along with her own daughter. In half an hour, Simon Berish would come by the department and drive her to the station.

'Mummy...'

Mila hated being called that, as she thought she didn't entirely deserve it. 'Yes?'

'Can I ask you something?'

She hoped to God the girl wasn't about to mention her father again. 'Of course.'

'Can we get another cat?'

Mila was taken aback by this request. 'Why? What's wrong with Finz?'

'She hates me.'

'No, she doesn't. Not at all. Besides, we're going to find her.'

'All right. Then can I have an iPhone? Jane's getting one for her birthday.'

Amazing how children's minds managed to flit from one annoying subject to another. 'You know how I feel about this,' Mila replied, still incredulous.

They had already talked about it, but Alice periodically returned to the offensive because her schoolmates had smartphones and she felt left out. Mila wasn't sure the girl was mature enough to have one of her own. She remembered the Andersons and their decision to get rid of electronic devices. We think we own them but, in reality, they own us.

'I saw Uncle Simon today,' she said, desperate to change the subject.

'Was Hitch there, too?'

Mila knew that the 'dog topic' would distract her. 'Of course. I might even invite them over one weekend – what do you think?'

She didn't know if it was a good idea to break her rule of not seeing her former colleagues again, but she reasoned that, at that moment, since Alice kept mentioning her father, she needed contact with a male figure, and Simon was the most generous friend she had.

'Uncle Simon is okay,' her daughter replied. 'But tell him to bring Hitch with him.'

'Will do,' she assured her before hanging up.

She walked down the long corridor in the deserted department. The agitation of a couple of hours earlier was now a mere memory and there was a faint odour of defeat in the air.

Her job there was over, as were the twelve hours she had agreed to give Shutton.

The Judge had barricaded herself in her office with her staff to try and work out how to respond to the earlier embarrassment at the hands of Enigma. An unprecedented volume of personnel and vehicles had been deployed just to find an empty room. The inscription on the wall, which had clearly been there for years, weighed on her like an unbearable prank.

Fishbone.

In Mila's head, this word echoed with the hissing, eerie intonation of the tattooed man during their interview at the prison.

'Fishhhboone . . .'

He had leaned towards her, drawing closer to the security glass with his penetrating eyes, and Mila had felt that this whisper alone had the power to shatter the barrier between them.

She decided to put it out of her mind because she was afraid that his voice had slipped something into her head – a sound virus or a parasite that could burrow into her thoughts.

On her way to the exit, she walked past the open door of a lab. Fifty or so computer technicians sitting at their work stations, analysing the old computers taken from Enigma's dump.

The ancient main units of the PCs were lined up on the floor, like headstones in a graveyard. They were connected with leads to more modern and advanced models that were scanning their residual memories and transmitting the results onto sophisticated LCD monitors. Every technician was focusing on his own task.

Curious, Mila took a step into the room.

All kinds of things were scrolling across the screens: emails, text documents, photos. There were faces of smiling, unknown people, unfamiliar landscapes, snapshots from holidays and everyday life. Happiness and sadness mixed together. There were love letters and business letters, contracts, insurance policies, wedding and birthday present lists, plane and train tickets, address books and phone numbers.

'Amazing how much life we throw away.'

Mila turned and saw Delacroix.

'We buy a computer, stick everything about ourselves into it, then get rid of it without thinking that, as well as the circuits, there's a part of us inside it.'

'Found anything interesting?' she asked.

'They're checking for the umpteenth time, but it seems there's nothing in those hard drives that relates to Enigma.'

Mila had briefly deluded herself that they could dig out something useful from that clutter of technological waste.

'So you're off?' Delacroix said.

'Apparently so,' she replied, shrugging her shoulders.

'We've probably found out all we're going to about this business, and the tattooed man will remain nameless.'

It happened more often than one would have thought: a blood feud, too few clues, the sparse evidence inexorably erased by the passage of time. Police officers knew that in a case like this, where all possible leads had been pursued to no avail, their chances of solving it were non-existent unless new evidence came to light.

'At least there's a culprit in jail,' Mila said, trying to comfort herself.

Neither of them mentioned the bodies of the Andersons, because they both feared that they'd never be found.

'It's been a pleasure working with you, Vasquez.'

She was sure that Delacroix meant it. After all, he'd been the only one among her former colleagues who hadn't made her feel like a stranger that day.

'Only next time, please keep your mobile on or else get yourself an email address,' he added, scolding her in a good-natured way. 'Yesterday, the Judge gave us hell because we couldn't find you.'

'I can assure you there won't be a next time. And Shutton can fuck off. If she wants to talk to me, she can come in person.'

Delacroix smiled. 'It's pouring outside,' he said, then turned away to resume overseeing the work being carried out by the technicians.

Mila handed in her visitor's badge to Reception. It was like reclaiming her freedom. She walked down the long entrance hall of the building. Through the glass doors, you could see the thunderstorm lashing the city. As soon as she stepped out, she saw Berish's car, waiting for her at the corner, engine running.

'So how was your day?' he asked as soon as Mila got in.

'I couldn't wait for it to be over,' she said, knowing that was exactly what Berish wanted to hear.

The rain was pelting the windscreen and the wipers couldn't keep up. It was nice and warm in the vehicle, but Hitch's wet fur gave off a pungent odour that mingled with the woman's perfume Mila had smelt that morning. There was nothing pleasant about the resulting miasma.

Berish got into the chaotic Friday evening rush-hour. Office workers were pouring into the streets, intent on getting home so they could start the weekend as soon as possible.

'They've involved you in the Enigma case, haven't they? You can tell me now . . .'

'The less you know about it, the better,' she replied, not wanting to talk about it. She changed the subject and said, 'I promised Alice I'd take her some Indian food for dinner but at this rate I'll miss my train. Can't you speed up?'

Berish ignored her request and went back on the offensive. 'Your opponent's sophisticated plan ended with his making a fool of you people,' he said, determined to have the final word.

He was right. After they'd deciphered the geographical coordinates, Mila had briefly thought that Enigma was an enemy with a fine mind. She had forgotten that he was just a cruel murderer of innocents. Or maybe she didn't want to accept it. Like everybody else, she had trouble admitting that evil was banal.

'I wonder why we always imagine the devil as a cunning being,' the father of her daughter, the best criminologist she had ever known, used to say. 'Maybe it's because otherwise it's too vexing that we've been unable to stop him.'

Meanwhile, a line of cars had formed in front of them.

'Shit, I shouldn't have gone through the city centre,' Berish said. He saw a parking space and pulled into it.

Mila was surprised by this manoeuvre. 'What are you doing?'

'There's an Indian restaurant along here and I'm sure they also do takeaway.' Before getting out, he turned and winked at her. 'You're not going to disappoint my little niece, are you?'

'Choose something vegetarian,' Mila said, watching him walk away in the thunderstorm, skipping between puddles, slouching as though his shoulders were heavy under the weight of the rain.

Left alone, she switched on the hazard warning lights. Hitch was asleep on the back seat, snoring softly. That billowing breath, in addition to the ticking of the warning lights and the pitter-patter of raindrops on the roof, soothed her nerves. In the calmness, a thought was taking shape. Mila withdrew from her surroundings and immersed herself in the silence of her mind.

The Anderson case was messy. None of the available data, none of the evidence, none of the clues fitted together. There was no way of identifying the 'purpose' concealed behind the slaughter.

Chaos reigned.

And yet the numbers were all about order, precision, cleanliness, she thought. A man with numbers can't have just given in to the killing instinct, driven by coincidence and chance. He must despise chaos, or he wouldn't have chosen to mark his skin that way.

So where was the purpose?

Without realising it, Mila was doing something she hadn't done in a long time: making connections between the pieces of information available to her, looking for patterns.

She shook herself for a second, suddenly feeling the need to take notes. She looked around and instinctively opened the glovebox, certain that, being a good policeman, Berish kept a notepad and a pen in his car. And so it was.

Mila glanced through the pad in search of the first available blank page and began to jot down a list.

– Blood
– Bodies

We know there's been a slaughter but we don't know where the victims are. In other words, there's a part of this story we don't know. But why would the murderer hide the bodies when the blood splattered all over the farmhouse tells of the carnage? Either the killer is trying to deny to himself that he's done something dreadful – which would make him one of those psychopaths who is tortured by guilt after committing murder – or else the actual removing of the bodies is essential to him. Enigma's behaviour suggested the latter.

– Angel Tear

From the victims' blood we go to the blood of the killer, which contains traces of a synthetic hallucinogenic drug.

– Tattoos – Numbers

Numbers are tattooed on Enigma's body and Karl Anderson's wrist. This led to the surmise that the two knew each other.

But what did the tattooed figures signify?

Enigma used them to give us geographical coordinates, which led us to a place where there was nothing except a piece of meaningless graffiti.

– Fishbone

What could it mean? Does it actually have a meaning or is it just a prank?

Enigma had uttered the same word during their brief meeting in the Grave, making her deeply anxious.

Mila wrote:

– *Fear*

Karl Anderson was afraid of Enigma, that's why he had taken his family to live on a remote farm. But, if you looked at it more closely, the Andersons had made themselves uncontactable, not inaccessible. Like me, Mila thought, when I moved to the lake. And this train of thought led to another item for her list:

– *Renounce technology*

Mila had refused to use a mobile phone or a computer with internet because she didn't want anyone from the past being able to contact her. Only this hadn't worked, because Shutton had gone to the lake in person.

Enigma had done the same. He'd gone to find the Andersons. The thought made her shudder and she finally wrote:

– *Old computers*

The Andersons had given up technology, while Enigma surrounded himself with old computers. There was a pattern but no logic.

Mila lifted the pen from the page and studied the list.

Nothing new had emerged, only a vague summary. Suddenly overwhelmed with frustration, she tore the page from the notepad and screwed it up angrily.

What am I doing? I should drop all this. So why am I still thinking about it?

The reason was all too evident.

Because that bastard tattooed my name on himself.

The fact that her name was permanently written on the skin of a murderer drove her insane. It was like being locked up in that cell in the Grave with him for the rest of her days.

How on earth did I get involved? She sensed that this business would become an obsession, and that frightened her. She wasn't like her old colleagues on the force; she couldn't leave her cases behind her. That was the real problem, her biggest flaw when she'd been working at Limbo. Missing people had followed her everywhere. She'd searched for them in the faces of passers-by, their interrupted lives were constantly in her thoughts, preventing her from living her own life fully.

Now the ghosts had returned. And yet she was sure she had left them at Limbo, in the maze of the Bureau of Missing Persons with . . . *her old life.*

Mila froze. She'd suddenly felt something – a tickling at the base of her neck. An idea had flashed before her but not long enough for her to grasp it. She opened the screwed-up paper again and read the last line.

– *Old computers*

She remembered the scene at the department, with computer technicians busy extracting data from the now obsolete units collected by Enigma.

'Amazing how much life we throw away,' Delacroix had said. So she added another item to her list:

– *Old life*

The reason Karl Anderson knew Enigma was connected to the past, a previous life. And where do people hold their lives? In technological items. That's where we store everything. It would be interesting to look into the Andersons' old computers and mobiles to see if there was any reference to their murderer. Unfortunately, that was impossible because they had got rid of all their technology.

Enigma has tattooed my name on himself, she repeated. He knows me but I don't know him. But what if that wasn't the case? What if there was a connection? The only way to find out . . .

' . . . is to search my own past,' she said out loud without realising it, giving substance to the latter part of that revelation.

'I was as quick as I could be,' Berish said apologetically, getting into the car, soaked from the rain, proudly handing her a bag with a picture of Ganesh with doctored sunglasses.

'What's the matter?' Berish asked, alarmed by the look on her face.

'We have to go back,' she told him. 'The answer is at Limbo.'

8

The Waiting Room.

The sanctuary-like place where photos of missing people were preserved. Final snapshots before their lives vanished into thin air. Smiling portraits, captured during joyous or carefree moments: a birthday party or an excursion, a graduation, a christening or a wedding. Because, Mila remembered, we take pictures of ourselves in times of happiness. And nobody could imagine that they'd end up on one of these walls.

She looked around and noted that in a year nothing had changed. The office was deserted because no police officer wanted to work on these cases. Too many mysteries and too few hopes of success.

'So what are we looking for?' Berish asked in an uncooperative tone.

Mila approached. 'Listen, I want you to go home.'

'You're joking, aren't you?'

'No,' she said. 'I'm not authorised to share the information in my possession: I'm just a civilian now.'

The truth was that she was afraid for him so didn't want to involve him. She was certain that Joanna Shutton was trying to offload the responsibility for her own failure and that there would soon be a hunt for a scapegoat in the department. Heads would roll, and Mila didn't want Berish's to be one of them.

'You're about to get yourself into a hell of a mess, aren't you?' he said.

'I have no authority to carry out investigations, but something's nagging at me and I need to put it to rest – you know what I'm like.'

'And what if someone finds you here? I'm in charge now, so I'd be involved anyway.'

'I can always claim I still had the office keys.' She smiled. 'And that I had a pang of nostalgia.'

'It's a crime,' Berish said sternly.

They looked at each other for a while without speaking.

'What about Alice? And the Indian dinner?'

She'd forgotten about it. 'Fuck,' she said, suddenly consumed with guilt.

Berish had no intention of rubbing it in. 'What's her schoolfriend's name?'

'Jane.'

'I'll call her mother and tell her you've been delayed.'

Mila gave him the number. 'Ask to speak to Alice. She'll be pleased.'

He shook his head in disapproval. 'Hitch hates vegetables, so I'll have to eat them all,' he said as he left.

Once alone, Mila went to the desk that had once been hers. The only light that illuminated the room came from there. She sat at the old terminal. Limbo's resources had always been limited. There was no glory in missing-persons cases, the majority of which remained unsolved. So the bureaucrats couldn't see any point in spending money on resources.

Mila switched the computer on and waited for the operating system to load. It took a while but then it immediately opened on the case archive.

She thought about what to key into the search engine, then typed the word 'tattoo'.

As expected, hundreds of links appeared, most of them relating to missing people who had got a tattoo at some point in their lives. A tattoo was a precious lead, especially in abduction cases: an immutable detail was more useful than an old photograph, especially when it came to identifying the victim after many years, by which time their physical appearance could have changed.

She refined the search by adding the word 'numbers', which reduced the list by three quarters but still there were too many cases. She looked at some of the photos in the files but the tattooed numbers were rather ordinary, since people tend to impress a date on their skin that's important to them. She needed another element to filter the results. Entering 'Angel Tear' allowed her to narrow the selection even further, although she was afraid that this detail would take her off course. Cases of disappearance involving drug dealers and addicts appeared.

That's when it occurred to her to type in 'fishbone'. The search engine yielded just one case. Here we go, she thought, let's see who you are. As she opened the file, she saw the gaunt, pimply face of a seventeen-year-old. It was circled in red in a picture taken at a school party, a summer ball. Timmy Jackson, a paper cup in his hand, was the only one who wasn't smiling. He made an odd impression on Mila. Because of his skinny build, height and slouching posture, they called him 'Fishbone'.

The police report, drafted after the notification by Vita Jackson in early March, seven years earlier, stated that the teenager had inexplicably vanished one Wednesday morning. His mother had gone to wake him up and found his bed empty.

Mila knew that this was what she'd been looking for when she read that Timmy had a prior conviction for vandalism and damage to public property after he'd defaced a metro carriage with spray paint.

A graffiti artist, she thought, remembering what they'd found in the abandoned refinery. According to his mother's statement, Timmy had been a quiet boy before being arrested and nobody would have imagined he'd turn into a vandal. He spent all day shut in his room, constantly on the internet, playing 'some kind of video game'. According to her, her son had become a hooligan because of the negative influence of someone he'd met online.

That meeting could account for his disappearance, Mila thought. Minors were often lured by malicious adults who took advantage of the anonymity of the internet.

Enigma immediately came to mind. That was why Karl Anderson had eliminated technology from his life. *He'd met his murderer online.* Only his decision hadn't been enough to save his and his family's life. Had Timmy met the same fate as the Andersons? She carried on reading.

Searching Timmy's room after he went missing, his mother had found blue pills, which turned out to be LHFD or 'Angel Tear'. Moreover, she said her son had tattooed a number on his calf using a ballpoint pen and a lighter. This had triggered violent arguments in the family.

'He's been missing seven years.' Mila thought again about the probable age of the graffiti on the refinery wall. It had been a long time ago and Timmy's case must have been worked by someone else at Limbo back then or she would have remembered the name Fishbone.

There was a final note in the file: at Vita Jackson's insistence, the police had seized her son's computer to analyse it and track his internet acquaintances. If anything had been found, it would surely have been included in the report, but the only thing recorded was an alphanumeric code. Mila knew what that meant: Fishbone's computer was still stored at Limbo.

The underground room was an eerie place. Low ceilings, only a row of basement windows on the west wall, but the light from them was blocked by panels of plywood. You had to be careful walking down the stairs because some genius had put the light switch next to the bottom step.

Mila reached out for the switch and the neon lights blinked, came on and revealed a maze of shelving units. The Limbo archive was divided into two areas. The first contained case files too old to feature in the database and the other, at the far end of the room, held the exhibits. These weren't pieces of evidence so much as items that had belonged to the victims and which it was hoped might provide a starting point for an investigation. You held on to everything just so you could discover something, because a search would often run aground before it even got under way.

Mila always thought the cops who worked in Homicide were the lucky ones. In addition to evidence found at the scene – blood, DNA and other organic materials, maybe even a murder weapon – in the majority of cases they had the corpse. Those who investigated missing-persons cases often had nothing at all to go on.

She headed for the far end of the room. The box with Timmy Jackson's belongings was on the top shelf, partly concealed behind similar containers. Mila had to climb up to get it and take care to avoid everything tumbling down on her.

She noticed the cardboard had become soft because of the humidity. Afraid that the bottom would fall out, she decided not to take the box upstairs. Instead she would open it here, on the table used for consulting paper files. She put it down and, before opening it, removed her leather jacket because all that exercise had made her hot and sweaty. She took a letter opener, cut through the duct tape and folded back the flaps.

The box contained an old laptop with stickers of punk-rock groups, a joystick and an early model virtual reality viewer. Mila took them out, put the box to one side and arranged them in front of her on the table. She studied them carefully, keeping her hands on the desk. Then she opened the laptop and plugged it into an electric socket to wake it after its long hibernation.

The first screen that appeared had a message from the departmental technicians, informing her that the computer had originally been protected by a password but that it had been decrypted. She therefore had free access to its contents. There was a photo of Joe Strummer from the Clash, smoking, on the desktop. It was studded with icons of old, obsolete programs, like ones for graffiti artists, that allowed the user to create inscriptions and drawings before reproducing them on a larger scale, and video games that were almost touchingly banal in comparison with those in the present day.

Basically, Fishbone's laptop didn't reveal anything out of the ordinary: it was the computer of Generation X teenager before Millennials came along. In a corner, there was a folder with the department's logo, containing the technicians' report on what they had found in the computer memory. Mila opened it and discovered that, before he went missing, Timmy Jackson had spent much of his time on a nameless video game. She couldn't work out what it was, so she looked for the corresponding icon and found it. It was a simple blue ring. She clicked on it and a warning immediately flashed on the screen: in order to gain access, you had to connect to the internet and plug in the joystick and the virtual reality viewer.

Mila followed the instructions and searched for the department's Wi-Fi connection, hoping the signal carried all the way down to the basement. She found it, typed in the password, praying it hadn't changed. Finally, she managed to connect.

A stylised, revolving globe appeared on the screen.

So is this where you got lost, Timmy Jackson? There was only one way to find out: do exactly what he had done. Mila sat down, positioned the joystick and was about to put the viewer on when the program finished loading and a new screen appeared. A box was flashing beneath the revolving globe, asking for data: latitude and longitude.

Mila gasped, remembering the geographical coordinates indicated by Enigma on his own body.

She lifted her hands from the keyboard and, hesitating briefly, keyed them in. The viewer next to her lit up. Mila picked it up slowly, not knowing what she would see and afraid to find out.

She put it on her head and was projected into an old-fashioned video game. Images and sounds came from a derelict, empty room. The walls and pillars were falling to bits and the floor was strewn with plaster. You couldn't see a great deal because it was night-time and the only light came from moonbeams filtering through the cracks in the ceiling. You could hear the noise of the wind and the odd metallic sound but far away. Despite being three-dimensional, the graphics were rather flat and the resolution anything but high. Not at all like modern video games. Mila wondered how old this program was. She tried to shift the joystick lever and the image before her also shifted.

I'm an avatar, she thought.

In practice, a duplicate of her was moving in that virtual room. She took advantage of this to explore her location. She stepped forward, wandered around the surrounding area and felt an odd sense of déjà-vu. It was as though she'd been here before. It's absurd, she thought. But then she turned and recognised the graffiti on one of the walls in the room. There was an inscription. *Fishbone.*

I'm in the abandoned refinery. How is this possible? What am I doing here? Before she could get upset, she heard foot-steps around her. She turned in the direction she thought they were coming from.

A shadow was coming towards her. A silent figure that was walking slowly. As soon as it stepped into a moonbeam, she recognised it.

Enigma smiled at her.

Mila froze. The tattooed man was naked, like when they had

arrested him. He said nothing and didn't stir for a few seconds. Then, with elegant, mesmerising gestures, he indicated a series of numbers on his body, the way he had done in the Grave. After he'd finished, he smiled at her again and vanished.

Mila removed the viewer. Her return to reality was abrupt and she had to look around for a few seconds to trust her surroundings again. She was still in the Limbo archives but something told her she wasn't safe.

She was still bewildered from her encounter with Enigma. *What did he want from me? Why does he insist on dragging me into this business?*

The screen with the revolving globe was in front of her. Mila had had time to memorise the new coordinates. Only she had a gut feeling: if she keyed the new position into the computer, she wouldn't be able to pull back again. This was the point of no return. But if she didn't press on and find out, she'd be haunted by doubt for the rest of her life.

What do you want me to see, you ugly bastard?

Her fingers shaking slightly, she typed the coordinates into the appropriate box and plunged once again into virtual reality.

It was still night. She recognised beyond the glass wall in front of her the view of the city. Only something was different. It was ghostly.

Where am I? I'm in a flat on the upper floor of a skyscraper. She looked around. The graphic effect wasn't perfect: the outlines of things were blurred and the pixels couldn't keep up with the movements, so the image was shaky or else black holes would form.

The furniture looked elegant and expensive. Mila realised

she was in a large living room with a big plasma TV, a built-in gas fireplace, white sofas and a drinks cabinet. Someone was singing somewhere in the flat. It was a female voice.

She followed the sound down a long corridor and saw a door ajar, through which a beam of light was filtering. She approached, pushed the door open and found herself in an elegant kitchen with black-lacquered furniture. There was a woman preparing food, standing with her back to her. She turned slightly, her shape poorly defined and the outline of her face vibrating, but Mila saw that she was the spitting image of Frida Anderson. There was a crystalline laugh and two fleeting shadows came into the room through another door. The twins, Mila immediately thought. Eugenia and Carla were playing, chasing each other. They ran a couple of times around the table, laid for dinner, then went out again.

Neither mother nor daughters noticed Mila. She wondered what was going on. Even though this was only a digital copy of reality, she was troubled by the sight of them alive when she knew what had happened to them.

That's when she looked down and noticed that she was holding a long, sharp knife.

Oh, my God, I'm Enigma.

An external force suddenly took possession of the avatar and seized control. Without wanting to, Mila was impersonating the killer. Before she could understand what was happening, she saw her arm lift and brandish the weapon.

It rushed at Frida, who was caught unaware, and started stabbing her violently. Plunging the blade into her outstretched hands as she tried to shield herself, then her breasts and her belly. And then her face, stripping off its flesh until she was unrecognisable.

Frida collapsed on the floor, dead, but Mila's avatar kept on stabbing her, over and over again, blood spurting out of her wounds, the splatter covering everything, including the avatar. Mila knew it was all fake and that what she had before her was the imperfect representation of a computer program. Even so, she wished she could stop there and remove the viewer, only she couldn't. She had to see. She had to know. She was sure Enigma wanted to show her what he'd done.

At that moment, she didn't wonder why they weren't at the farm and why there were still technological items in the house, items the Andersons had relinquished. She didn't have time to work it out because Enigma stepped back from Frida and moved on. Mila knew where he was heading. He was looking for the twins.

They were playing hide-and-seek and weren't aware of the danger. One was curled up behind an armchair in her parents' bedroom. When she saw the killer, she stared at him in terror. She didn't have time to scream; instead, she made such a natural gesture that Mila felt as though there really was a little girl before her: she covered her eyes with her hands, as though that would be enough to blot out the horror of the world.

Once again, the knife was raised pitilessly and began to strike at the innocent flesh. More blood but no tears. Once Enigma was sated with the spectacle, he went to her sister.

She was in their bedroom, hiding among their soft toys. She greeted him with a frozen expression but there was something in her eyes that did not understand and was discordant with the situation.

It wasn't fear but, if anything, amazement. It's as though she knows me, Mila thought.

The little girl was about to say something but her head was

cut off in a single blow. Mila moved the joystick, instinctively trying to stop, to save her, but it was pointless. The severed head rolled at her feet, and the vacant eyes met her gaze.

I killed her, Mila thought. No, it was Enigma, but impersonating the killer made him absurdly vivid. In the silence of the room, all you could hear was the murderer panting, the satisfied exhaustion after the slaughter.

Something unexpected happened. A shadow brushed past her.

Look at yourself.

There was someone else there, with her.

Mila touched the joystick, realised she could control the avatar again and immediately looked away from the carnage. When she turned, she saw a pale pink dressing table, the kind little girls play with in the privacy of their room, pretending they're an adult.

Look at yourself.

Mila decided to obey the instructions of the whisper and gingerly approached the dressing table. She looked at herself. For the first time, she met her alter ego and froze.

It wasn't Enigma who was staring back at her in the mirror but Karl Anderson.

Suddenly, the scene vanished and a black veil fell without warning. And while Mila was being disconnected from the virtual world, she managed to say it.

'It was the father.'

9

She was hungry. When had she last eaten? She'd had a frugal, hasty breakfast and then only a couple of coffees for the rest of the day. Moreover, she felt she was coming down with a cold.

She rummaged through the pockets of her leather jacket in search of a tissue but found something completely different in her hand – the photo of Enigma's face, doctored to eliminate the tattoos. The face of a normal man.

For the first time, Mila realised she knew him.

Tell me you're not who I fear you may be.

She was sitting on a very uncomfortable plastic chair in the corridor of the Violent Crime Unit office, the VCU. She was waiting for a response. They hadn't given her the visitor's badge again because her current position was uncertain. They'd have to assess her actions and decide whether there was sufficient data to charge her with investigating without the appropriate authority, and in particular with using the department's resources.

Her fate rested on what was taking place elsewhere, far

away. And on what they would find there. She'd told the Judge where they would find the bodies of the Andersons. Not because she harboured any hope that Frida, Eugenia and Carla were still alive – she knew that was impossible – but for her own sake. Even if that might lead to being charged.

Tell me you're not who I fear you may be, she repeated to herself.

She knew the wait was over when she saw Delacroix at the end of the corridor, walking towards her. As he approached, Mila could clearly see in his face the answers to her worst questions.

'It was just as you said,' he told her.

That's right, the nightmare was real. They'd found the bodies of the Andersons in the flat where they'd lived before moving to the country.

'Karl took them there after killing them at the farm,' Delacroix continued. 'He put his daughters into their beds and tucked them in as though they were asleep. Then he lay down next to his wife's body in the master bedroom, slashed his wrists and died with his arms around her.'

He didn't say this in a cold, detached manner, the way police officers usually did to show they weren't emotionally involved.

'The fact that we didn't immediately find Karl Anderson's blood at the farm should have made us suspicious,' he added, shaking his head.

They'd thought Karl had been murdered first, in the yard, and that Enigma had then headed into the house to finish off the job. They'd assumed that his blood had been washed away by the thunderstorm that had raged over the area for much of the night.

'We'll now have to review the role of the tattooed man,' Delacroix said, disheartened. 'We have to work out if he took an active part in the carnage or if he just drove Karl and the bodies to the flat in town, then went to the abattoir where we arrested him, thanks to the anonymous tip-off.'

That would reduce his sentence, Mila thought.

Delacroix put his hand on his forehead. 'This is all crazy,' he said.

'It's not, trust me,' she replied to reassure him.

He noticed the picture of Enigma in her hand and his expression hardened. 'How would you know?' His tone was aggressive. 'You shouldn't be here. You're no longer one of us,' he added, deliberately trying to hurt her.

He'd always been kind to her up till then and it was understandable that his attitude should have changed after the recent developments, but Mila couldn't accept reality becoming distorted. 'I didn't want to be involved,' she said. 'I don't want your damned case. A year ago I made a decision: to put an end to this shit for ever. You're the ones who dragged me here.'

Delacroix pointed a finger in her face. 'It was Shutton. We didn't want you.'

Mila reacted with a smile. 'Of the two of you, I thought Bauer was the arsehole.'

He didn't comment.

'I'll be happy to tell you people what happened then leave you for ever so you can devote yourselves to your precious case all by yourselves.'

'No matter what you have to say, two little girls and a woman are dead, killed by the one who was supposed to protect them,' Delacroix replied. 'The only person who'll benefit

97

from your contribution is Enigma, whose charge might be downgraded from murder to accessory.'

'I don't think so,' Mila replied, surprising him. 'Because I know who he is.'

In Shutton's office, Corradini, Bauer and Delacroix were again in attendance. Mila was sitting in the middle of the room, while the others were revolving around her, waiting for answers.

'What I saw through Timmy Jackson's computer was a kind of ... of *simulation*.'

'I don't understand,' the Judge said. 'Was it real or not?'

'It was ... Or rather it eventually became real.'

Mila was trying to explain what she'd seen or, actually, experienced. It wasn't easy because as soon as she'd been disconnected against her will she hadn't been able to access the strange program any more.

Karl Anderson had gone into a sort of virtual reality. A faithful copy of the world around us, Mila thought but didn't say out loud; only darker and more ghostly. 'I still don't understand exactly how it works but it's a kind of online video game.'

Bauer rolled his eyes. 'A video game?'

'A game without a name, where you can make your forbidden wishes come true and test yourself and your very nature.'

Timmy Jackson, for example, had found the courage to become a graffiti artist and vandalise a metro carriage.

'A game where you can try to be somebody else,' Mila continued. 'Maybe even a killer. Only I think that over time Karl Anderson truly became the character he was playing.'

How many times had Karl experimented with his fantasy

of eliminating his own family in the video game? There was no way of knowing.

'By the time he realised it, it was already too late.'

Moving far from the city and abandoning technology had been useless. The demon he had been fleeing was inside him.

'I still don't understand Enigma's role in all this,' Shutton said, using the name she herself had banned.

'Karl Anderson met Enigma inside that video game.'

'Why, can more than one person play?' Corradini asked, confused.

Mila was surrounded by deep scepticism. Delacroix was watching her, his arms folded, saying nothing.

'I suppose so. I felt a presence while I was there,' Mila tried to explain.

Look at yourself.

'A presence?' Shutton said.

'Yes. It arrived just before I was disconnected. I can't describe it exactly, but I had a feeling someone was watching me . . .'

'A feeling?' Bauer said mockingly. 'Are we really going to listen to this drivel?'

Delacroix wanted to hear the rest, so gestured at his partner to calm down, then folded his arms again.

'Enigma and Karl Anderson met inside the game,' Mila reiterated. 'Maybe for Karl it really is just a pastime in the beginning, but then he starts doing things he can't explain.'

'Like massacring his own family?' Shutton asked, stupefied.

'Exactly,' Mila replied. 'When Karl realises he's about to cross a dangerous boundary, that he's about to enact in real life what he's only been expressing in the virtual world up till then, he severs all connection with the game. Only to discover that disconnecting himself won't be enough because something has wormed its way inside him. A kind of *temptation*. So he convinces his wife to give up their gilded lifestyle – and especially technology, which, according to his by now warped reasoning, could prompt him to go back into the parallel reality.'

'This is ridiculous,' Bauer said.

Mila ignored him. 'Only Enigma manages to unearth him and, this time, goes to see him in person. While his wife calls the police, Karl goes out to talk to him. Maybe he asks him to leave him alone, or perhaps they don't argue at all. Somehow Enigma persuades him to finish what he started in the game. He hands him the sickle he's taken from the tool shed and watches him go back into the house . . . We know the rest.'

'So according to you, Enigma is some kind of instigator,' Delacroix finally said.

Mila stared at him. 'Enigma looks for people who are brittle, like Karl Anderson.'

'Brittle?' Shutton protested.

'Killers who don't know they're killers,' Mila replied with conviction. 'Those who harbour a dissatisfaction or a weakness. Enigma is able to spot them, intercept them and approach them. He's able to flatter them and knows how to win their trust. Then he persuades them with his lie—'

'What lie?' Corradini asked sceptically.

'That they can be anything they wish. That their fantasies, no matter how sick, are not wrong. That even if inside them they cultivate a secret kernel of violence, there's nothing wrong with them.'

'Are you saying that the tattooed man is innocent?' Bauer asked aggressively.

'No, what I'm telling you is that Enigma is a *whisperer*.'

10

They were called 'whisperers' or 'subliminal killers', and the most famous among them was Charles Manson.

They surrounded themselves with followers and formed 'families'. They killed by using others. They'd choose go-betweens, subjugate them and persuade them to indulge their darkest instincts.

Whisperers had no relation or contact with the victims and didn't touch them. Often, they didn't even know them because it wasn't they who selected these victims. They'd let their followers choose them by delving in their own desires or anger. Whisperers were almost never present at the killing.

Often, they were nowhere near the scene of the crime, and this made them immune to any accusation. They could not be charged or punished. Above all, it usually proved difficult, if not impossible, to identify them. Their goal wasn't death or, paradoxically, even harm. On the contrary, the latter was a secondary consequence to their true motivation.

The power to change people, to turn them from harmless individuals into sadistic killers.

Mila knew this very well since she had already met one whisperer in her life.

This was partly the reason she didn't want to hear about Enigma and this whole business any more. She could admit it now: she was terrified.

She left the department at 11 p.m., hoping never to set foot there again. It hadn't stopped raining since the afternoon. She hailed a taxi and went to the station. The last train was at midnight and she had no intention of missing it.

She wanted to return to the lake, she wanted to get her daughter back.

Jane's mother had told her on the phone that Alice was sleepy and that she could make her a bed on the sofa. Mila had thanked her and said she'd come and pick her up anyway, since tomorrow was Saturday and the girl could lie in as long as she liked.

She arrived at the station reasonably early, so had time for her umpteenth coffee that day. The only open bistro had three customers, all men.

Mila got an Americano in a paper cup and took it to one of the tables by the window. It had no flavour but at least it was hot and she was cold. She was afraid she might have a temperature. It would have been nice to curl up in Alice's blanket shelter and try to sleep, shielded from bad dreams.

She should call Simon Berish and apologise for getting him in trouble with her foray into Limbo, but she wouldn't tell him anything. She was still sure it was better to keep him out of all this.

As far as she was concerned, she would forget about this

day. She wanted to return to her routine by the lake, even if that meant coming to terms with the letter she kept in the kitchen drawer.

The patient's general condition remains incurable.

As she raised the cup to her lips for another sip of dark liquid, Mila realised one of the customers was staring at her.

The man, who was leaning on the counter, immediately looked away. He was wearing a black raincoat, grey trousers and worn brown shoes. He smoothed his straight, greasy hair behind his ears with his hand.

It was a fraction of a second but Mila noticed a dark mark emerging from the collar of his threadbare shirt. She gave a start and gasped. Was it a birthmark or a tattoo on his neck? Did it look like a number or had she merely imagined it?

She kept an eye on the stranger, waiting for him to turn to look at her again. He didn't, but neither did he go away. So she decided to get up and make her way to the platform.

The kiosks and shops all had their blinds drawn and there was nobody around. Mila walked without turning, but with her ears on alert, listening for movement behind her. All she could hear was the echo of her steps dissipating in the vast east wing of the station, as well as the motor of the sweeping machine cleaning the floors somewhere.

She saw that her train was already standing at the platform and boarded the last carriage. She stood by the automatic doors to check if the man from the café was coming, too. It was possible, since this was one of the last trains to be departing that night. But the stranger in the raincoat did not come.

The doors closed and Mila felt a sense of relief. Now she could look for a seat. She was spoilt for choice, since the carriage was empty.

I'll be there in less than half an hour, she thought. She wanted to take off her wet clothes and return them to the cardboard box in the cupboard.

I'm not a hunter any more. I'm a mother.

Even though she hadn't worked for a year, she still had a decent sum of money put aside that could allow her to take over a small kiosk next to a shop on the lake shore that sold bait and fishing equipment. If business was good, she could even get a boat and take tourists fishing for rainbow trout that they would then have embalmed for display over the mantelpiece.

Yes, she could definitely see herself in that role.

For a moment, she remembered what had happened a little earlier, when she'd got scared of the stranger in the raincoat, and she felt embarrassed. She wouldn't have felt like this in the past. But perhaps it was a good sign and meant that her old instinct for chasing after shadows had almost disappeared. That maybe what had prompted her to accept Shutton's invitation was mere curiosity and this had somehow been a positive thing because it confirmed that she was becoming 'human'.

I come from the darkness . . .

As she thought about all this, she could feel her neck and shoulders finally relaxing after hours of tension. She was gently rocked by the motion of the train and the almost hypnotic rhythm of the wheels on the rails. Without even realising it, she let her eyes half close.

A sudden noise made them fly open again. At the far end of the carriage, somebody had flushed the toilet, sending down the drain her reverie about the kiosk by the lake and the fishing boat. Mila waited with trepidation for the toilet door to open, but the occupant was taking their time. She started mentally to count the seconds, waiting for them to emerge. Though she knew that stress had a tendency to slow time down, after four minutes, she decided that the wait was excessive.

She heard the click of the lock and just as the toilet door opened, she thought she saw the individual in the raincoat but it was in fact a young man with very white skin and hair.

The young man with albinism, who wore a windcheater and a shoulder bag, looked like a student. He met her eyes for a moment, then went to sit ten seats away from her, facing in the direction of travel, but on the other side of the aisle.

The train was speeding through the night with the occasional noisy bump when it changed tracks. Mila watched the other passenger closely, afraid she'd sense something that would catapult her back into terror. The sounds of the train, which she'd previously found relaxing, now made the silence between her and the passenger unbearable.

The young man opened his bag and began to rummage inside it. Mila wished she had her pistol on her, but she'd left it at home knowing that she couldn't take it into the department.

Finally, the albino took out a diary, lifted it up to his face and began jotting something down with a pen. He was very focused on writing. Or maybe he was just short-sighted.

A couple of minutes later, the train began to slow down. The young man looked away from his diary and through the window. From the loudspeaker, a pre-recorded voice announced their arrival at an intermediate station.

Mila carefully watched the young man's movements, hoping he'd get off there. She saw him get up again, zip up his jacket and adjust the strap on the shoulder bag. Then he walked past Mila to the automatic door behind her. As he passed her, she smelt a familiar perfume on his clothes. Lily-of-the-valley and jasmine – the same as in Berish's car.

How is this possible? Mila wondered, troubled. She was confused. Was this fragrance a figment of her imagination, a strange coincidence, or was someone sending her a subtle warning?

We know everything about you, you can't escape us . . .

I'm an idiot, she said to herself.

What was happening to her? Why had she become so paranoid? She was well aware of how absurd her behaviour was but, even so, she couldn't keep her anxiety under control.

She decided to change seats so she could see her stop more clearly. She didn't know why, but she was now afraid someone might be waiting for her there. Someone unexpected. She'd soon find out: the loudspeaker announced she had reached her destination.

It wasn't raining and the station was deserted at that time of night. Mila was the only passenger to get off. She looked around. She needed to take the underpass to get to the car park where she'd left her Hyundai that morning.

She looked at the stairs that plunged underground. A yellow light came from the abyss. She tried to assess any potential dangers. She was hostage to her own imagination and no longer knew if she could trust herself.

The train doors closed behind her and the train departed. At this stage, she didn't have many options; it was a choice between spending the night on a bench or facing the demon of fear.

She made her way down slowly. As soon as she'd reached the bottom step, she glanced around. The tunnel was a hundred or so metres long to her right. It was straight except for a bend at the very end. She picked up her pace.

The sound of her combat boots produced a metallic echo, like a hammer on an anvil. She covered the distance, trying not to think about what she might find at the end of her journey, but her mind was too adept at dodging good intentions and presenting worrying scenarios. As she drew closer to the blind spot, she slowed down and listened out for the slightest sound. She turned left and glimpsed the car park exit. As soon as she was out of the underpass, her car came into view – the only one left there at this hour.

The damp chill ambushed her like a spiteful elf, grabbed her face and hands and locked her in a vice from which there was no escape. As she headed to her car, she could feel her lips trembling, her eyes tearing and her breath condensing into small clouds that speeded away from her.

She put a hand in her pocket and took out the keys, which, naturally, she nearly dropped. She unlocked the Hyundai at the first attempt and got in. The inside of the car was so freezing, it made her think of a grave.

She quickly shut the door and started the engine.

She drove to Jane's house with just one thought in mind: to hug Alice. She was sure it was the only way she would get warm and not freeze to death. The chill she felt didn't come from outside but from within her. It was the breath of death. They said that after investigating murders for a while, police officers developed bad breath. Mila had inhaled that putrid air, pregnant with death, for years. Even now, she still had a bitter taste in her mouth and was sure the smell would never go away.

That was another reason she never kissed her daughter. She was afraid the girl would notice it.

Despite what she'd promised herself, Mila didn't hug Alice when she saw her. In any case, the girl knew not to expect it.

'I talked to Uncle Simon on the phone today,' she said, sleepy, as soon as she saw her mother in the hall of the small detached house where Jane and her parents lived.

She didn't ask her where she'd been all day or why she was late. That was Alice's nature. She was still wearing her school clothes and Jane's mother had sat up with her to wait for Mila to arrive. Mila noticed that she did not look pleased but was polite and didn't rub it in.

'Are we going home?' Alice asked.

'Of course,' Mila replied. Where else could they be going at that time of night?

She had been anxious on the drive from the station and nothing had happened in the end. No suspicious encounter, no car following her. Even so, she couldn't stop thinking that the tattooed stranger in the café and the scent of the albino man were some kind of message.

She took Alice to the back seat and fastened her seat belt, certain she would be asleep within the first kilometre, and restarted the car.

As expected, the girl fell asleep almost immediately, head back, leaning against the window, mouth open, her red hair over her face.

Mila was tired but the adrenaline accumulated during the day was keeping her awake. Her eyes were travelling back and forth between the road and the rear-view mirror, searching the surrounding area for any change.

A bolt of lightning flashed behind her in the sky, illuminating the trees and the mountains for a second. That's when Mila noticed a motorbike following them, its headlights off. This confirmed her worst premonition. This time, she hadn't imagined it. It was real.

She took her mobile from the pocket of her jacket to call the local police, although she already knew there was no signal in that uninhabited area. She quickly ran through her options. The road to the lake went through the woods and there were no side roads she could turn into to try and evade her pursuer. Other than taking a dangerous U-turn and driving at the mysterious biker in the hope of catching him off guard, the only thing she could do was to keep driving ahead.

What do you want from me? Who sent you? She already knew the answer but wouldn't admit it to herself.

Her only hope was to head for home and try to get there first so they could barricade themselves inside. At least there was a pistol there.

Mila suddenly changed gear and put her foot on the accelerator. The Hyundai recoiled for a second before the engine gave it a shove forward. Alice gave a moan in her sleep but didn't notice anything.

The asphalt flowed fast in the headlights. Mila kept her hands firmly on the steering wheel: there were some difficult curves on the way to the lakeside road and at this speed she risked losing traction.

She took the first turning too hard, skidded slightly but managed to avoid ending up off the road. She took the next bends with ease because she was focusing on her driving rather than what would happen when she got home.

She checked the rear-view mirror a couple of times but

couldn't see the motorbike. I hope you drive into a tree, you son of a bitch.

Fear and anger alternated in her. She feared for her daughter but was also furious at the prospect of what could happen to her.

At last, she saw their house.

The porch lights had come on automatically, as they did every night. She couldn't tell if it was safe to go there, because all kinds of danger could be awaiting them. But there was no other choice.

The Hyundai raised a cloud of dust as it reached the court-yard. Mila slammed on the brakes. Fortunately, Alice had her seat belt on but the wrench woke her up anyway. Mila got out of the car and checked there was no one behind them as she went to get her. She couldn't hear a motorbike and that at least reassured her.

'Come on, we have to get inside,' she told her daughter, who didn't want to walk. 'Alice, do you hear me? Hurry up.'

With an arm around her shoulders, she managed to lead her to the front door. As she unlocked it, she looked through the glass windows. Everything inside the house seemed in order and there were no signs of intrusion.

As soon as they were in, Mila shut the door behind them, switched on the lights and let Alice collapse on a chair. She gave her a couple of shakes to wake her. 'Alice, listen: you have to help me, OK?'

The girl's eyes opened wide. 'What's going on?'

'We have to check that all the doors and windows are locked.'

Alice realised from her mother's tone that something was wrong. 'What's going on?' she repeated, confused.

Mila didn't have time to explain. 'Stay close to me and everything will be all right.'

She grabbed the poker from the fireplace and they did a quick tour of the house. The back door and the ground-floor windows were locked from the inside and there was no sign of a break-in. They then went upstairs to the bedrooms. Mila switched on the lights: everything looked the way she'd left it that morning. She rushed to the bedside table where she kept her pistol, checked it was loaded and felt much better holding that than the poker.

Meanwhile, outside, there was no sign of the motorcyclist. Mila ran downstairs and again checked the area around the house through the windows. The two lime trees were swaying calmly, like two bony hands dancing in the black sky. The lake and the night were one and the pier looked suspended in mid-air. The shadows among the trees in the forest were deceptive and Mila was afraid that one of them would shift at any minute and reveal a human shape.

The mobile phone had a signal in the house and Mila considered informing the police immediately. Before calling, however, she told Alice to go back upstairs.

The girl protested. 'Why?'

It was safer, although Mila couldn't tell her that. She thought briefly about Frida Anderson and her desperate attempt to keep the twins safe by taking them to the upper floor of the farm. It didn't stop her husband from climbing the stairs and starting the slaughter.

In Mila's case, however, there was a pistol. Her years of experience had taught her that no ill-intentioned person would face a firearm in an open space, and that not even the craziest of them would risk his own life like that.

'You have to do as I say now – is that clear?' she said in a tone that brooked no argument.

Alice whimpered something then did as she was told.

Mila dialled the number of the local police station. A recorded voice put her on hold. Damn it, she said to herself. What could they be doing that was so important they couldn't respond to an emergency call? She hung up and was about to call the department when she saw Alice at the bottom of the stairs again and froze. 'I told you to—'

'I know,' the girl interrupted her, a strange smile on her face.

Mila grew suspicious. 'What's the matter with you?'

'You won't believe it,' the girl replied, her eyes sparkling. 'Daddy's come to pick me up.'

Mila felt her throat constricting. Alice didn't even know what her father looked like. The only time she'd ever seen him he was in a hospital bed and she was too young to remember that.

'Where is he now?' Mila asked, trying not to alarm her.

'Upstairs, in my shelter.'

Mila walked up the stairs, aiming the pistol ahead. The blanket shelter was the only place she hadn't checked. But if Alice wasn't hallucinating, how had an intruder got into the house? She swore to herself that if it turned out to be yet another of her daughter's fantasies, she would punish her like never before. And fuck any guilt trips – she wasn't a good mother.

She reached the top of the stairs, the small landing outside the attic door, and stood facing the shelter made up of blankets clipped with clothes pegs to ropes. The entrance was closed by the red-and-green tartan.

Mila slowly approached, feeling stupid about what she was

about to do. Her footsteps made the floorboards creak. The slightest sound sent a shudder through her. She stretched her hand towards the plaid door, slid her fingers through the gap and felt the soft fabric under the tips. She pulled the blanket aside and aimed her weapon at the same time.

Inside, there was a darkness consisting of shadows and fears – children's stuff, she thought. Now Alice was in for a real scolding. Mila was about to step back when something stopped her.

There was a pair of eyes staring at her in the darkness.

PASCAL

11

She was awakened by the early morning chill.

She opened her eyes and immediately recognised her living room ceiling. She was lying spreadeagled on the sessile-oak floor. What am I doing here? she wondered, the way you do when trying to remember your dreams after you've just woken up.

She couldn't remember anything. She was still clutching her pistol. She tried to sit up but her head was spinning and her whole body was aching. Outside, day was breaking. A rosy glow filtered through the windows and there was a light mist hovering over the lake.

She heard noises from the kitchen. Saucepans, plates and glasses. Alice must already be up, she thought, and I forgot to make breakfast again. And Finz must be back and starving.

She stood up and went to the door. As she approached the sounds, she grew increasingly certain that her daughter and the cat were there, but she couldn't believe her eyes when she stepped into the kitchen.

A powerful stag stood before her.

His coat was glossy and his bearing regal. Mila realised where the chill that had woken her up was coming from: the animal had entered the house through the wide-open back door, perhaps driven by hunger. He lifted his muzzle and his antlers hit the central light fitting, making it sway. He then looked at Mila.

As she gazed back at him, transfixed by the absurdity of the scene, she kept telling herself, 'There's a large stag in my kitchen.' It seemed like a sign.

That's when she suddenly remembered. I've been drugged, she thought, only the animal wasn't a hallucination, nor had the eyes in Alice's blanket shelter been.

She darted towards the stairs, still clutching the pistol. Her sudden movement frightened the animal and Mila heard him skidding on the floor, looking for an escape route, while she headed in the opposite direction.

Despite her dizziness, she launched herself up the stairs, holding on to the railing so she wouldn't fall. Once upstairs, she rushed to Alice's room and flung the door open with a single prayer in mind.

But the bed was empty and intact.

The nightmare was starting to take shape around Mila but she didn't lose heart. 'Alice!' she called out. 'Answer me, Alice!'

She went to the blanket shelter. After all, her daughter often spent the night in there.

On the attic landing, she saw the same scene as the previous night. The hut was there, its entrance closed. She recognised the unmistakable voice of Elvis Presley in the soft babble of a song. Alice fell asleep with the iPod again, that's why she hasn't heard me.

This time, she pulled the tartan blanket aside without a second thought. The iPod was, indeed, among the cushions, playing. But Alice wasn't there. Mila looked around, trying to understand, overwhelmed with despair. Why can't I remember anything about last night?

She went downstairs and wandered around the house in search of clues to help her reconstruct the events. When they came home, the doors and windows were locked – she had no doubt about that – but she hadn't checked the attic. Had he got in through there?

She was beginning to wonder if there really had been an intruder. Could the eyes in the darkness have been a product of her imagination? She was no longer sure of anything, not even herself.

She went out through the back door and ran to the pier. How many times had she warned Alice not to get too close to the lake? Mila wasn't sure what would be worse: if she'd been abducted or if she'd drowned. There was no sign of a body in the clear water, however. She registered this information but it didn't make her feel any less anxious.

I have to calm down, she said to herself. Calm down and think. Because I know what you have to do in these cases. I'm a hunter of missing persons. I speak the secret language of objects, recognise the evil scent concealed in things, see shadows others can't, and follow their steps in the dark world.

I come from the darkness ...

She went back into the house. She had to comb it carefully for anomalies, signs of struggle, bloodstains left by Alice or the possible abductor. Evidence evaporates, she thought. It's absorbed by its surroundings and vanishes for ever.

That's why an initial examination of the location was

increasingly important. And a stag had already contaminated the scene.

As she wandered through the rooms, she heard a phone ringing: her mobile was calling her from somewhere in the house.

Who could it be?

She immediately dropped what she was doing and went looking for the phone. She found it where she'd left it the night before, when Alice had interrupted her attempt to call the police.

You won't believe it. Daddy's come to pick me up.

Her heart filled with apprehension, Mila answered. 'Hello?'

'Good morning, Ms Vasquez,' a male voice said. 'Last night you left a message on the voicemail to report your daughter's disappearance – is that correct?'

Mila was confused. She could remember calling and being answered by a recorded voice that put her on hold but wasn't at all sure she'd left a message. 'Yes, probably,' she said.

'I apologise if we haven't called you back sooner but we have few men available in the winter and at night they go out on rounds to deter burglars who target summer holiday homes—'

'No problem, never mind,' Mila broke in. 'Do you have any news of my daughter?'

'I'm afraid not,' the police officer replied. 'But could you tell me exactly what happened?'

'Someone broke into the house last night and took my daughter Alice away.'

'Can you describe the intruder?'

'No. I must have been drugged, because I can't remember his face.' Only his eyes, she thought. Then, a total blank. She shuddered again.

'And your daughter? Can you describe her?'

Her years of experience had taught her that people who reported a missing relative often provided information that was totally useless to the investigation because they were in a panic or bewildered. Mila therefore concentrated on what she considered details essential to an initial description, stripping them of any adjectives or comments that could distract who-ever was recording them.

'Ten years old, one metre thirty-eight tall, thirty-five kilos, medium build,' she said slowly to allow her interlocutor time to write. 'Green eyes, shoulder-length red hair. Last time I saw her, she was wearing blue cord trousers, a knitted navy-blue sweater, a white blouse and a pair of white Nikes.'

Mila then noticed that Alice's pale-coloured anorak was still hanging on the coat rack in the hall. She'll be cold, she thought, entirely irrationally, as though this was the real problem at the moment.

'Any distinguishing marks?' the policeman asked.

'Sorry, what do you mean?' Mila couldn't see the point of the question.

'Does the little girl have any distinguishing marks on her skin, like a birthmark or a scar? Any missing teeth or fillings?'

'No,' she replied, irritated. Maybe the local police weren't used to missing-persons cases, she thought. 'None of the above.'

'Are you sure?' he calmly insisted.

She was annoyed. 'Sorry, but how would any non-evident distinguishing features be useful?'

'In case we have to identify a body.'

Mila suddenly felt cold. What kind of a manner was this? She'd never come across such an amateur. She was about to protest when she heard something on the other end of the line.

A restrained giggle.

'Ms Vasquez, are you still there?'

There was someone else with him and they were laughing. 'Madam, would you like to complete your statement?' the policeman insisted.

Mila noticed that he, too, was struggling not to giggle.

'Who am I speaking to?' she asked, tensing up.

He replied after a brief hesitation. 'The local police.'

She was beside herself. 'And who the fuck are you?'

There was a vulgar laugh on the other end, then they hung up.

Mila took the phone away from her ear and stared at it in her hand. What was happening? What was all this about?

At that moment, she noticed something written on her right wrist, partly hidden by her jumper. She pulled up the sleeve.

Six numbers. More geographical coordinates.

It wasn't a tattoo. The latitude and longitude were traced with a felt-tip pen. As she processed the information, her mobile rang again, startling her.

She was about to hurl it far away but stopped herself. She didn't know what to do. Her heart was pounding and she was scared of finding out who was on the other end of the line. A part of her was sure she'd hear Alice's voice, that her daughter would appeal to her in tears and that she wouldn't be able to help her.

'Hello . . . ?'

A few seconds' silence. Then a male voice again.

'You have to get out of there.'

It was a different man from the one she'd spoken to earlier.

'Who—'

He cut her off, his tone insistent: 'Now. Meet me at the end of the path leading to the observation point.'

Mila no longer knew whom to trust but the stranger spoke again. 'You must hurry, they're coming.' Then he added, 'Bring the pistol if you like, but leave the mobile at home.'

She didn't walk along the path. She didn't trust it. Instead, she followed the lake shore and kept an eye on the undergrowth, trying to detect any movement or somebody's shadow. Naturally, she had the pistol with her.

She came to the observation point but there was no one there. She looked around. A form popped out from behind a rock.

Mila pointed her gun. 'Freeze!'

It was a man in a red balaclava. You could just about see his eyes and mouth. 'I'm unarmed,' he said, raising his arms in full view.

He was stout and clearly unfit, wearing a pale-coloured, shapeless suit. His jacket, trousers and tie were speckled with grease stains accumulated over time. He had latex gloves over his stubby-fingered hands, which were too small for his build. And flat feet.

He didn't look threatening, only bizarre.

'I want to help you,' he said.

'Take off that fucking balaclava.'

'No. That's my only condition . . . Anyway, if you shoot me or force me you won't get anything out of me.'

Mila considered this for a moment. It was a paradoxical situation. 'Where's my daughter?'

'The customer with the black raincoat, in the bar,' he said. 'The albino boy and then the motorcyclist.'

Mila didn't understand. How could he know about those three? 'Are they a gang?' she asked.

'Actually, they don't know one another. But all three had the same task: to scare you.'

'Why?'

'Because that's what's expected in their game.'

'What game?' she said, irritated.

'I don't know,' the man replied. 'It's like in Monopoly: you pick a card and it tells you what you're entitled to. And that's what you're entitled to, I'm sorry.'

Mila thought. 'Enigma sent them, didn't he?'

Yes, it was the whisperer, she was sure of it.

The man in the balaclava didn't reply. Instead, he asked, 'Can I bring my arms down now? They're starting to ache.'

She motioned to him that he could. The stranger rubbed his sore elbows.

'Thanks.'

'Are you going to tell me what's going on?'

'It's not safe to stay here,' he replied. 'I'll tell you everything I know, but you have to come with me.'

'You're out of your mind. I'm not going anywhere with you.'

'You can call your police friends, if you'd rather. But don't use the phone you left at home. They've hacked into it.'

'Who?' Mila was exasperated.

The man grew evasive again. 'If you go to the police, you won't see your daughter again.'

'And how do you know that?'

'I don't, but it's easy to predict how this will go.'

Mila was bewildered so he tried to convince her.

'Look, he's chosen you.'

He meant Enigma. How could he know about the tattoo

124

with her name? The department hadn't circulated the story to the media.

'You know things you shouldn't,' Mila said. 'Can you prove to me that you're sincere? For all I know, Enigma might have sent you.'

'You're right. I wouldn't be too trusting, either. But think about it: what's the alternative?'

Mila pondered this. She moved the pistol from one hand to the other without taking her eyes off him. Then she pulled her sleeve up with her teeth to uncover her wrist.

'When I woke up a little while ago, I found this ...' she said, showing him the inscription with the geographical coordinates.

'All right,' the stranger said in a tone of concern after taking in the information. 'Let's go.'

This time, Mila decided to follow him.

They headed down the path, she a few paces behind him to keep him within range of her pistol. They reached an unpaved open space where camper vans parked in the summer. There was a beige Peugeot 309 from the nineties. Just like Enigma's green Passat, she thought.

'I'll tell you what we're going to do now,' the man said. 'As you know, I don't want you to see my face. Only I can't drive with the balaclava on: I'd be too noticeable.'

'I'll drive.'

'Yes, except that I don't want to tell you where we're going either.'

'So what are we going to do?' Mila asked.

The man fell silent and it dawned on her what he had in mind.

'I'm not getting into the damned boot. Never. So forget it.'

125

'You have a pistol and I'm unarmed,' the stranger pointed out. 'Or is it my driving you don't trust?' he added jokingly.

Mila looked at him sideways. 'I hope for your sake that your information is as important as you say it is,' she said menacingly before walking towards the back of the car.

Shut up in the boot, Mila tried to register what was going on around her during the journey.

They drove through a residential area because she heard children's voices in a playground. They must also have travelled past an industrial plant, because she picked up a powerful metallic smell that most likely came from blast furnace emissions. Moreover, the man in the balaclava had sneezed repeatedly.

'I'm allergic to cats,' he said apologetically.

Mila thought she might have Finz's hairs on her and that had immediately brought Alice to mind. She was afraid of what her daughter must be going through and wished she could bombard the stranger with questions, but refrained from doing so.

It took them almost an hour to reach their destination. They parked in a place where there was no sound. Then Mila heard a rolling shutter closing and the man came to free her. When the boot was opened, she saw that they were in the garage of a house.

'Are you all right?' he asked, proffering a latex-gloved hand to help her out.

'Fine,' she replied without lowering her guard, since she had no idea where they were.

'I'll lead the way,' the man said.

Shortly afterwards, they stepped into an informal living

room and were greeted by a strange chemical smell, like plastic or burnt rubber, perhaps the stench of a tyre set on fire.

Mila heard the door close behind her and realised it was too late to run away, so she studied her surroundings instead. The house looked like a detached family house in the residential suburbs of a large city, although she couldn't be sure of that because the windows were blocked with heavy black curtains. The furniture was simple and, above all, looked as though it hadn't been used for a long time. There was no sign of any other residents.

'This way,' the host said.

He took her to a door at the top of a flight of stairs that led to the basement.

Mila hesitated. She had no wish to end up like those victims that foolishly trust their murderer so much they even follow him to the trap he's set them.

'You still have your pistol, don't you?' the man said, noticing her hesitation. Then, without waiting for an answer, he preceded her down the stairs.

When she'd reached the bottom step, Mila realised she was in a basement that served as a storage and laundry room. But amid shelves crammed with furnishings and crates there was also a camp bed and a kitchenette. A strange collection of work overalls were hanging in a see-through closet, next to elegant suits, youthful T-shirts and old coats. Mila was surprised to see also a dressing table with a mirror, polyester heads for holding various wigs and a shelf full of cosmetics.

This was where her eerie host lived. An odd choice, given that he had an entire house at his disposal upstairs. She then turned and saw a threadbare armchair in front of an old iMac with a cathode-ray tube and bright-blue trimmings. She remembered that this machine had been revolutionary when it had been put on sale, back in the late nineties. This modern antique must still be in working order, though. On the table where it stood, along with a mouse and a keyboard, there was also a joystick and a virtual reality viewer. Everything you needed in order to access a nameless game, Mila immediately thought.

'Welcome,' the man in the red balaclava said. 'And now you can ask me anything you like.'

'Where's Alice?'

'I don't know,' he promptly replied. 'But even if I can't guarantee it, I'm almost certain she's all right.'

'What makes you so sure?'

'Because your daughter is the stake.'

That game again – what did it mean?

He removed his discoloured jacket and laid it carefully on the camp bed before sitting down, his gloved hands on his lap, as though waiting. 'Second question . . . ' he said.

'Who are you?'

'My name wouldn't be any use to you,' he replied calmly. 'And nor would seeing my face. Anonymity is a little neurosis of mine, I hope you don't mind.'

'That rather depends on who you are,' Mila said. 'I could shoot you in one leg and force you to show me your face. Bullets can be very persuasive and I'm sure you'd tell me everything in order not to bleed to death.'

'You could, but you won't . . . '

Mila fell silent. A few seconds of silence lapsed.

'All right,' he said, since she wasn't relenting. 'Years ago, I decided to erase all traces of my identity. Even if I told you my name or showed you my face, you'd find no reference in any archive or database. Besides, no one's ever seen me and no one knows me: I severed all contact with the rest of the human race a long time ago.'

Exactly like Enigma, Mila thought.

'How do you avoid being caught on security cameras when you're out and about? Do you become invisible?'

'I often change my appearance and dress up to blend in with the crowd,' he said, indicating the dressing table with the make-up and the closet. 'I don't leave fingerprints or DNA,' he added, raising his latex-gloved hands. 'It's not easy, you have to be disciplined, but I can assure you: it can be done.'

Mila was struck by his level of dedication.

'I have no mobile phones or electronic equipment that could allow someone to locate me or reach me. The only technology I use dates back to the nineties, when multinationals weren't yet permitted to insert tracking cookies in their products.'

Mila thought about his car and his computer. Enigma, too, used similar precautions.

'It took me a long time to achieve this result,' he finally boasted. 'But in the end I succeeded . . . I don't exist.'

'So what shall I call you?'

'Pascal.'

'Pascal,' Mila echoed. 'Like the programming language, I suppose,' she said, tapping into her scant knowledge of IT.

The man didn't comment, so Mila decided to cut to the chase and pointed at the viewer.

'Tell me about the nameless game.'

The man in the balaclava went to put the kettle on the electric stove in the kitchenette.

'The game is called Two,' he said. 'But some people call

it Elsewhere. It was put online shortly before the start of the new millennium, that's why the graphics aren't as sophisticated as those in modern video games. But I find its vintage appearance makes it particularly beautiful, don't you think?'

Mila did not reply. It wasn't relevant.

'In any case, it would be an unforgivable error to consider Two as just a game, because in the beginning it was primarily an extraordinary utopia.' Pascal's tone was nostalgic. 'The creators of Two chose to remain anonymous and there are lots of legends about them. What's important, however, is that they imagined a parallel world, a virtual place that was an exact replica of the real one, and where you could carry out a revolutionary social experiment . . . Elsewhere was supposed to be a dress rehearsal for a future world, a way to test new models and new formulas for making humanity progress.'

Pascal appeared convinced by what he was saying, but Mila still couldn't work out whether he could really help her or was just a lunatic.

'What was amazing was that everybody could be a part of this great dream: as soon as you accessed Two, you had to get yourself a job where you could earn money, buy a house and acquire possessions – all in the game. It couldn't be just any job but one that would benefit the growth of this new society, because the rule of Two was that each person's well-being should benefit all. You could have a career, success and accolades, but only on condition that it would be beneficial to others . . . There was no unemployment, class war or social injustice in Two.'

'Could you be anybody or did you absolutely have to be yourself?'

'You'd pick an avatar and were free to play any role you

liked. But the lesson everyone soon learned was that honesty was always the best policy.'

Mila did not believe humans could be honest. Everyone lies to get the upper hand, she thought.

'Two was created to facilitate the interaction among individuals. You met, got to know one another, and there was a constant exchange of ideas and suggestions. It was equally extraordinary on the relationship front. You'd often date and even marry people who were different from the ones you had beside you in real life. But there was no malice in it, it wasn't on a par with cheating on someone. As a matter of fact, many people's real-life relationships became stronger precisely because in Elsewhere they'd learn things about themselves they hadn't even imagined.'

The kettle whistled and Pascal took it off the ring. He poured the hot water into two cups and dropped in teabags.

'The first time I went into that world was through the computer of a missing seventeen-year-old,' Mila said, remembering Fishbone. 'All I saw was a ghostly city.'

'Two used to have houses, cars, shops and bars. You could go to the cinema or dancing, buy yourself a nice dress or stand for elections. Many artists – painters, musicians and performers – would showcase their new creations in Two. There was no crime, no selfishness, no cruelty: anyone who didn't abide by the rules would end up excluding themselves from the game of their own accord . . . People were happy.'

'So what happened?'

Pascal's voice grew sad. 'While trying to imagine the perfect society, the creators of Two forgot to take into account an essential variable of human nature.'

'Evil,' Mila said, pre-empting him.

Pascal nodded. 'Excluding evil from the outset was a mistake and they realised it too late. They should have foreseen it to allow the parallel universe to create antibodies to defeat it on its own. In the long run, the world we had generated out of thin air was no longer attractive. People no longer aspired to be perfect. On the contrary, they wanted to feel free not to be ... And so the Two attendees gradually lost interest and started to leave the game.'

Mila realised that, as well as being nostalgic, Pascal was disillusioned.

'Those who used to travel in Elsewhere now prefer to surf any social media network,' he said with bitterness. 'You think you're interacting with others but you're actually surrounding yourself with false friends just so you can peep into other people's lives and put yourself on show – without modesty, without shame ... You're no more than a hamster in a cage that spends its time looking into the cages of other hamsters.'

The man in the balaclava checked that the tea had brewed sufficiently, then handed her one of the cups. Mila accepted it.

'According to the department's reports, the "Shutton Method" is working beautifully,' he said. 'Crime rates are falling significantly, murders are drastically diminishing and people feel a lot safer ... '

Mila remembered Berish saying something similar, and the data rattled off by the Judge during her brief speech in the operations room just before the raid on the abandoned refinery.

'Instead of being pleased with these results, we should ask ourselves a question: what happened to evil?'

Mila was afraid of the answer.

'The internet is a huge sponge: it absorbs what we are,

especially the worst in us. In real life, we are forced to adapt to coexisting with others, reach compromises with our nature, and accept laws and conventions. Sometimes, we even have to wear a mask, but that's inevitable: otherwise, we couldn't be a part of society . . . While on the net we feel liberated from all this hypocrisy but it's only an illusion: they've simply left us alone with our demons. And Two is proof of that.'

'What happened after people left the game?' Mila asked impatiently.

Pascal leaned against a beam and loosened his tie. 'After a time when it had been deserted, Elsewhere started to be populated again. Picture a no man's land that's an exact reproduction of the world in which we live, a place where people can do things they wouldn't do in real life for fear of the law but also out of shame, because they'd incur social judgement. Think of a place without any rules, where the only god is selfishness and the only law is the survival of the fittest.'

Mila could easily picture it. A world that frightened her. 'Yesterday, while I was exploring Two through the computer of someone called Fishbone, I felt a presence around me . . . Then it spoke and said: Look at yourself.'

Pascal dismissed it. 'Everybody was watching you.'

'The other players, you mean?'

'Enigma invited them to the performance, so they all saw it. I did, too. That's how I found you.'

Mila wasn't at all convinced by his explanation and studied Pascal. 'I think the numbers on my wrist are saying that if I want to find Alice I must return to the game . . . '

'I'm afraid so,' the man replied, also looking at her. 'It's the only way you'll understand how it really works.'

*

133

Pascal went to the iMac and switched it on. 'Don't worry, I have an encrypted connection so no one will be able to locate us,' he reassured her, sitting at the terminal and typing hurriedly on the keyboard. 'I'm creating an avatar for you.'

Mila still didn't know if she'd agree to this. Meanwhile, the man in the balaclava kept typing away.

'Favourite song?'

'What?' she asked.

Pascal looked up at her. 'I have to be able to get you out at any time and the music is a kind of safety rope.'

'Last time I came out by myself.'

'Trust me, this time will be different.'

'In that case, anything by Elvis Presley,' she said, remembering what Alice liked.

'The King is always an excellent choice,' he said approvingly.

Once he'd finished, he stood up to fetch a large map of the city and unrolled it in front of her. 'I'd hazard a rough guess that the coordinates they wrote on you mean that you'll enter Two through here . . . '

He showed her the spot.

'Chinatown,' Mila immediately said, remembering the excitement, smells and colours of that district.

The man with the balaclava handed her the virtual reality viewer then gave the back of the chair a couple of taps to let her know everything was ready and that it was now up to her.

'You know you can't take that with you, don't you?' he said jokingly, indicating the pistol.

'Aren't you coming with me?'

'I don't think the invitation is for both of us . . . And I won't even be able to see what's going on down there, so you'll have to pay attention.'

Mila placed the weapon on the table, next to the computer. She figured if Pascal had really wanted to kill her, he would have found a way by now.

She sat down. On the iMac screen, the Two portal appeared, with the stylised spinning globe and the box for keying in the latitude and longitude. Pascal entered it on cue by reading what was on her wrist.

'One final detail,' he said. He rummaged in the pockets of his trousers then opened his gloved hand in front of her. There was a small blue pill in his palm.

'Angel Tear,' Mila said, recognising it. 'Why do I need a synthetic drug?'

'As you saw with your own eyes when you were there, the graphics in Two are almost elementary.'

Mila could remember the low definition, with missing pixels and black holes, blurred outlines and flat images despite the 3D.

'Many players take the Angel Tear so they can have a more realistic experience.'

Mila had no intention of taking the pill. 'I'm out to investigate, not play.'

'There's a component of Elsewhere that's not written in the program codes: an emotional, sensory experience that can't be explained . . . And if you don't fully understand what I mean, you'll never get into Enigma's head and you won't understand what his design is.'

'Design' was a word used by criminologists and profilers, Mila thought. I don't know who Enigma is but neither do I know who you are, Pascal: anyone could be under that balaclava. Once again, she looked, undecided, at the pill lying on the latex surface. 'Earlier, you said that Alice was the stake.'

'Enigma has started a new game,' Pascal said. 'And you're his opponent.'

'What's my game?'

'I'm afraid you'll have to discover that on your own.'

Mila took the blue pill and threw it into her mouth without a second thought. 'I'm ready,' she said. 'Let's go.'

12

It was very different from the first time.

She was propelled into a black tunnel. It was a fast trip – under a second – but there was a feeling of total disconnection: she no longer sensed Pascal next to her and the sounds and smells of the basement also disappeared. At the end of the tunnel, she landed in an alleyway between two buildings, and could see a deserted street at the bottom of it. It was night-time, which surprised her since, in the real world, it was morning.

The visual effect was astonishing. The reality around Mila was still artificial but the overall image was surprisingly sharp. Edges that had been blurred on her previous trip were now better defined and the movements were more fluid – like being in a vial. Above all, the colours were no longer faded but so bright they were almost disturbing.

Thanks to the Angel Tear.

Mila looked at her hands. They were well-cared for, elegant, with tapered fingers. She'd never had hands like these.

She usually trimmed her nails very short and her skin was damaged. Strange. She was curious to see the rest of herself.

She noticed a window a metre away from her and approached so she could see her reflection in the soot-coated glass pane.

She was wearing dark clothes, like she usually preferred. Her eyes travelled up to her face, the memory of seeing Karl Anderson's image still vivid. Her hair was fluttering in the wind slightly and the skin on her face was smooth. Mila was surprised that the avatar Pascal had created for her was a familiar stranger. She couldn't put her finger on it at first. She was like her, only different.

That's not me, she thought. That's Alice as an adult.

The resemblance was natural, after all, but Mila often forgot how much she and her daughter had in common, and she found this thought painful.

At that moment, her attention was diverted by a feeling she'd already experienced in the past: a light mist was falling on her face and the back of her hands. She looked up at the jet-black sky. It was raining. It was a fine drizzle and she could feel it clearly on her. Only then did Mila understand what Pascal had meant.

There's a component of Elsewhere that's not written in the program codes: an emotional, sensory experience that can't be explained . . .

The sense of moisture was another trick – the most successful so far – of the Angel Tear.

She headed to the top of the alley and, once on the road, looked around. Chinatown was a long enclave of short buildings towered over by the city centre skyscrapers. These were usually lit-up giants, but in Elsewhere they seemed like monoliths made of black Bakelite.

The colourful shop signs of the Chinese district were switched off and the red lanterns were swaying like sad vestiges of the past. A gloomy silence weighed heavily over the place, which wasn't the one she remembered and enjoyed going to. It was as though it had been contaminated with something evil.

A breeze blew past her, brushing her leg. Mila turned to look but there was no one there. Once again, as in the Andersons' flat, she had the definite impression of not being alone.

'Everybody was watching you . . . ' Pascal had said.

She walked down the road. She could see nothing but darkness through the shop windows. There was that breeze again, only this time it spoke to her.

'*Save yourself*,' said the same gentle voice she'd heard in the room of the twin girls.

Mila froze and looked around to see who'd spoken. There was no one. She did, however, notice a change in front of her.

There was a cinema at the end of the block. The door opened and a shadow stretched onto the pavement. She decided to go and see what it was.

Inside the building, there was a long, dark corridor, and a clock was ticking somewhere at the back.

For a moment, she was afraid to continue. It's all pretend, she reminded herself. It's silly to dither. No one can really hurt me, she repeated to herself as she walked into the darkness. And yet the less rational part of her had a foreboding.

There was a room at the end of the corridor. It reminded Mila of the living room in her grandmother's house. The ticking sound that had led her here came from an old grandfather clock. There was a velvet sofa and armchairs, a rug with geometrical patterns and a floor lamp with a burgundy shade that emitted a warm light. A sideboard and coffee tables strewn with porcelain figurines. A lit cast-iron stove and a rocking chair. The wallpaper with pretty red flowers was so realistic Mila approached and tried to touch them.

The flowers moved and she pulled her hand away.

There was a painting hanging on the wall. A country landscape. Like the wallpaper, the painting wasn't at all static. The water flowed peacefully in the stream and the grass was waving, caressed by the wind.

In the middle of the field, there was a beautiful black rose.

Pascal had mentioned artists who used to experiment with their talent in Two, and Mila thought this might be a digital display. She was tempted to pick a flower, but the painting dissolved and turned into a mirror. She recognised her avatar but didn't like what she saw behind her in the reflection.

The rocking chair moved as though somebody had sat on it. The light bulb under the lampshade flickered and the light dimmed. The cast-iron stove went out and she suddenly felt bitterly cold. These few dissonances were enough to make her realise that everything was the same as before and yet *everything* was suddenly different.

The reflection of her avatar was sucked into the frame by a liquid abyss. Mila turned around. The flowers on the wallpaper had wilted. She realised she was no longer alone, or perhaps she never had been.

Save yourself . . .

No, she thought. It's too late, they're already here. A human-shaped shadow came away from the wall and took three steps towards her, then stopped. It did nothing, said nothing. But its very presence was frightening, and Mila knew who had sent it.

'Have you got something to say to me?' she asked to break the oppressive silence.

No reaction.

'Come on, I'm here . . . What do you want from me?'

She was getting annoyed but only because – even though she didn't want to admit it – she could feel fear swelling inside her.

Nothing happened for the next few seconds. Then it was all too quick. The shadow leapt with the elegance of an ancient predator and was immediately on top of her. Mila didn't have time to get out of the way or run. The shadow grabbed her. *None of this exists, it's not real. It's just inside my head.*

She was lying down but not on the ground: she was floating in mid-air. The shadow was over her, and two black eyes emerged from its head. The same eyes she'd seen in the blanket shelter.

The shadow spoke. '*Mummy . . .*'

It was Alice and she was frightened. Her child's voice was in contrast with the monster's mouth. Mummy – Mila had hated that name so many times.

'*Mummy, help me, please . . .*'

My daughter is calling me. My daughter needs me.

The missing-persons hunter, the woman with no empathy suddenly felt something inside her after many years. An unfathomable turmoil. How was this possible? Was it what her daughter was feeling at that moment?

Suddenly, someone threw their arms around her neck.

It's Alice, she's clinging to me, she wants me to save her.

Shame she couldn't respond. She would have liked to tell her that she wouldn't abandon her.

But then the embrace grew tighter and tighter. It wasn't happening just to the avatar but to *her*. Mila realised she was struggling to breathe.

She was wrong. It wasn't her little girl hugging her but the monster strangling her.

She could clearly feel a claw clenching her throat. The creature was too strong for her. This isn't really happening, she kept repeating, but she was choking.

She looked to her left and saw a face in the mirror from earlier. A young woman with delicate features and youthful skin. With blue eyes framed by a pair of glasses and long blonde hair in a ponytail. She was in the same condition as Mila. Supine, turning blue in the face, a stranger's hands around her neck. She was pleading for help with her eyes. There were purple bruises growing larger on the throat of the young woman in the mirror, a network of broken capillaries spreading all the way up to her temples. She was dying, and Mila realised the same thing was happening to her.

I can't die, not now.

'*Mummy . . . Don't go, Mummy . . .*'

I'm sorry, Alice. If I stay here, I'll certainly die. I have to get out of here.

'*No, Mummy, please, stay . . . Stay with me . . .*'

I'm sorry, I'm sorry, I'm sorry . . .

When she saw the young woman in the mirror yield to the fury of her killer, she knew that it was over for her, too. As she clung to her last breath, she recognised a gentle, distant piece of music . . . The unmistakable voice of Elvis Presley singing 'You Don't Have to Say You Love Me', soon afterwards dominated by Pascal's voice . . .

*

'Breathe,' he said.

Mila opened her eyes and found herself lying on the floor in the basement.

Pascal was over her – exactly like the shadow that had attacked her – and was shaking her.

'Breathe,' the man with the red balaclava repeated, slapping her breastbone with the palm of his hand.

Only then did Mila remember that she could still do it. She opened her mouth and inhaled as much air as she could. It took her a while to catch her breath. There were black dots floating before her eyes. At last, she understood the danger she'd been in.

She pushed him away, sending him sprawling. Then she grabbed the pistol she'd left on the table and aimed it at him. 'What did you try to do to me?' she roared with anger, her voice hoarse.

Pascal raised his arms but remained where he was. 'You'd stopped breathing,' he said.

'You wanted to kill me,' she said accusingly, while Elvis kept singing.

'It wasn't me,' he replied. 'It was the drug.'

Mila could still feel the grip of her assailant and put her hands to her throat. Much to her surprise, it wasn't hurting. How was this possible?

The music stopped – the one that was now just in her head, too. She realised she'd made a mistake: if the rain effect in Two had been so realistic, she should have imagined what would happen with the rest. Fiction could become real.

There's a component of Elsewhere that's not written in the program codes . . .

'You can die in Two,' she said, furious. 'Is that what you wanted me to discover for myself?'

'The mind sees what the mind wants to see,' was Pascal's answer. 'The sensation is as real for the victim as for the attacker: that's why Two is successful . . . Sex, violence, pain, death: you can experience everything. And the extraordinary thing is that you're breaking no laws: no one can punish you.'

Mila thought of Karl Anderson. She'd wondered how a father could brutally murder his own flesh and blood. The answer was simple: he was already familiar with the feeling. And he liked it.

'It's a fairground for fucking maniacs,' she said without moving the pistol away from Pascal.

'Please, calm down—'

'I'm not going to calm down.'

'If I hadn't been with you, you would have suffocated,' he replied, getting up, a hand on his sore back. 'Instead, you should thank me.'

Mila felt her knees give way. She was dizzy and about to collapse on the floor. Pascal rushed to her and caught her just in time.

'You're still very shaken,' he said, then gently removed the pistol and led her to the camp bed.

Mila let him.

'The game spoke to you, didn't it?' he asked.

'Yes, I think so,' she replied. 'But I still don't understand what it's all about.'

'Don't worry, you will,' Pascal said, then went to get a small bottle of water. He was about to take a sip but then handed it already open to Mila instead.

She accepted it and it was like an act of peace. 'Now I know how it works, send me back down there so I can finish the game.'

'You don't know a thing and you can barely stand. Besides, you can't take another pill so soon: that stuff turns your brain to mush, you know?'

She didn't care: Alice needed her.

'If you go back there now you wouldn't know where to go. You must first find other geographical coordinates in the real world.'

Mila remembered the numbers they'd written on her wrist. She realised it had been a welcome gift, that the rest wouldn't come free.

'You'll have to focus on what you saw while you were there,' Pascal explained. 'The details of the setting are crucial for understanding what your game is: they're like the pieces of a puzzle, each of them has a meaning.'

'Alice talked to me – does it mean she's still alive?' she immediately asked.

'I'm sorry to have to tell you this, but I think your daughter was a red herring: she was there to distract your attention from more important things.'

Nothing was more important for her, but maybe Pascal was right. Mila took a large sip from the bottle and thought. 'In the beginning, a voice warned me about what was about to happen . . . '

Save yourself.

'You won't find any friends there,' was his response.

'And yet it's true: I also sensed its presence at the Andersons' home,' she insisted. 'There was nothing threatening about it, on the contrary: it was a positive presence, not sure how to explain it. It was like . . . *a ghost.*'

Pascal shook his head. 'I can't explain it either but sometimes, in Elsewhere, you see and hear things that aren't there because they're a product of your mind – especially if you're under the influence of LHFD.'

'And then, of course, there's the monster and the girl . . . '

'Describe them.'

'The former is made of shadow, I only know it tried to strangle me . . . But the girl looked like a student, maybe because of her glasses. I saw her in the painting that was also a mirror because her face was a reflection of my face . . . '

'A painting, a student . . . ' Pascal summarised.

'There was some old furniture and a black rose,' Mila added. She felt dizzy again, propped herself with her arms on the camp bed and closed her eyes.

Pascal brought her another bottle of water. 'You have to drink to flush out what's left of the Angel Tear. And you should also try and get some sleep.'

'There's no time,' she replied, forcing herself to react. *Alice has no time.* 'Besides, I'm too wound up to sleep.' That too was because of the drug, she thought.

'There's a remedy for everything . . . ' Pascal said.

He searched his pocket and produced another little pill.

'Niacin is the antidote of LHFD: four grams to snap out of the trip.'

Mila swallowed it with a gulp of water. He then laid his latex-gloved hands on her shoulders and made her lie down on the bed. She put up no resistance, she had no strength for it.

'When you wake up, you'll think a lot more clearly,' he said. 'And we'll concoct a plan to free your daughter.'

Mila felt her eyelids grow heavy. In the mist of her senses, everything became rarefied. She glimpsed Pascal removing his red balaclava. But before she could see his face, her eyes closed completely.

146

13

She had barely fallen asleep before waking up again after a few seconds. At least so she thought. But then she discovered that she was in the dark and that the only light filtering through a small window in the basement was coming from the moon. It can't be night-time already, she thought.

She was cold. She sat up and tried looking around. 'Pascal . . . ' she called out.

There was no reply.

Only then did she notice that the iMac, the strange wardrobe, the make-up and the wigs had all gone. The food supplies had also been taken away. The basement was empty, as though the man with the red balaclava had never lived there. In fact, as though Pascal had never existed.

Mila shook her head, confused. Another one of Enigma's tricks? If I don't want to go mad, I have to get out of here.

She put on her leather jacket and climbed the stairs to the dining room of the small detached house. The curtains were still closed and she recognised the chemical odour of burnt plastic she'd smelt on coming in. I never would have imagined this, she thought.

In the garage, there was no trace of the old beige Peugeot 309 in which she'd arrived with her mysterious guide. She shut the door behind her, immediately looked back and realised where the stench in the house was coming from: the upper floor had been devastated by fire. It no longer seemed strange to her that nobody lived here.

The house was surrounded by a tall hedge. The gate at the end of the path was secured with a padlock and Mila had to climb over it. As she had imagined, the house was in a residential area on the outskirts of the city. All the houses looked alike: with a garden, a lawn, a sloping roof and a garage. There wasn't anyone around: unless Mila had slept more than twenty-four hours, it was still Saturday.

I have to get out of here, she repeated to herself, chilled and huddling in her leather jacket. She looked for a car she could 'borrow' among those parked along the tree-lined street. She remembered Pascal's words about how vehicles could be traced. She hadn't yet decided if she trusted that man but, either way, spotted an old grey Beetle.

She picked up a brick from the ground, approached the car and hurled the brick at the window on the driver's side. This triggered an alarm that echoed through the street. Mila quickly slid her arm into the cabin and released the safety lock. Then she got in and started to fiddle with the wires beneath the steering wheel.

Less than thirty seconds later, the siren stopped shrieking and the engine started. As she quickly drove away, she decided that there was only one place she could go.

*

'There's no one I can trust,' she said as soon as the door opened.

On the threshold, Simon Berish stared at her in disbelief. He was wearing an elegant white shirt and giving off a perfume that was too heady – lily-of-the-valley and jasmine again. He could see at a glance that Mila's situation was serious.

'Go for a walk and come back in fifteen minutes,' he said before closing the door again.

Instead, she huddled in a dark corner on the landing and waited. The door opened again shortly afterwards and a woman emerged; Berish appeared, and the two of them kissed, then she turned to leave. From where she stood, Mila could see her face. She was very attractive. She finally understood who that heady scent she'd smelt on Simon belonged to. On Simon and on the albino boy on the train, she recalled with a shudder.

'I knew you'd get yourself in trouble,' he said in a scolding tone after letting her into a softly lit room. Hitch came looking for cuddles, but Mila wasn't in the mood.

'Where's Alice? Did you leave her with a friend again?' Simon added while taking two goblets with red wine into the kitchen to put them in the sink.

'Alice is missing, Simon. They've taken her away from me.'

He froze, still holding the glasses. Mila let herself drop on the sofa and dug her fingers into her hair. He went to her.

'What happened?' he asked sternly, forcing her to look him in the face.

She lifted her head and met his hard look. She deserved it. This whole mess was her fault. 'Enigma is a whisperer.'

Incredulous, Berish stared at her in silence for a few seconds. There was something Mila had never told him, so she took advantage of the moment and told him now. 'My daughter's father and I met thanks to a whisperer, ten years ago.' And it was as though he'd brought them together. 'Alice was the gift of evil. And now the darkness has come to get her back.'

She could see that Simon wanted to comfort her, to hold her, but he knew that Mila didn't like physical contact. 'We're going to discover new horrors, aren't we?' he asked in a faint voice. 'And what happened at the Andersons' farm is only the beginning . . . '

Mila didn't know what would happen; she'd only once had dealings with a subliminal killer and was still scarred by it. Should they expect a spiral of violence? She couldn't rule it out. 'I want to make something very clear straight away,' she said sternly. 'I know you care a lot about Alice and would do anything for her, but I must warn you: the cost is very high. So I'll understand if you don't feel up to it.'

'Damn it, you know me,' he snapped. 'How could I stand back? Don't worry about me: I don't have a wife or children, I have nothing to lose.'

'Doesn't your girlfriend, the one who was with you tonight, mean anything to you?'

'I know what I'm going up against,' Simon replied.

Mila got up and grabbed him by the shirt. 'No, you don't know, and you can't even imagine it. Last time, the team came out of it in pieces: I remember well how we were at the start of the investigation, and above all what we became afterwards.'

She could never forget the marked faces of her colleagues, or what had happened. The missing little girls, the graveyard of arms. The horrors came one after the other without their being able to stop them. Every time they thought they were

150

close to a solution, they discovered that it was a blunder and they were forced to start again. Even Alice's father, the criminologist who led them, had been tricked.

'The whisperer's goal isn't just to show you his amazing plan of death and destruction,' Mila said emphatically, sarcasm masking her fear. 'He wants to get inside your head . . . Whatever you do, however prepared you may be, you can't stop him. Trust me. And even when you think it's over, it isn't: the horror around you disappears but he's still here,' she said, touching her temple.

He has the power to change people, she remembered, because she could still hear the manipulator's persuasive voice inside her.

'Nobody escapes a whisperer,' she concluded gravely.

Mila didn't notice a small tear breaking out of the fortress erected inside her a long time ago and now running down her cheek. Berish looked at her. 'I won't let you face all this alone.'

Berish took out a bottle of Scotch and Mila spent the next hour bringing him up to date on the Enigma case, revealing the details she hadn't wanted to give him earlier, which she was supposed to keep to herself. She told him about the tattoo of her name, found among the numbers, and that was where it had all started. She explained how she'd come to discover Karl Anderson's guilt and the reasons why he'd rejected technology, and that the connection between her and this issue was concealed in her past at Limbo. The story of Timmy Jackson, alias Fishbone: she'd taken her first trip to Elsewhere through the seventeen-year-old's laptop, stored in the archive among the possessions of the missing people.

She tried to be specific in order to help him understand the game fully, often resorting to Pascal's words. The geographical coordinates as access keys; a place where it was always night-time, dominated by evil.

'How come the department hackers have never come across it?' Berish asked at one point, sceptical.

'From what I gathered, you can't access Two with more recent computers: you need a model that dates back to when the game was created, between the late nineties and the start of the new millennium.'

'Digital obsolescence,' Berish commented, referring to the phenomenon by which the speed of technological evolution presented a problem of access to data stored in past hardware. 'People from my generation have lots of cassettes they can't listen to any more. Progress should preserve memories, but instead it relegates them to oblivion.'

Then came the hardest part of the story for Mila: the account of how Enigma's men had followed her to the lake and abducted Alice. Finally, she told him about the previous twelve hours. The meeting with the stranger in the red balaclava and latex gloves, the basement and the second trip to Two to play the whisperer's game and get her daughter back.

'Angel Tear, a parallel world, a mysterious character who first says he wants to help you then disappears . . .' Confused, Berish was pacing up and down the room.

'He told me to call him Pascal,' Mila said. 'Like the computer programming language. I think he's a hacker.'

But at that moment Simon wasn't interested. 'There's only one thing to do: you have to tell Shutton.'

'No,' she stated vehemently, getting up from the sofa.

'She's the one who dragged you into this, so she owes you. You'll see, she'll bring all the department's resources together.'

'No way,' Mila replied. 'As far as they're concerned, Alice is just another missing-persons case, and you and I know what happens to those files: after a while they get forgotten.'

'You can't tackle this thing on your own,' he said, trying to convince her.

'Why not? How long did I spend dealing on my own with adults who'd vanished into thin air and children who seemed never to have been born? And how many times did I succeed in bringing them home?'

'You know perfectly well why not! Because you're not lucid, you're not objective, you're directly involved in this case ... This way you condemn Alice, do you understand that, yes or no?'

Mila slapped him without even pausing. She wasn't angry with him, she just didn't want to hear things she already knew.

Berish fell silent. Hitch looked up at them, trying to work out if everything was all right.

Mila should have apologised, told him she was sorry. Instead, she searched in her pocket and took out the doctored face of Enigma without tattoos that she'd been given at the department.

The face of an ordinary man.

'This is what the whisperer really looks like,' she said. 'Look at him carefully and tell me what you think ... '

Berish took it and looked at it. 'Why doesn't Shutton broadcast this image to the public?' he wondered. 'Someone might recognise him.'

'I asked her the same thing. She said they don't want to fuel the myth of Enigma. But the truth is that the department don't want to risk another embarrassment after Karl Anderson. They'll leave things as they are: Enigma will get life in the Grave for incitement to crime and aiding and abetting, and everybody will soon forget about him . . . That's why, as far as the Judge is concerned, this case is closed.'

At last, even Berish understood. 'All right, we'll do as you say.'

After her outburst, Mila poured herself another glass of Scotch. She realised her hands were trembling. 'I know what I have to do.'

'Where shall we start?' he asked, seemingly forgetting about the row and even the slap.

Mila felt uncomfortable about what had just happened but tried to keep her focus. 'On my way here, I was thinking again about the elements of my second trip to Two: Chinatown, old furniture, a black rose . . . A killer who likes to strangle his victims and, finally, a blonde female student wearing glasses: I get the feeling I've seen her before.' Mila omitted the part about the ghost who had advised her to leave, because she didn't know if it had really happened or if it was just her unconscious trying to warn her.

Save yourself.

Berish filled a bowl of water for Hitch and got ready to go out. Mila made him leave his mobile at home and they took the stolen Beetle. Berish clearly couldn't understand the reasons behind so much caution, but she was grateful he complied.

'I'm sorry about your date,' Mila said while Berish drove.

'She's a clever woman; she understood the situation straight away.'

She was glad Berish had someone at his side. In the past, she'd feared he would get too attached to her: if she'd had to push him away, their relationship would have suffered from it. Fortunately, he had never made that kind of move, and so had spared her the trouble of explaining one more time to someone she cared about that the feelings he and the rest of humanity considered normal were for her an unfathomable mystery.

Even so, something had changed in the past few hours. She couldn't tell if it was related to the emotional impact of Alice's abduction or the Angel Tear effect.

In Elsewhere, Mila had felt something.

An incomprehensible turmoil when her crying daughter had called her.

Mummy, please, help me . . .

She couldn't stop thinking about it and it frightened her.

To be on the safe side, they abandoned the Beetle in the square outside the train station. There was a van with volunteers giving out used clothes to the homeless. Mila took advantage and partly changed her outfit. She was copying Pascal's behaviour. She swapped her leather jacket for a black duster coat and the roll-neck jumper for a hooded top, also black. She and Berish then took the metro and headed to Limbo.

Lea Mulach's face was one of the many in the Waiting Room. But it took Mila less than twenty minutes to find it among thousands of missing persons.

A first-year university student studying Oriental languages, Lea Mulach had vanished into thin air in spring 2011.

'According to the other girls in her dorm,' Berish read in the police report, 'Lea was supposed to meet a young man and go to a cinema in Chinatown that Saturday evening. She never got to the cinema.'

Mila wasn't wrong; she did remember her. 'Her disappearance was a mystery for about a year, until the Violent Crime Unit took the case away from me.'

The VCU – which included Bauer and Delacroix – dealt with serial killers, spree killers, mass murderers and all killers who were driven by a motive that couldn't be attributed to normal criminal logic, which almost always had money as a goal. Instead, the motive that animated these kinds of killers resided in the darkest, most perverse recesses of the human mind.

'Lea was listed among the victims of a serial killer,' Mila remembered. 'As a matter of fact, they said she'd been the first.'

During the two years following Lea Mulach's disappearance, two other girls had gone missing. Students, blondes, wearing glasses.

'The three of them didn't know one another, but the last two had a mutual friend: a young man called Larry, a very nice guy,' Mila said. 'They'd met him on UniC.'

'UniC' was an acronym that stood for 'University Campus' and was the most popular social network among the nation's students.

'Larry would post photos on his page, with his friends, his dog and even his grandmother,' Mila said. 'He claimed he was studying law and liked rugby. Both victims were courted online for a long time, in true gentlemanly fashion. After they went missing, it turned out to be a fake profile: the "Larry" in the photos was a model in advertising and was unaware of everything.'

'The UniC killer,' Berish remembered.

The advent of social media had made life easier for serial predators. Modern maniacs, Mila thought, could hunt under the cover of anonymity and, above all, without risk. In the past, if you didn't want to be caught, you had to stalk your prey from a distance, study her habits, her movements. But now, serial killers had access to all the information they needed to stage a suitable performance. And this was provided by the victims themselves. So all the killers had to do was take on the appearance of their dream man.

The mind sees what the mind wants to see, Pascal had said.

As usual, Berish wasted no time. 'Why was Lea Mulach added to the list of victims if there was no evidence she'd been chatting with Larry?'

'Because her profile corresponded to that of the killer's favourite victims: a blonde student with glasses,' Mila suggested. 'The VCU people needed a third victim so they could elevate the status of the killer from occasional to serial, that's why they took the case away from me.'

Mila was very familiar with this convention. One day, criminologists had ruled that a serial killer could be defined as such if he performed the same ritual or modus operandi at least *three times.*

'But if Lea Mulach is dead, how come her picture is still on the Limbo wall?' Berish asked.

'Because, unlike the other two students, her body has never been found.' Mila thought about the sadness of this situation: some missing persons were destined to roam in the void without peace.

And yet Lea had been the first in the killer's series.

'If we'd found the body,' Mila added, 'we'd immediately have had confirmation that there was a killer ... ' And the other two victims might have been saved, she thought bitterly.

'How did the other girls die?'

'Strangled,' she replied and unconsciously put her hand on her throat: her brain hadn't yet processed the memory of the shadow man's claw squeezing her carotid. 'The bodies were both found abandoned on the edge of a road.'

Strangling belonged to the 'violent mechanical asphyxiating syndromes'. Unlike garrotting and choking, it didn't use tools such as ropes, hoods or cushions. It was carried out with bare hands. The killer didn't resort to a mediating object because he wanted to experience the pleasure of feeling someone else's life ebb away in his fingers – their breath weakening, their heartbeat slowing down until it stopped. Physical contact was essential and, as well as cruelty, this illustrated a certain determination. In fact, not everyone realised what strangling a person consisted of. The victim thrashing about in despair, the release of the sphincter muscle, eyes protruding from their sockets. For normal people, this was a dreadful sight, but it could be extremely exciting for some psychopaths who would achieve orgasm this way.

Mila came up behind Berish to read what else that was written in the file. 'The series of murders by the UniC killer stopped in April 2013 . . . Strange,' she said.

They both knew that the compulsion to kill couldn't be controlled, let alone independently stopped by the serial killer. The need to repeat the modus operandi was unstoppable. For it to come to an end, an external cause was necessary.

'Our man could have ended up in jail for some other crime,' Berish suggested. 'He might be serving a sentence for having snatched an old lady's bag and is just waiting to come out so he can get back to work. Or else the good Lord decided to bring his trip to hell forward.'

'I don't think he's dead,' Mila said. 'There's still something we don't know about this story.' Otherwise, why had Two made her experience Lea Mulach's death?

'It says here that a suspect was arrested in 2013,' Berish read on the screen, leaning on the desk.

'Where? Let me see . . . '

'A certain Norman Luth turned himself in to the police and gave a full confession of all three crimes.'

So he'd been the one who gave the VCU the tip to connect Lea to the other two, Mila thought. Otherwise, they wouldn't ever have noticed. 'No one informed Limbo. Why?'

But Berish hadn't finished, and the reason immediately became apparent. 'It seems the man provided details only the killer could have known . . . And despite that he was cleared.'

They looked at each other, incredulous.

He'd been supplied with a cast-iron alibi by a priest.

14

Father Roy lived in a suburb made up of red-brick houses that had sprung up around a large steel factory.

The houses dated back to the glorious era of the steel industry, when town planners longed to build communities, and workers were seen as an elite to be rewarded with a lifestyle, as well as generous wages. But then the world recession in the construction industry had destroyed every dream, every utopia. These incomplete cities had quickly become ghettos for imprisoning political failure as well as the ensuing social resentment.

To drive there, Mila and Berish had taken an anonymous saloon from the department, normally used for stakeouts and therefore untraceable.

Through the windows, the view was desolate. Houses up for sale or else long abandoned. Children playing in the street like stray dogs on a tedious Sunday morning. Men loitering at the corners of blocks of flats, trying to read the future in the bottom of a beer can. Behind the windows they saw women grown old too soon who had by now stopped hoping – you could immediately tell from their expression, dulled by poverty.

Father Roy lived in the rectory next to the church. Beyond it they could see an old garage beneath a flat with a TO RENT sign, while in front of it there was a garden with a rusty slide and a couple of swings that swayed, solitary, in the wind. The reason there were no children playing was obvious from the signs on the surrounding walls.

Insults and threats were a clear invitation to leave.

Berish pulled up on the opposite side of the street. 'So we have an understanding,' he said to Mila. 'Follow my instructions to the letter: remember we're here unofficially and if he kicks us out, we won't get another chance to find out more.'

The plan was for Mila to go and talk to the priest alone. Berish thought that the presence of two people might make Father Roy feel outnumbered and therefore defensive.

Everyone wanted to talk to Simon Berish, Mila remembered. She trusted him blindly: he was the most experienced agent in the department when it came to interrogations.

He reached into the inside pocket of his jacket, removed a small black imitation leather case and unzipped it all the way, revealing what police called 'the informer's kit'. Two invisible earphones and as many pinhead-sized radio mics, each connected to a transmitter with a 12V battery able to cover a two-hundred-metre radius. It was used to communicate with undercover operatives in the field, allowing them to receive precise instructions based on what their interlocutors were saying.

Berish helped Mila to put the kit on, then did the same himself. 'This little jewel has just one drawback,' he warned her. 'Sometimes, the signal gets lost, so keep away from radios, TVs and microwaves.'

Mila indicated with her eyes the signs on the rectory walls. 'Do you think he'll be willing to talk?'

Simon shrugged. 'Just play your part and make sure you deliver the lines we prepared: if that doesn't work, then at least we'll have tried.'

Mila stepped out of the car and, as she crossed the road, mentally summarised what she had to say.

The door was covered in rotten egg residue. Mila had to knock several times before she made out a form behind the frosted glass.

'Who is it?' a shrill voice asked suspiciously.

She tried to be reassuring. 'I'm conducting a private investigation and I need your help. Can we talk?'

'I've nothing to say,' he replied.

Mila turned to Berish and he nodded from behind the windscreen. As agreed, Mila crouched and slid a banknote under Father Roy's door, but only halfway. She stood staring at the protruding part, like a banner in the wind. After a while, it was absorbed from under the door. The door opened, although only a little. 'Hurry, come in.' Mila slipped through the gap and the door shut quickly behind her. It was dark inside and her eyes took a little time to get accustomed.

Meanwhile, the slight voice kept talking. 'They won't leave me alone, I can't show my face outside without someone throwing something at me. The postmen get beaten up and now there's no one left who's willing to deliver my shopping.'

Mila finally focused on the man in front of her. A sixty-year-old with an untidy beard and dishevelled, thinning hair.

He was wearing a threadbare dressing gown open on a prominent belly, and a pair of slippers. He gave off an unpleasant smell – cigarettes and cabbage – that also stank out the house.

'Get away from there,' he told Mila. 'You're too close to the window.'

She followed his instruction, even though the curtains were closed. She looked around. It wasn't a nice place, messy and with rubbish everywhere.

'I've done as I was told: I'm attending therapy and I've been toeing the line for months, but it won't do much good for as long as I stay here,' the priest mumbled, heading to the kitchen. 'Come, we'll be more comfortable next door.'

They went in and he immediately sat in a wrecked armchair in front of a television that was off, huddling in what Mila imagined was his favourite spot. He took a cigarette from a packet lying on one of the armrests, put it between his lips and lit it with a match.

Mila chose one of the chairs by the dining table, which was cluttered with dirty plates and old newspapers. 'Aren't you even going to ask my name?'

The priest was sucking his teeth, making an annoying sound. 'Frankly, I'm only interested to know if there are more banknotes like the first one.'

'It depends on what you can tell me.'

'These damned hormones keep me awake most of the night and make me constantly listless, so I don't know if I'll be able to answer your questions correctly.'

Mila connected the words 'therapy' and 'hormones' and understood the reason for his high-pitched voice. Some called it 'chemical castration' and it was offered to some sexual predators as an alternative to jail.

'As I was saying, Father Roy, I'm conducting a private investigation.'

'Never mind the "Father" – just call me Roy,' he said, dismissing formalities with a hand gesture. 'The Roman Curia has suspended me *a divinis*, but until they reduce me to a layman, I can still live here.'

'All right, Roy,' Mila replied, to make him happy. 'I'd like to talk about Norman Luth.'

The name dropped between them like a stone in a pond. Father Roy stayed silent, perhaps assessing the situation, trying to gauge if it was worth his while answering.

Mila took another twenty from her pocket and placed it under the dirty glass, in full view.

'I never touched Norman,' Roy said, defensively. 'I met him when he was already an adult.'

'I'm here about another matter,' she reassured him. 'I'd just like to know why you provided him with an alibi when he'd already admitted killing three female students.'

'I didn't provide him with any alibi, I only told the police what they should have known, anyway. That Norman Luth couldn't have been involved in those murders because he was hospitalised in a psychiatric facility.'

'Luth admitted it of his own accord,' Mila replied, familiar with the story. 'Because he knew he had aggressive tendencies that derived from his inability to relate to others, women in particular. He wanted to be in control of his own demons, only it was his demons that controlled him.'

Roy inhaled his cigarette smoke deeply. 'So you're claiming Luth was the real killer.'

'I read the confession. It was too detailed . . . Luth described meticulously the way he strangled them with his bare hands and the feelings he experienced . . . He mentioned details that had never been circulated by the press: only the police and the real murderer were aware of them.'

'So that gives us two possibilities,' Roy said ironically, revealing a yellowed smile. 'Either Luth is the true culprit or else he was a clairvoyant.'

'Someone I used to know would say that you can cheat anybody except yourself,' Mila replied, quoting her daughter's father. 'Luth wasn't a pathological liar: he knew who he really was, he knew he was capable of terrible things, like brutally killing an innocent person . . . That's why he committed suicide before he was released. And do you know how it happened?'

'He put a plastic bag over his head,' Roy said promptly.

'That's right . . . He experienced a death like the one he reserved for his victims.'

Roy took one last drag from the stub in his hand, then crushed it in the heaped ashtray next to him. 'If you know and are so sure of everything, why have you come to see me?'

As he lit another cigarette, Mila slid another banknote under the glass. 'You were Luth's friend and know about his past . . . I want to understand how one becomes a serial killer.'

Berish checked the time: it was nearly nine o'clock and the conversation between Mila and Father Roy had been going on for twenty minutes. Judging by what he could hear on the radio, his friend was managing quite well. She had highlighted the controversial aspects of the event immediately and was now getting ready to pick up on the slightest inconsistency in the priest's story.

If Enigma has brought us all the way here, there must be a

good reason. He wants us to see something or reveal a fact no one has ever unearthed.

'Norman came from a normal family,' the priest was saying. 'His father had a button factory and his mother was a housewife. He was an only child. At primary school, he was a polite little boy and a good learner; as a child, he never gave any sign of the mental disorders that would eventually ruin his life.'

The priest was using cigarettes to try and make his voice harder, Berish thought, but the result was ridiculous. He sounded like an old clown. The kind that visited children's nightmares.

'I get the feeling you're about to tell me some terrible drama wrecked this idyllic picture,' Mila said provokingly.

Careful, Berish mentally warned her. If you start doubting his every word, there's a danger he'll tell you only what you want to hear. He's already admitted that he's only doing this in the hope of grabbing a few more banknotes from you. Nevertheless Berish refrained from intervening by radio for the time being. He didn't want to distract her.

'When he was nine years old, an event took place that would change everything,' Roy confirmed. 'Norman came home from school and discovered that his father had got back from work early and that his parents were arguing in the living room. The little boy hid so he could listen to what they were saying . . . In a nutshell, Gregory Luth was accusing his wife of repeatedly cheating on him. She initially denied it, but in the end gave in and admitted everything: except that, instead of showing contrition, she told her husband she was glad to have humiliated him by going with other men. Blinded by rage, Gregory put his hands around her throat and strangled her.'

This last detail was not negligible, Berish thought, since the UniC maniac resorted to the same method of killing. Everything fit perfectly and corroborated the theory that Norman Luth was the true culprit, although there was still the issue of his alibi for the three murders.

Berish figured Luth must have found a way of temporarily absconding from the psychiatric hospital. Or perhaps someone had helped him leave then return.

'After Gregory had killed his wife, he noticed his son. He ordered him to pack a suitcase because they were leaving. Norman obeyed and, shortly afterwards, got in the car with his father. After less than eight kilometres, as they were crossing one of the bridges that led out of the city, Gregory stopped the car in the middle of the traffic, got out and walked silently to the parapet.'

'Good God!' Berish involuntarily exclaimed, thinking about the devastation of the poor child who, in such a short space of time, had witnessed the violent deaths of both his parents.

'Who took care of Norman after that?' Mila asked.

'His closest relatives did for a while, but then they offloaded him onto social workers, with the excuse that this way he'd be given better psychological support after the tragedy he'd experienced . . . In the end, the judge ruled that he could be fostered and potentially adopted.'

'Only he couldn't adapt to any family, right?'

'No one wants a child who saw his father kill his mother before taking his own life,' was the priest's bitter reply.

Berish knew he was right. They were called 'the children of horror' and were marked for life by the sins of those who had given birth to them.

'Norman ended up in a psychiatric institution for minors. In reality, he was of perfectly sound mind, and was parked there only because there was nobody willing to take responsibility for him.'

That's absurd, Berish thought. They had assumed that Norman was irreversibly marked by what he'd experienced. And so, after spending time with the mentally ill, he'd become mentally ill, too.

'How did you meet Norman Luth?' Mila asked.

'When he turned eighteen, the doctors decided he could be released.' The priest gave a sarcastic snigger. 'The only place where he could go and live was the house he'd inherited after his parents' death.'

Unbelievable, Berish thought. To go back to the place where his tragedy had begun can't have been very good for him.

'Norman didn't want to stay there . . . So, one day, he read in the paper that I was letting a two-room apartment above the vicarage garage and came to see me.'

Berish shifted in his seat for a better view of the building he'd noticed on their way here, at the bottom of the alley that skirted around the playground. Once again, he noticed that there was a flat on the upper floor with a TO RENT sign.

If no one was living there, then it had probably been Norman Luth's last home. It might be worth going to take a look.

Mila was pleased with how her interview with Father Roy was proceeding: it didn't even feel like an interrogation. Since Berish hadn't yet intervened, it meant he was pleased, too. Meanwhile, the priest coughed hard and spat a lump of phlegm into the already-used tissue he took out of his pyjama pocket.

Mila continued with her questions. 'How long did Norman live in the apartment above the garage?'

Father Roy looked up at the ceiling, trying to go back in time. 'From 2011 to 2013, the year he died.'

It was the exact time frame during which the students had been murdered. Moreover, 2011 was the year of the probable killing of the young woman who would subsequently be classified as the UniC murderer's first victim, Mila thought. Luth and Father Roy's acquaintance coincided with Lea Mulach's disappearance and was yet further confirmation of the theory she was developing.

'As I've already mentioned, every now and then, Norman would decide to get himself admitted into a psychiatric hospital in the hope that doctors would restore order to the mess in his head. He'd spend some time there and, when he'd had enough, he'd come back to me. The periods of his admittance coincide with the three murders by the UniC killer. Do you think that's pure chance?' He laughed provokingly.

Mila had formed quite a specific notion of how Norman Luth could have dodged the hospital's surveillance, gone and killed his victims, then returned. She suspected Father Roy himself had helped him. Norman hadn't mentioned his accomplice in his confession: was that out of gratitude or just fear? One thing was certain, however: one day, Luth's psychiatric disorders, linked to the experience of violent death in his childhood, had met the urges of a children's predator. A lethal association. Maybe that was precisely the mystery Enigma wanted her to discover. Only, Mila didn't have documented proof of that yet and didn't know what Two had to do with this.

'There's one thing I really don't understand, Roy. Since

you insist Norman was innocent, I find it odd that you're not asking yourself a question . . . '

'What question?'

'Have you never wondered how come the series of crimes Luth confessed to stopped with his suicide in 2013? Since then, no blonde female student with glasses has been murdered . . . '

The priest said nothing and gave a faint, involuntary smile. Mila had followed Berish's instructions to the letter and waited until this moment to pick up on an inconsistency. She thought she had cornered him.

'Norman was an obsessive writer, did you know that?' Father Roy said, a total non sequitur. 'He filled one journal after another . . . I kept a few – would you like to see them? Who knows, you might find something useful for your investigation.'

Mila couldn't tell if this was just a way of diverting her attention or of syphoning more money. 'Bring me these journals,' she said, adding a fifty to the stack of banknotes under the dirty glass.

The priest paused briefly, apparently studying her. She didn't like that.

'They're in a closet,' he said, getting up from the armchair. 'Come, I'll show you.'

Mila stayed where she was. He saw her hesitation.

'What, changed your mind?' he asked, amused at having made her nervous.

'Not at all: let's see them,' she replied, sniffing, even though she didn't have a cold.

Berish stood at the foot of the staircase outside the garage, which led to the apartment above. On the radio, he'd heard

Mila throw her most important card on the table: the fact that Luth, as well as knowing details he shouldn't have known about the murders, had put an end to the UniC killer's feats by taking his own life. This move meant almost the end of Mila's performance, so he didn't have much time left for a search. But then he heard the priest mention Norman's diaries.

'Okay, give him more money and go see,' he said into the mic. 'Meanwhile, I'll take a look at the apartment above the garage.'

Mila sniffed. The signal that she'd understood and would proceed.

Berish climbed the stairs and reached a white door with a small window, only you couldn't see through it because it was obscured by a yellow blind. He probed the lock and opened it with an ordinary credit card. A strong, pungent smell immediately swept over him. He looked down and saw a dead rat on the carpet. He decided to leave the door open behind him to let some air in.

The two-room apartment was actually one large room partitioned by a folding wall, which was now completely open. The front section had a single bed. At the back, there was a kitchenette and a door, probably to the bathroom. There were clothes strewn around the place, as well as tins of food, porn magazines and all the rest. Given the layer of dust over everything, Berish deduced that they had been there for a long time. But the confirmation that these items belonged to Norman came from a framed photograph on the bedside table. A smiling little boy in his parents' arms, on an outing to the seaside.

Berish forced himself to forget about the dead rat and the stench, and started rummaging around.

*

The priest walked down the corridor dragging his slippered feet, which made an unnerving sound. Mila followed him reluctantly through the maze of the dark, smelly house. The religious paintings and crucifixes on the walls instilled no sense of peace or comfort. A noise from the floor above put her on the alert: it sounded like footsteps. She looked up at the ceiling and saw a little dust fall from the timber beams. For the first time since she'd been here, she got the feeling they weren't alone in the house.

Discreetly, she pushed her duster coat aside and laid a hand on the grip of the pistol. They walked past a kind of study and her eyes met those of a bearded man. She froze, but then realised she was looking at a life-sized wooden statue of a saint.

Realising the misunderstanding, Father Roy gave a sardonic laugh. 'St James the Great, patron saint of armies . . .'

As she resumed walking, Mila noticed an old PC in the corner of the room. No joystick, no visor. But the keyboard had an odd shape: the number keys, usually on the right-hand side, were located on the left.

'Here we are, it's all in there,' the priest said, opening a door and switching on the light inside.

Mila saw that it was a narrow cavity, at least four metres deep.

'Norman's stuff is at the back. You'll find two large boxes on the bottom shelf. You can't go wrong: his name's written on them.'

Mila was hoping Berish had heard: if Luth's things were there, maybe he shouldn't be wasting his time in the apartment. But the truth was she had no wish to venture into this bottleneck. She looked up at the ceiling again, wondering if it had only been her impression or if there really was someone else there.

All right, let's get on with it, she said to herself, determined to defy her claustrophobia.

She removed her black duster jacket and rolled up the sleeves of her hooded top, ready to venture into the cavity. Meanwhile, Father Roy leaned against the door jamb of the closet and, to enjoy the show better, lit another cigarette.

The dead rat was stinking out the apartment and Berish was trying to breathe only through his mouth, but it wasn't enough. Moreover, his search wasn't yielding the hoped-for results, there were just useless knick-knacks. He suppressed a retch, but he had to hurry and get out of here or else the stench would permeate his clothes. At the second warning from his stomach in turmoil, he realised he would shortly be vomiting. He headed to the bathroom door, tried to open it but couldn't. Strange, there was no lock, only the handle, which meant something was obstructing it from inside. He forgot about his nausea and tried forcing it: there was indeed an obstacle on the other side. He gave the door a few shoulder pushes. When a gap was finally created, he put his head through to look ... but retreated immediately.

A stench worse than that of the damned rat, and it was coming from a body in an advanced state of decay. Berish covered his nose and mouth with his hand and forced himself to put his head through the gap again.

The body was lying on its side, in an almost foetal position. It took up almost the entire floor of the small bathroom. The skin on the face was taut and black because of the putrification process. You could see the teeth and the eye sockets were hollow. It had a man's clothes on: a dark shirt and trousers.

The flies were undone.

Berish leaned forward to get a better view. There was a puddle of congealed blood at the level of the pubis, but only when he looked at the hands did Berish understand what had happened.

One was clenching a knife, the other his own penis and testicles. He had castrated himself and bled to death. He'd done it to punish himself.

While Berish was drawing these conclusions, he caught sight of a detail on the shirt and was paralysed by what he saw. On the left pocket, at the level of the heart, was a pin with a crucifix.

Mila had opened the first box: it contained only an alarm clock radio, a toaster, a couple of saucepans and a hairdryer: no sign of the diaries mentioned by Father Roy. She was now about to open the second box, hoping Father Roy hadn't taken her for a ride.

It contained clothes.

As she rummaged among old jumpers and flannel shirts, she thought she heard Berish's voice in the earpiece. Except that the signal was distorted and she could only hear fragments of words. The damned cavity was preventing the radio signal from reaching her. Berish's voice stopped altogether and, at the same time, Mila was distracted by something at the bottom of the box.

Three diaries with colourful covers, like the ones used by children. Each had the relevant year on the spine: 2011, 2012 and 2013. One for each victim, Mila thought.

If Norman Luth really was a compulsive writer, as Father Roy claimed, perhaps they contained an account of the student murders. She picked up the first one, hoping the UniC killer might have also written down where he had concealed the only body that had never been found. Maybe Lea Mulach would finally be laid to rest. But when Mila opened the diary, she saw a different reality. The pages, densely written in tiny handwriting, were only full of numbers. She had evidence that Norman Luth was connected to Two.

Once again, there was that tickling at the back of her neck. But that wasn't the reason. The discovery had reminded her of the numbers on Father Roy's computer keyboard.

Berish had torn down the stairs from the apartment and was now running to the vicarage, hoping he was in time.

'Mila, can you hear me? That's not Father Roy,' he was screaming into the radio, but was unable to get a response. 'The priest is dead, you have to get out of there now!'

All he could hear was his breathing blending with the wind. Then a muffled explosion. Berish slowed down without realising it. It could have been his imagination, but his instinct was telling him that it was the sound of a shot being fired.

I didn't imagine it, he thought. It came from the house.

When he entered the vicarage, holding his pistol, he began searching for Mila. It was too quiet, which wasn't good. Then he heard a suffocated cough and followed it through the maze of the house.

The cough belonged to the fake Father Roy, who was lying on his back on the floor of the corridor. Mila was next to him, trying to plug a wound in his stomach with her hands.

'Where's my daughter?' she was asking gently, softly. 'Tell me where she is, please.'

The man coughed again and blood spurted from his mouth, staining the white hairs on his chin. Then he smiled.

Berish understood what had happened, because Mila had put down on the floor the weapon she had fired to defend herself and next to it was the knife with which she had probably been attacked.

She noticed him and turned to him with pleading eyes. 'Call an ambulance,' she said. But Berish had too much experience of wounds and bullets not to know immediately that the man was done for. A few seconds later, he saw an evil light going out in the man's eyes.

'We have to leave,' Berish said, lifting her by her arms.

'The computer keyboard,' she replied, devastated.

He did not understand.

'It's a left-handed keyboard, and he smoked only with his right.'

While looking at the numbers in the diaries, she remembered what she'd seen in the priest's study – there was a tickle at the back of her neck. Whoever this bastard was, he'd been sent by Enigma.

They heard footsteps upstairs. Berish was immediately on the alert, ready to shoot. Through the ground-floor windows, they saw two figures come down the fire escape, run to a parked car nearby and disappear.

Mila hadn't been wrong: there really had been someone else in the house.

'Fuck,' Berish said. He picked up the diaries by the closet door and placed them in her still-bloodied hands. Then he gave her instructions on what she had to do. 'Take the car and go to my flat.'

'What about my gun?'

'Leave it here. I'll take care of it.' He then looked at the body and added, 'And of everything else.'

15

She'd cleaned her hands with wet wipes she'd found in the glovebox in the car. But she still felt soiled with the blood of the man she had shot, so as soon as she reached Berish's apartment, she stepped into the shower. She stood there for a long time, turning the cold tap to the minimum setting in the hope that the flow of scalding water would do her good.

Mila Vasquez was always trying to heal pain with pain.

The first thing she did once she'd left the bathroom, wearing Berish's towelling robe, was to fill Hitch's bowl with food. Then she found something for herself, too, because she was very hungry. A sandwich loaf and pickles. She took them with her to the sofa.

Outside, it was raining.

Sitting cross-legged, Mila began looking through Norman Luth's diaries, hoping those numbers would reveal something. It was like solving a complex mathematical problem, one of those impossible questions that occupied scholars for a lifetime.

No, she thought. It's the sick fruit of a murderer's mind. There's no logic in these numbers, only chaos and death. Because that's the whisperer's only creed. Mila was confused. Perhaps the answer lay concealed in her second trip to Elsewhere: *the old furniture and the black rose*. But she wasn't sure any more.

It was almost midday by the time Berish returned. He threw his rain-soaked coat over a chair and poured himself a drink.

'Is everything all right?' she asked tentatively.

He took a gulp before replying. 'Yes, everything's all right.'

Hitch went up to his owner, sensing a strange smell on his clothes. Berish pushed his muzzle away.

Mila didn't ask how he'd managed to remove the traces of their visit from the vicarage that morning, or how he'd disposed of the remains of the castrated priest and the stranger who'd pretended to be him. She knew that a police officer who'd spent so many years in the force was bound to have developed contacts in the criminal world that might turn out to be useful. But Simon was upset, and she didn't like that.

'What's in Luth's diaries?' he asked, eager to change the subject.

Mila picked one up and quickly showed him the pages. Berish shook his head. 'It was pointless . . . '

'If we'd found the solution to the mystery, we should also have come across the new coordinates to access Two.'

'So we have to start from the beginning again . . . '

'Why?' Mila challenged.

'Because now we have to question everything the fake priest told us: did he lie to us to throw us off the track or tell us the truth the real Father Roy could no longer share because he'd been dead for a long time?'

'We have to start from the facts again . . . ' Mila said. 'And the facts tell us that Norman Luth confessed to the murders in minute detail because he *knew*.'

'Except that his alibi holds up.'

'But no other female student has died since he committed suicide.'

Simon gulped down the rest of his drink. 'There has to be an explanation.'

'The numbers in the diaries may be comprehensible only to an insane mind,' Mila replied, 'but they're definitely not a coincidence. They're proof that Norman frequented Two and maybe knew Enigma.'

'They still don't constitute evidence,' Simon said, even though he was reluctant to contradict her. 'We have to *turn* them into evidence . . . '

Mila was frustrated. 'But how?'

'By investigating,' Berish replied, almost angrily. 'By going to look where we haven't yet, sticking our noses where we haven't yet, and plunging our hands in the shit we haven't stirred yet.' Mila had never seen him so fired up. 'Convention stipulates that we have a serial-killer case where the murderer has killed at least three people using the same method. But who says it absolutely has to be that way? We've decided that only because we always notice his existence too late, after he's already struck. It's an excuse for being unable to stop him sooner!'

Mila couldn't see what he was getting at.

'And what do we do when we discover a new serial killer? We wait for him to kill again and hope that this time he commits an error . . . '

The *unfortunate* thing about serial killers was that they couldn't stop. The *fortunate* thing was that they couldn't stop.

'Well, that was exactly what we did today,' Berish concluded, not forgiving himself. 'We went to question a priest. Instead, we should have asked the real question of ourselves . . . How does a serial killer learn to kill?'

Mila understood at last. 'His first victim teaches him.'

What characteristics did serial killers look for in their victims? It was one of the crucial questions for criminologists.

Often there was no actual choice at the basis of the murder. All it took was for the victim to be female and in the right place. Right for the killer, that is. At other times, the designation was purely accidental. Mila recalled a serial killer who raped and cut to pieces only waitresses. When he was caught, he admitted that there wasn't a specific reason for that: since the first woman he'd killed happened to be a waitress in a bar and that time he'd got away with it, he'd decided to carry on with that category. For superstitious reasons, if nothing else.

But there was also a more deep-seated reason: as far as a serial killer was concerned, a repeated modus operandi is as much a source of satisfaction as the actual murder. It meant for him that he's doing a good job. The notion that they'd come up with a method of killing without being caught was fulfilling to their ego, Mila told herself.

'If a cake comes out well, why change the recipe?' the man who'd taught her these things would always say. 'In time, you can perfect it by learning from experience. Every now and then, you can even afford to substitute an ingredient. But you don't go turning it upside down, risking failure.'

Lea Mulach, the blonde student with the glasses, had been the prototype for the UniC killer. The one who would become a progenitor to the others. Because every murderer has his ideal victim, Mila remembered.

The young woman's mother lived in an attractive apartment block in the bay. After her daughter's death, she'd got divorced and, a year ago, had got remarried, to a lawyer.

Mila and Berish knocked on her door, hoping the rainy Sunday would have kept her at home. A maid admitted them to the spacious living room overlooking the sea. After her daughter's disappearance in 2011, Barbara Mulach had called Limbo almost daily asking for updates. A few months later, her calls become less frequent. And when the police decided to include Lea among the UniC killer's victims, her mother stopped contacting them altogether.

No sooner had Barbara Mulach stepped into the room than Mila realised she'd been immediately recognised. I'll have the same expression if I can't find Alice, she thought.

Powerlessness and shock.

The woman was wearing a grey chenille tracksuit. She still had blonde hair, but it was now dyed because of her age. She had it tied in a ponytail, which made her look strikingly like her daughter.

She burst into tears. 'Have you found her?' she asked in a faint voice.

Mila went to support her. 'Unfortunately, no . . .'

'Then why have you come here?' she asked, confused.

'Because I'm looking into the case again,' Mila replied, lying in part.

The goal of her unauthorised investigation was not to find Lea's body, but Alice.

'This is Officer Simon Berish, the new head of Missing Persons.'

After the introductions, they sat on pale leather sofas by the terrace. Outside, the sea was stormy, but it was a silent spectacle, since the sound of the waves couldn't filter through the windows.

'She would have been an extraordinary woman,' Barbara Mulach said, indicating the photos in silver frames on a small table. They showed her daughter at various moments of her short life. As a newborn baby, a small child blowing out the candles on her birthday, on a ski track, riding a horse, dressed as a majorette and, finally, smiling, holding her school diploma.

'She was always number one at everything, she never wanted to come second.'

And so she had been also in death, Mila thought. The first of a series.

'I know that when you speak of the dead, in particular when they're young, it's easy to say that they were wonderful people, and everyone loved them,' the woman said. 'It's quite pathetic, after all. But Lea didn't even have time to go wrong.' She took a breath. 'When she told me she wanted to study Oriental languages, I encouraged her. Her father would have preferred her to get a degree in economics. But Lea wanted to travel, which had also been my dream as a girl.'

Because she lacked empathy, Mila was unable to feel compassion for this woman, but she knew only too well what a sense of guilt was.

We call obstacles on the road to destiny 'if's.

If she hadn't forced Alice to live in a secluded house by the lake, if she hadn't agreed to take on Shutton's assignment, if she hadn't met Enigma, maybe now things would also be different for Mila.

'Mrs Mulach,' Berish said. 'As you're well aware, Lea was included in the list of the UniC killer's victims ... but there are important differences from the other murdered girls: your daughter's body has never been found and there's no evidence that she was lured on social media by the mysterious young man called Larry. Of course, this may not mean much: the killer may well have used a different profile ... But I must ask you: was Lea the kind of girl who would have dated a young man from the internet? She was very attractive, and I understand many young men were after her.'

'You're right, Officer Berish, but that bastard came into her life at the worst possible time. Lea had just come out of a long relationship with a boy from high school. You know how some things go when you start university: you drift apart, your habits and your friends change ... I think my daughter felt lonely, but she didn't have the courage to start a new relationship.'

In that case, the university's social network must have been a kind of therapy, Mila thought. A way of socialising with someone again without needing to make a commitment.

'She went to the cinema with that coward only because she thought it was a harmless thing to do ... After she disappeared, there were a pair of jeans, a jacket and a T-shirt missing from her wardrobe: if Lea had considered it a date, she'd never have dressed like that.'

'As you know, a few years ago, a man called Norman Luth claimed responsibility for the murders, including Lea's,' Simon reminded her.

'Ah, yes, the psychologically unstable pathological liar,' the woman replied dismissively. 'Let me tell you something: the police were right not to believe him. That son of a bitch Luth was lying, because he would never have been able to trick my

184

Lea. A man who's always in and out of mental institutions can't fool a beautiful, brilliant young woman.'

About that, Barbara Mulach was wrong, Mila thought. Unfortunately, reality was entirely different and many maniacs who went hunting on social networks weren't in the least cunning or charming, all they had to do to lure their prey into the trap was look interesting. The victims usually did the rest, by believing the lie they told themselves. She also recalled the words of her mysterious friend in the red balaclava.

The mind sees what the mind wants to see.

'We're not here to build up your hopes, Mrs Mulach,' Mila said. 'We're trying to reassemble the pieces of the case and thought we'd start with Lea precisely because that's also what the killer did.'

Berish intervened. 'The fact that Lea's body has never been found could be a revealing clue to the murderer's personality ... After killing her, he didn't abandon her on the side of a road, like the others.'

Simon was trying to make her understand that perhaps the killer had made the body disappear because deep down he was still able to feel ashamed of what he'd done. In time, he would lose that sensibility, but back then he would still have wished to take care of Lea's remains. You couldn't, however, persuade a mother of the possibility of remorse or care amid the horror.

'What's revealing in the spite of not allowing parents to mourn over the grave of their daughter?' the woman did indeed reply, offended.

'Officer Berish is only trying to say that the murderer may have chosen Lea for a reason,' Mila said. 'If we discover what it is, perhaps we can get to him.'

Barbara Mulach looked at them. The prospect of contributing to catching the monster who'd ruined her life and broken up her family had reawakened a positive anger in her. 'How can I help you?'

'Do you still have Lea's computer?' Berish asked. 'We'd like to take a look at it.'

'Yes, I have it. I was able to cope, to start anew. My ex-husband, on the other hand, can't find peace. You know, after we separated, he brought me our daughter's things because he couldn't bear to have them at home. Except that he then regretted it, but her things are still here . . . .'

The woman stood up from the sofa and went to a different wing of the apartment.

'What do you think?' Berish asked softly.

Mila shook her head. 'I don't know, I only hope you're right . . . '

Barbara Mulach returned a few minutes later with a notebook in a red case covered in small gold dragons. 'It's been intact since Lea disappeared.'

Mila recognised it because when she'd been in charge of the case, before it had been taken over by the VCU, she'd analysed the laptop, searching for useful clues that could explain Lea's disappearance.

'Do you really think you can still find the killer? Your fellow police officers say it's been too long, and after the other two poor girls the murderer vanished into thin air . . . '

It often happened that the parents of victims of violent crime would adopt their killer in place of the children they'd lost. In their hearts, hatred would take the place of love. Mila didn't want to have given her false hopes.

'It's just a lead,' she made sure she said to clarify. 'It could

186

take us somewhere or nowhere ... In any case, Lea won't be forgotten. I haven't forgotten her.' And that was true.

'We're so desperate, three years ago we placed a headstone in the cemetery ... We're aware there's no one under it, but people will walk past the grave and read her name. So they'll know that there was once a beautiful young woman called Lea Mulach and remember her even after the two of us are dead ... '

This mother's true tragedy wasn't that her daughter had died, but that, given her young age, she had lived in vain.

'I don't know if it's a joke or an act of genuine charity ... I even told the police but they couldn't explain it ... Perhaps it's of no importance.'

Mila couldn't understand what the woman was referring to. She exchanged glances with Berish and he, too, looked puzzled.

'What's of no importance?' Mila said encouragingly.

Lea Mulach's mother turned to look at her. 'Ever since we placed the headstone, every year, on the anniversary of her disappearance, someone has left a black rose.'

16

The modus operandi of a serial killer was like a cake recipe.

Mila repeated the effective comparison to herself. If something works out well with a specific procedure, why try and do it differently? But, even in keeping to recurring elements, the modus operandi of a serial killer could vary from one murder to the next: the murderer, like a pastry chef, tends to perfect his art, since he learns from experience.

That's why many criminologists considered this an outdated criterion when attributing crimes to the same serial killer: as a matter of fact, most probably, there would be so many differences between the first and the last murder that they would appear as the work of different hands. And this represented a risk, especially in court, where a sharp lawyer could highlight the discrepancies so that the charge against his client would be dropped. That's why profilers had started relying primarily on another trait of the serial killer's behaviour. Something that remained unchanged over time.

His signature.

'The serial killer uses murder in order to satisfy a need,' Mila explained to Berish as he was driving in the rain. 'In order to be fully satisfied with a murder, there's something he must absolutely do. For example, if his need is to inflict pain or dominate the victim, he won't be able to resist sadistic or humiliating acts, and these will then be his signature.'

The common denominator of his crimes.

'But the distinction between the modus operandi and the signature can be very fine,' she said.

Mila remembered the case of a bank robber who photographed his hostages after forcing them to strip naked. This behaviour was neither useful nor necessary to the success of the robbery but, on the contrary, increased its risks, since it made the robber spend longer in the bank.

That was his signature, the symptom of an irrepressible need.

Another robber, on the other hand, would get the hostages to strip but without photographing them. His reason was merely practical: once naked, they would avoid looking at him because they were embarrassed, therefore less likely to describe his appearance to the police.

Still, Berish wasn't following. 'What does a serial killer's signature have to do with the black rose Lea Mulach's mother finds on her daughter's artificial grave every year?'

'Let's go to Limbo and I'll explain: I get the feeling we've made a mistake,' Mila said, without adding anything else.

The traffic flowed easily despite the bad weather. The temperature had dropped by quite a few degrees and the forecast heralded nothing good for the coming hours.

Mila and Berish arrived at the department at around four.

There wasn't much activity in the building on a Sunday afternoon, but they were still praying that no one would recognise them and blab to Shutton that they'd seen them together.

In the missing-persons room, Mila put Lea Mulach's notebook on a corner of the desk and plugged it in to charge, since it probably hadn't been switched on for ages.

'We'll look at the girl's computer later,' she said to Berish.

She immediately sat at the old terminal to seek the confirmation she was hoping to find.

On the murder database, there was a section devoted to so-called 'minor victims'. It wasn't politically correct to talk about people who had died because of their lifestyle, but that's what it was, effectively. Anyone who dealt drugs, prostituted themselves or was a member of a gang was more likely to be killed than others. Some even called it 'an occupational hazard'.

Mila was focusing on prostitutes and, after refining her search by keying in 'blonde hair', 'glasses' and 'strangling', she obtained a list of six murders from 2013 to the present day.

'Here's the signature,' she announced triumphantly. 'The serial killer hasn't stopped killing: he's just become more cunning.'

In order to act undisturbed, he'd changed one ingredient in the recipe, Mila thought. No more students, but prostitutes. A strangled student is an exception, while a prostitute is seen as the umpteenth predestined victim.

'I don't understand,' Berish said. 'So was Norman Luth innocent or were there two serial killers from the outset?'

Mila indicated the chair next to hers. 'I have a theory, let's see if you buy it . . . ' She was excited by the discovery and couldn't wait to share it with Berish. 'Norman Luth used to visit Two – this is confirmed by his diaries full of numbers. In the virtual world, Luth witnesses the staging of another player's fantasy: one who enjoys strangling blonde female students with glasses.'

Mila had had a taster of what it meant to enter someone's sick fantasies: she wouldn't forget what she'd felt when impersonating Karl Anderson as he was slaughtering his wife and daughters with a knife.

'Luth is mentally unstable, and when the killings keep occurring in the same way in the real world, he becomes convinced that he's the murderer: he goes to the police and makes a detailed confession . . . But since he was always at the psychiatric hospital when the killings took place, they decide it can't have been him, so he's cleared.'

'Only the incident with Luth, which culminates with his suicide, teaches something to the real killer,' Berish said, finally following her thread of thought. 'If he doesn't want to be caught, he has to change his modus operandi just enough to make it look as though the serial killing has come to an end . . . That's why he replaces the students with prostitutes.'

'His signature is the victim's appearance. In order to fully satisfy his need, it must always be the same: blonde hair and glasses.'

Berish gave it some thought. 'And what about the black rose? What does that mean?'

'It's not necessarily a gesture of compassion or reformation,' Mila replied. 'It could be a way of proving to himself that he hasn't forgotten his first victim.'

All serial killers were grateful to their first victim, Mila remembered. Like a first love, they couldn't forget it.

'If Norman Luth was in touch with the real murderer through Two,' Berish said, 'then all we need to do is look at his computer. Only, there was no computer in the flat above the garage,' he recalled with frustration.

It seemed like a dead end, but Mila had an idea. 'The fake Father Roy told me that Norman inherited the house from his parents. But because of the unpleasant memories, he refused to live there and so had rented the two-room apartment. Luth's computer is probably where he lived as a child.'

'The fake priest may have lied,' Simon said, warning her. 'Or else someone else now lives in that house.'

But Mila did not agree. 'Nothing's stopping us going to check . . . Then we'll devote ourselves to Lea's notebook,' she said, unplugging the laptop charger, ready to leave.

The rain that had been pouring down on the city all day had declared a truce, but there was still a mass of threatening black clouds hanging over their heads.

As sunset approached, the light was quickly fading. Soon, another long night would begin for Alice and this thought troubled Mila. It was like having to live with a dull ache in the middle of her chest, a punch that would slowly sink between her ribs, pushing through with tenacity.

Norman Luth's parents had left him a lovely Art Nouveau villa in the hills, surrounded by a large garden fenced off by an iron enclosure. But Berish was right: the house was inhabited. Even though the curtains were closed, you could make out lights inside.

'What shall we do?' Mila asked, assuming it was now pointless knocking on the new tenants' door.

'I don't know,' Berish replied.

Their move was proving unproductive, but then Mila noticed a cobalt-blue Lancia Beta, partly hidden by the knotty branches of a pine tree, at the back of the villa.

Enigma and Pascal also drove cars that dated back to the

previous century. Pascal had, in fact, explained the reason for that: these cars did not have the electronic devices that could allow them to be located.

'I don't know if it's just a coincidence,' she said, 'but I think many Two players use that precaution.'

Berish considered this. 'What do you think – shall we ring the bell and ask if they still have Luth's computer?'

'I don't think so.'

'That's what I figured.'

Berish took two pistols out of his coat pockets and handed one to Mila to replace the gun he'd disposed of after the fake Father Roy's murder. 'It's a clean weapon,' he said, meaning it couldn't be traced to them.

Shortly afterwards, they were climbing over the enclosure in a spot where they couldn't be seen from the house. Then they headed towards the villa across a lawn strewn with wet leaves that muffled the sound of their footsteps. Gusts of chilly wind suddenly blew down from the hill above and bounced off the trees in the garden, swaying the foliage before dropping.

Berish indicated a back entrance that led to a conservatory. All you could see through the frosted glass was a tangle of branches, like skeletons in the darkness. Pushing on the jamb was enough to get the better of the elementary lock. Within seconds, they were inside, welcomed by a pleasant warmth coming from the house. They stood for a moment and listened, trying to detect the presence of whoever lived there, but heard nothing.

Berish took a step towards the inside of the villa, but Mila held him back by the sleeve. He turned and saw what she had seen.

The conservatory was home to a rose garden. The most beautiful and valuable bush had black buds sprouting from it. If confirmation were needed that they were in the right place, this was it.

Berish walked ahead of Mila as they explored their sur- roundings. The old parquet creaked under their feet, so they carefully calculated the weight of their every step. They weren't sure if there was anyone there, but the house was lit up. Table lamps covered with damask scarves and golden wall lights that stood out from amaranth-red wallpaper seemed to show the way with their amber glow. Vintage furniture gave off a pleasant smell of antiques – beeswax and expensive wood.

They reached a staircase with an inlaid balustrade that led to the upper floors. Berish motioned to Mila that he would follow that direction while she would stay downstairs. So they split up in order to search the rooms better.

Mila held the pistol with her arms stretched out in front of her, as she'd learned to do as a new recruit at the academy. Her eyes and the gunsight had to move almost in tandem and cover a safety area of a hundred and eighty degrees.

She walked past a pale yellow kitchen with copper pans hanging from a grille on the ceiling and a white lacquered sideboard. Just next door were the servants' rooms, then a library with a transistor radio made of walnut root. Mila thought that this house must have been passed on by Luths for generations. Norman, however, had preferred to live in an apartment above the garage of a depraved priest. The reason for that was held in the living room, where the ghosts of Norman's parents still lingered. Mila stepped in.

An old grandfather clock ticking calmly in a corner. A

velvet sofa and armchairs. A rug with geometrical patterns. A floor map with a burgundy lampshade at the top. A sideboard and coffee tables strewn with china statuettes. A cast-iron stove and a rocking chair. Wallpaper dotted with pretty red flowers.

Mila realised she'd already been here, only in Elsewhere.

It was the place where the shadow had tried to strangle her, but years earlier a real-life act of violence had taken place within these walls: an unfaithful wife had been strangled by her husband, before the innocent eyes of their nine-year-old son.

Norman saw his mother's face drain of blood, her eyes pop out of their sockets, and a puddle of urine spread beneath her, Mila thought as she pictured the scene. Even after all this time, every item in the room held a secret of death. But there was also something she hadn't come across in its virtual twin in Two. A desk with an angle-poise lamp, its beam illuminating an old PC in sleep mode.

She went closer to get a better look, in the hope that it was the one Luth used to access the game. And as she walked around the table, she did indeed notice a joystick and a visor on the desk. Her eyes froze on the keyboard.

There was a red balaclava lying on it.

Her lungs were like a pair of pistons, taking in more air than they needed. She was hyperventilating and her heart was beating so fast, the palpitations turned into a sort of tinnitus.

Pascal lied to me. He's the UniC killer.

Through the ceiling, she could hear Berish's steps creaking as he surveyed the floor upstairs. I must warn him, she thought.

She retraced her steps through the rooms she'd already seen as far as the wide staircase with the inlaid balustrade. Carefully trying to pick up on the slightest sound or change around her, she began to climb the stairs, preceded as ever by the barrel of her pistol.

When she'd reached the first landing, she tried in vain to glimpse Simon. Her back flat against the wainscoting, she realised it concealed a secret door perfectly camouflaged by the wall.

Strange that Berish hadn't noticed it.

She pushed the skirting board with her foot and what opened in front of her was an ordinary cupboard with a vacuum cleaner and detergents. She was about to close it when she heard a sound. Like a moan.

She listened intently and mentally counted the seconds until a minute had gone without anything else happening. Still, she wouldn't give up, certain that she'd heard something.

There was another, albeit very brief moan.

The ghost, she thought, remembering the voice she'd heard in Elsewhere.

Look at yourself . . . Save yourself . . .

Mila crouched because she realised where the weeping in the cupboard was coming from. There was an air vent covered by a grating.

It's coming from under the house, she thought.

She would have liked to warn Simon, but she was suddenly overwhelmed with anxiety: she had to find out if someone truly needed help. So she went back down the stairs in search of a way into the basement. Imagining that it would be through the kitchen, she went back there.

As it happened, there was a grey door with a brass handle

behind one of the tables. She shifted it and tried the lock. It was open. Before her, an abyss of stairs.

Mila hesitated. So many times in her career as a hunter, she had explored dark, dangerous places. Places ordinary people could only imagine and where nobody with an ounce of caution or self-respect would have ventured. Not even a police officer. But it had never been a problem for her.

I come from the darkness. And to the darkness I must sometimes return.

But at that moment, a different thought crossed her mind, restraining her.

If I die now, it's all over for Alice.

Only, if she didn't go and see what lay beneath, she wouldn't get the answers she was searching for either.

That's not my daughter, she told herself, remembering the moan. But it could still be a trick.

Putrid, dank air was wafting from the basement. Mila decided to go towards it and went down the first step that led to a familiar darkness. She didn't have a torch – nothing except the pistol. And in such pitch-black, a weapon was of no use anyway. As she went down, she could feel the kitchen door grow distant behind her: light and the familiar world were confined up there, while she was descending into a different dimension, made up of unavowable horrors and laments concealed in the darkness.

Mila counted the steps until she'd reached the bottom of the stairs. Twenty-six. The darkness was so dense down there that she could feel it on her skin, like an unwelcome caress.

She banished thoughts of death from her mind, because only with total blankness could she forestall events. She went ahead, using her instinct like a sonar.

Then she heard breathing.

Somewhere near her, a creature was waiting for her. It was crouching in the shadows, searching for her.

The breathing turned once again into a moan.

'Alice?' Mila asked the darkness.

No response.

'Who's there?' she asked again.

This time, the darkness replied. 'Look on the floor.'

An adult male voice. Mila froze. Then she took a couple of steps and the tip of her combat boot bumped into a metal object. She bent forward and, her weapon still ready, extended her hand over the dusty floor until she found something. She felt it to try and work out what it was.

A gas camping light.

She pressed the switch and heard a series of tiny discharges, then the hiss of the gas. She kept her finger pressed on the switch until the lamp began to come on. The opaque light revealed that the basement had been dug out of the rock: foundation pillars rose around her.

A man was chained to one of them.

Mila lifted the lamp and extended it towards him. The stranger immediately shielded his face with his hand, but, through his fingers, she saw a pair of frightened eyes.

He was a little over twenty years old. There was a heavy cuff clasped around his ankle. He was barefoot and dressed in a kind of tracksuit – pink, like the one Enigma had worn in the cell in the Grave.

'Who are you?' Mila asked.

He hesitated before answering. 'My name is Timmy Jackson.'

But another name immediately came to Mila's mind.

Fishbone.

17

'We have to take him to hospital,' Berish said to her softly.

After his reconnaissance, he'd joined her in the basement to say that there was nobody else in the house except them. Mila had stopped him on the stairs to prepare him for what he was about to see. Berish had turned white at the sight of the prisoner. But at that moment, they had different views on what to do with Timmy Jackson.

'He needs a doctor,' Berish said, indicating the young man.

He was curled up on the floor in an almost foetal position, staring into space, his ankle still in the grip of the chain. Berish couldn't take his eyes off him, but Mila forced him to look at her by turning his face. 'You're not listening. Timmy Jackson has been missing for seven years. There's no knowing how much he could tell us.'

But Berish was upset and disagreed with her. That was why she hadn't yet told him about the old PC in the living room or the red balaclava she'd found on the keyboard.

'I'm going to look for a pair of clippers and set him free,' he said.

Mila grabbed him by the arm. 'No way.'

Fishbone was in an indeterminate emotional state because he still hadn't realised he'd been saved. What happened afterwards, with the return to normality, to a world that no longer abided by the rules of violence, was what psychiatrists called 'survivor's shock' and was an actual trauma. A disturbance that tainted memories by triggering a process of erasing the events: that was the main reason many of those freed were then unable to accuse their jailor. On the contrary, they tended to justify him so as not to have to admit that the horror they'd experienced had been real.

Mila knew that the minutes that followed the discovery of a missing person were the most important in terms of obtaining useful information. 'You must question him,' she said to Berish. 'And you must do it now.'

Clearly, he didn't feel like doing that.

'If you don't, Alice will suffer from it.'

'Don't you dare,' Berish said, menacingly.

Mila didn't wish to be unfair towards her old friend, but she had no alternative.

'Besides,' he protested, 'this isn't the sort of interrogation I'm trained in. This is a job for a psychologist, someone with the skills to get into a victim's mind ... But there's no need to tell you because you know that perfectly well,' he added, annoyed.

The psyche of an abduction survivor was a minefield. The principal danger lay in unleashing a sense of shame in the victim: many felt guilty for having fallen into the monster's trap and caused suffering to their loved ones. After being saved, many committed suicide.

Mila had no intention of giving up. 'Sometimes, you have to make choices,' she said. It sounded cynical, and perhaps it was. But she knew she had to be pragmatic if she wanted to obtain something. Pascal had told her that she would have to discover what 'her game' was on her own, but up till now she had only endured the situation, letting herself be tossed around by events and never in control – not even for a moment. Now she was tired and wanted to score a point to her advantage. Change at least one rule in the game.

'Look at him,' Mila said. 'He's clean and has been well fed all this time. That means the jailer has been looking after him.'

This gave Berish an idea. 'All right, but I'm only giving you twenty minutes before we call for aid.'

They approached Fishbone.

'Timmy, Officer Berish wants to talk to you. Is that all right?'

The young man nodded.

Berish sat down on the dusty floor, facing him: by placing himself on the same level as his interlocutor, he communicated that from the outset everything would be proceeding in a relaxed manner. During interrogations, on the other hand, he would often remain standing, looming over the person being questioned, who was generally handcuffed to a chair.

Berish had brought Lea Mulach's notebook from the car and put it down next to him, so that Fishbone might see clearly the red cover with the gold dragons.

'Would you prefer me to call you Timmy or Fishbone?' Berish asked, trying to strike a friendly note.

'I don't know ... Whatever you prefer, makes no difference ...'

'Is there anything you'd like to ask me before we start? Anything you want to know, or you're not sure about ... '

Fishbone thought for a moment. 'How long have I been here?'

Throughout her career as a hunter of missing persons, Mila had had occasion to answer this question more than once. It happened when she saved someone who'd been snatched away from his or her life years – but also a few days or hours – earlier. Time would expand and even a few minutes spent in captivity could seem endless.

'Seven years,' Berish replied.

Mila thought again about the spotty teenager passionate about rock and graffiti.

Fishbone paused to think about that figure. He didn't appear especially upset by it. He had yet to process the idea that in that time the world had forgotten him.

'Who brought you here?'

'He's gone, he won't be back,' he said to reassure them.

'How do you know?'

Pascal was waiting for us to arrive, Mila thought, then he fled.

'I know because he gave me these before he left . . .'

Fishbone opened his palm and showed them a handful of blue pills. Berish took them and gave them to Mila. Angel Tear: the only freedom granted by the fleeing kidnapper to the prisoner was the option of taking his own life with an overdose.

'Would you be able to recognise the man who used to live here?'

Fishbone stared at them, his eyes filled with fear, then shook his head. 'He always covered his face.'

Mila was disappointed: she wouldn't discover what the face under the balaclava looked like. Berish dropped the subject and moved on.

'Timmy, can you tell us what you remember before coming here?'

'I don't know how I ended up in that video game,' he admitted hesitantly. 'I was a total idiot back then . . . I'd read stories online, but they sounded so absurd: like one of those myths that circulate on the internet.'

Mila knew many of them, from the one about Slender Man to the Blue Whale.

'I downloaded the game and went in. And once you go in, you can't come back out any more, but I didn't know that . . . Mum always told me I spent too much time on that fucking computer and I'd get angry with her. But I could feel something was happening to me, because I wasn't myself any more. I couldn't tell any more what was real and what was only in my head. All because of those fucking blue pills . . . '

Fishbone was still speaking like a teenager, as though his intellectual development had been halted seven years earlier. It was one of the effects of captivity, Mila thought.

'How did you meet the man who kidnapped you?' Berish asked.

'He's the one who found me in the game, so I ran away from home because he said he'd take care of me.'

'And what was this man doing in the video game?'

Fishbone bit his lip before answering. 'He enjoys killing.'

Mila and Berish said nothing, just registered the information.

'He wants only blonde women, but they have to wear glasses,' Fishbone then added. 'I don't know why.'

Berish leaned towards him. 'Timmy, did you see this man hurt young women?'

Fishbone was silent.

Berish insisted, gently. 'It's all right, you can tell us . . . '

Fishbone started to cry. 'He forced me to watch . . . '

Berish allowed him to let it out for a while, then resumed, 'Have you ever heard of a Norman Luth?'

'This used to be his house, didn't it?'

'Yes, that's right.'

'And does the name Alice ring any bells?' Mila asked, perhaps rushing things a little.

While Berish gave her a sharp look, Fishbone snivelled and shook his head.

For a moment, Mila had harboured the hope that he might know something about her daughter.

'Timmy, I need to ask you a question, but I'd like a definite answer . . . ' Berish began. 'Have you ever wondered why you were abducted?' The young man seemed disorientated. 'What I mean is, if your kidnapper enjoyed killing blondes with glasses, why did he take you and keep you down here?'

'I don't know . . . '

Berish didn't insist, simply took note of the reply and changed the subject once again. Mila wondered what he had in mind.

'How did this man entice these young women?'

'He'd find them on the internet . . . The students on a site called UniC, the prostitutes on dating sites.'

'And then they'd come here?'

'Yes, that's right.'

Berish leaned towards him again. 'Are you telling me the truth, Fishbone? Are you saying that these women came into this house of their own free will?'

Mila noticed that the young man had lowered his eyes.

Berish continued. 'And I'm expected to believe that a killer who's managed to trick the police for years would take the risk and post this address on the internet?'

Fishbone began sobbing again.

'He'd give them an appointment somewhere else, right?' said Berish. 'And so he wouldn't have to show himself, he'd send you.'

Fishbone shook his head determinedly, but he wasn't convincing.

'You didn't just watch, he used you as bait.'

Mila understood why the kidnapper had taken care of his prisoner.

'What could I do?' Fishbone burst out, crying from despair. 'If I hadn't done as he said, he'd have killed me.'

His eyes were red and a trickle of saliva was dribbling from his mouth, but Berish had no time for pity. He picked up the notebook with the red cover and the gold dragons, placed it on his lap, opened it and switched it on.

'The owner of this laptop was called Lea Mulach,' he said as he waited for the computer to start. 'As you know, before our friend began devoting himself to prostitutes, he had a soft spot for students. Lea was the first to be killed but, unlike her two successors, her body has never been found. Moreover, while the other two girls were lured with a fake profile in the name of a young man called Larry, we don't know what he did with Lea.'

Mila recalled how they'd discussed the same topic with Barbara Mulach, and wondered if the serial killer had used another false identity that was still unknown to the investigators. The fact that he'd changed it in favour of Larry might reveal an important weak link in his strategy, something defective in the modus operandi he would then have wished to correct. Thanks to this slip, they might discover his true identity.

'Now you're going to show us how the killer contacted her ...'

'I can't remember,' Fishbone immediately said.

'Yes, you do,' Berish replied calmly, cornering him. 'You were already here.'

'It was too long ago,' Fishbone said, trying to protect himself.

But Berish was determined. 'We're going on the UniC site and you're showing me, that's it.'

Berish took a pair of reading glasses from his coat. The desktop image was that of a night view of Hong Kong, and the program icons popped up over it. He put on his glasses and opened the internet browser. He looked through the browsing history and froze. The date and time of the most recent view was marked next to every site on the long list. These dated back to 2011, the year Lea had disappeared. But, as he scrolled up that list in reverse order, UniC never featured. The only possible reason for that was that the young woman had never joined that social network.

Berish and Mila asked each other the same question with their eyes. *Then how did the killer lure Lea Mulach?*

When it came to them, the answer took their breath away. 'Shit,' Mila couldn't help exclaiming. 'He knew her personally.'

'How could the VCU not have realised?' Mila wondered, upset.

'Norman Luth unwittingly tricked them with his confession,' Berish said. 'He was the one to point Lea out to them, because he'd witnessed her murder in Elsewhere.'

'All they needed was one more name so it would make three victims and they'd be able to embark on an official serial killer hunt.'

'Since the modus operandi for luring and killing the second and third student was identical, the VCU guys took it for granted that the same had been true for the first victim.'

'The only difference being that Lea Mulach's body hasn't been found – but they must have thought that was a minor detail,' Mila added with a blend of sarcasm and anger. She was furious and Berish didn't want her to lose her concentration.

'What are we going to do?' he asked, trying to be practical. 'Because we've ascertained that the boy isn't able to provide a description of his jailer.'

They were once again standing by the staircase so as not to upset Fishbone with their conversation. But the young man was still lost in his personal hell and was paying no attention to them.

'The black rose is a sign that there was a specific connection between the killer and his first victim,' Mila said with certainty, returning to their initial theory. 'He didn't pick Lea Mulach because she had blonde hair and glasses, but he did pick all the others because they looked like her.'

Lea had been what criminologists called 'the prime victim'.

Mila's certainty had been reinforced after she'd seen the rose bush with the black buds in the conservatory. The care devoted to these flowers, as well the act of marking every anniversary of Lea's disappearance with a rose placed on her fake grave, could have turned into bitter hatred.

Berish, too, was coming round to this theory. 'That's why the killer makes no distinction between students and prostitutes: what's important to him is that his victims look like Lea.'

'We must find out why she's so important to him.'

'I agree.'

'I think the killer is gripped by an obsession he can't free himself from.'

'Now we know that they knew each other,' Berish said, 'perhaps we should look for someone who was at university with her.'

Mila was sceptical about this. 'You heard her mother: Lea had only just started university. She was new to that world, she hadn't had neither the time nor the possibility to become the object of someone's sick fantasies.'

She knew very well that an obsession doesn't spring from a casual acquaintance but requires years to take root. Years of stolen glances, of gestures never understood. The victim is often unaware of this attention. And when the obsessed individual finally finds the courage to reveal himself, she doesn't understand his true intentions. Then every reaction on her part, however small, is interpreted as a rejection. The disappointment becomes unbearable and the person in love eventually turns the idealised woman into an enemy to be destroyed. Because if he destroys her, she won't belong to anyone else and will forever be his.

'Were you thinking that Lea may have perhaps become, without knowing it, the obsession of a family member?' Berish asked, trying to trace the serial killer's profile.

'I don't know, but, yes, I was thinking of someone in her circle in the past, when she was still a minor. Someone who found the courage to make a declaration once she was at university and who came forward only so he wouldn't lose her.'

They mustn't get sidetracked by Lea's appearance, Mila thought. It had turned out to be an essential element in connecting the other victims, but might not be all that vital for whoever was obsessed with her.

'Often, the victim is idealised not because of specific physical characteristics,' Mila said, 'but because in the killer's eyes she represents something unattainable ... something *forbidden*.'

'It could be someone who couldn't reveal himself before Lea was of age because of his role.'

'What about a high-school teacher? I remember that at the time of her disappearance, there had been reports of female pupils being stalked at school, and the culprit was never found.'

'Why wasn't that noted in the Limbo file?' Berish asked, doubtful.

'It was just a rumour and, besides, the VCU took the case from us before we could look into it.'

'Still, it makes sense that it should have been an adult,' Berish said, persuading himself. 'I'll go to Lea Mulach's old school and do some research on her teachers. You never know, something interesting might pop out.'

Mila was pleased, because that was exactly what she wanted.

'Meanwhile, call someone about the boy,' he added, indicating Fishbone with a glance. 'Then leave before emergency services get here. They absolutely mustn't find you here.'

'All right,' Mila answered. But she had no intention of obeying.

18

Mila had made up the story about the stalker at Lea's school just to throw Berish off the track. There had been no such rumour. And she had no intention of calling emergency rescue for Fishbone. At least not straight away. She still had something to do in this house. For a start, she wanted to investigate the PC next to which she'd found Pascal's balaclava. She was certain that it was an invitation to switch on the device.

Even if Berish didn't agree, Timmy Jackson was a valuable resource and Mila couldn't lose him before she found out what was on that computer. Now that she'd got rid of Berish, she had all the time she needed.

She gave Fishbone a cushion, a blanket and a bucket in case he needed the toilet, and promised she'd be back soon. She should have felt sorry for this young man, still chained like an animal, but, in this case, Mila was grateful that her alexithymia inhibited every emotion. Her priority was to save her daughter.

Mila took off her black jacket and threw it on one of the antique armchairs in the living room. The clock tolled eleven times. She started the computer and waited for the operating system to load. A single icon appeared on the screen: Two. She clicked on it. On the first screen, the stylised globe was rotating but, unlike the other times, numbers had already been inserted in the box for latitude and longitude.

I knew it, Mila thought.

The room smelt of the past. Outside, it had started raining again and drops were falling on the plants in the garden, producing a cacophony of sounds. She felt a sense of comforting solitude.

Once again, she was ready.

She put her pistol on the table to have it nearby, in case, rubbed the palms of her hands against her jeans to wipe off the sweat, breathed in and out a few times. She took out of her pocket one of the blue Angel Tear pills the jailer had left Fishbone so that he might commit suicide. She looked at the red balaclava and popped the pill into her mouth. Then she picked up the joystick and put on the visor.

A kaleidoscope of colours propelled her into the alternative world at the speed of light. During the uncontrollable descent into that hyperspace, she felt her heart rush down to her belly. It was so true, so real.

But then everything suddenly slowed down.

A pleasant calm took her over as the pixels started forming the new reality in an orderly fashion.

In the silence of the night, the echo of distant explosions. Concrete ramparts rose over an inland harbour and tall metal cranes soared into a jet-black sky. On the extensive sandy shore, at the mooring, the wreckage of large ships, lying on their sides or leaning against one another – the iron groaned, making them look like giant disorientated cetaceans that had been washed up.

Another explosion.

Mila turned to look, but all she saw was debris in the distance, with hydrocarbon smoke rising above it. She could sense its acrid smell, just as she could see the condensation of the breath from her mouth because of the cold.

The first thing she did was look for her reflection in a puddle: the avatar had the appearance of the black shadow that had tried to strangle her in Chinatown. The UniC killer.

Another rumble.

A dust cloud rose over the city: one of the skyscrapers in the centre had collapsed. She wondered what was happening.

The artificial universe was breaking down.

She walked down the road, which was shiny from the rain. On her left, there was the river, a thick, dark, oily substance that flowed slowly. On her right, a row of abandoned shops. She didn't know where to go or what to look for, but then heard blues music. Once again, Elvis was singing. It was a distorted version of 'That's All Right, Mama'. Like a demon inviting her to a party.

The meaning of the song was clear; Mila followed it and reached the door to a bar. She was curious to know what trick of the whisperer awaited her inside.

She pushed the door open.

A gust of air came in and stirred wind chimes hanging from a beam. A series of gentle high-pitched sounds welcomed her in. In the dark room, there was a long counter and, on top, a large bottle rack. A jukebox was switched on in a corner, and that was where Elvis's song was coming from.

In front of it, a man was standing with his back to her, tapping his foot in time with the music. He was wearing a velvet jacket and a pair of deformed Clarks, and his hair was tousled. Even before he turned towards her, Mila recognised him by the scruffy appearance that had attracted her ten years earlier.

Her daughter's father looked at her with strange, bird-like eyes, dark and expressionless.

You should be in a coma, damn you. 'The patient's general condition remains incurable.' And yet he was carving a piece of wood with a small knife. No, it isn't wood, Mila corrected herself. It's a bone.

He cocked his head to indicate the room next door. An archway led to another room, with tables and booths. Next to these stood a cradle rocked by a skeletal hand.

Mila followed his directions, but terror made her sway at every step. Of the nightmares Enigma had created for her, this was definitely the worst.

When she reached the booth, she saw that the hand belonged to a woman with a black veil. The dark cloth also covered the cradle, making it hard to see the baby. All that was visible were its little legs kicking.

The veiled mother was laying tarot cards on the table. The skin on her arms, uncovered by the cloth, was covered in old scars. Razor-blade kisses, Mila called them when, at the age of sixteen, she'd started cutting herself. She realised that the black mother must be her, so Alice must be the baby in the cradle. The entire family reunited, she thought, sitting across the table from the woman and waiting for her to finish.

'Follow him.'

Once again, the voice of the ghost quickly and unexpectedly swept past her, like a whisper in her ear. Mila turned in

213

the direction she thought it had fled. She saw a bamboo tent moving and, inside, possibly a child – he must have been ten years or thereabouts, Alice's age, and wearing a red T-shirt.

Follow him. Who was she supposed to follow? She didn't understand.

They looked at each other for a long moment, then the veiled mother slammed her bony hand on the table to get her attention.

Startled, Mila got distracted. When she looked at the bamboo tent again, the ghost of the child had vanished.

After she'd finished spreading her cards, the woman began turning them over, one at a time. They were faces. Women, men, old people, young people, children. They were smiling. They were the photos of missing persons, like those on the Waiting Room walls in Limbo – their last image before being swallowed by the darkness.

As Mila wondered what she was trying to reveal to her, the woman turned over a card that was different from the others: it wasn't the picture of a person but that of a beautiful, emerald-coloured snake.

Then something unexpected happened. The black mother began to cry under her veil. Quietly at first, but then increasingly louder. Her lament soon became devastating, like the sobs that shook her chest. At the same time, she stopped rocking the baby. Not understanding what was going on, Mila glanced at the cradle.

Alice was no longer kicking, but lying motionless.

Mila felt dismay. It was as though Elsewhere was telling her that in order to finally be able to cry, she'd have to see her daughter die.

At that moment, she realised she was unable to move. She

214

was paralysed. She couldn't fathom the reason for this but then saw it. The emerald snake had slithered out of the tarot card and was coiling around her.

This isn't real, she told herself. It's like last time, when I felt someone strangling me. I must just convince myself that this isn't real.

The snake was sliding up her body. Mila turned her head towards the window of the bar.

She saw them coming, in groups and alone. They were shadows, they were monsters. They were approaching slowly, like a procession. They'd been summoned by the veiled mother's lament. They're coming for me, Mila thought. She wanted to run away, but the snake's embrace grew tighter and tighter.

The child in the red T-shirt had tried to warn her of the imminent danger. Once again, she hadn't listened. But she didn't intend to give in.

I can do this, she persuaded herself. It doesn't take much, I just have to drop the joystick and then I'll also be able to remove the visor. All I need to do is open my fingers around the handle and I'll break this evil spell in my head.

No effort was actually necessary to take her hand off the lever. She even managed it quite easily. But it wasn't enough, because the feeling of constriction persisted.

Soon, the monsters will be here, she thought, picturing the horrible things they would do to her.

The mind sees what the mind wants to see.

To make the situation worse, Mila heard someone laughing in the middle of the weeping. The repulsive snake had wrapped all the way up around her neck, so she could move only her eyes, and therefore couldn't work out where the laughter was coming from.

What's the joke? Who's laughing?

But then there was a male voice. 'No point in looking for me,' it said, amused. 'I'm not in the game.'

Mila realised what was happening. The laughter and the voice were not in Elsewhere, nor were they caused by the Angel Tear.

In the reality outside the game, the snake was a rope and Mila was tied to a chair in front of the computer. And there was someone else in the room with her.

It had started raining heavily again. Berish was driving along the bypass, leaning forward on the steering wheel, the windscreen wipers going at full speed.

He was thinking about his situation. He'd planned to spend a romantic weekend, with good food and pleasant conversation. Instead, he was in a nightmare with no visible way out.

I'm doing it for Alice, he repeated to himself. He felt sorry for the girl, but also angry with Mila, because she stubbornly refused to understand that, if they failed, she would bear the weight of remorse for the rest of her life.

He was fond of her, but he also knew that she was at times obstinately hostile. Moreover, she had a strange attraction towards the darkness and, even though he'd never admit it to her, that frightened him.

Berish drew comfort from the thought that his relationship with Vanessa wasn't at such an advanced stage that she would be involved in this descent into the abyss. He couldn't have forgiven himself if his new girlfriend paid the price for the case he was on. Because he wasn't sure he'd come out of it alive.

His relationship with her was only a few weeks old, but

Berish felt he'd found the right person for him. Before they met, he'd been almost resigned to spending the rest of his life in perfect solitude. He'd realised that he didn't need a family or a wife. He had his dog, his books, a collection of Scotch, Thursday-night poker with friends, and a whole series of honed habits that made him into a contented man.

But Vanessa, with her gentle ways and attentions he hadn't received for ages, had planted the seed in his mind that perhaps what he had wasn't enough. It was still too soon to tell whether the elements were really there to take things a step further, like, for instance, moving in together. Hitch would object, but only because he didn't like change. But Berish had to consider the fact that his Hovawart was ageing faster than he was and that, sooner or later, he would leave him on his own.

He'd met Vanessa in a club, since they shared a love of jazz. She'd come up to him with a Bloody Mary and asked if she could sit at his table. The evening had turned out to be surprisingly pleasant.

She was about his age and had confessed to having been married. Once the fact that there were no children had been established, Berish hadn't asked her anything else about her previous relationship, partly because he'd sensed that it wasn't an easy topic for her. Other than that, they got on perfectly well. They had the same tastes and were in sync with each other. He'd received proof of the complicity between them the night before, when Mila had shown up on his doorstep and, grasping the situation, Vanessa had had no problem about leaving without even asking about the emergency.

Berish could still smell her perfume on him – lily-of-the-valley and jasmine. At this time, they would have been in

217

bed, in each other's arms, enjoying the teeming rain and the secret sweetness of a tedious Sunday night. Instead, drenched to the bone, he was driving into the past of a young woman murdered many years earlier, probably by a person she trusted. Or unaware that they were dangerous, he thought. We let someone into our life, suspecting nothing, and unwittingly become prisoners of another person's obsession.

He took the exit that led to Lea Mulach's old district, then slowed down and pulled up next to a bus stop to check the address on the map he'd found in the glove compartment. He'd promised himself he wouldn't turn on the satnav. He wasn't sure whether he really did need to take these precautions or whether they were just the fruit of Mila's or that Pascal fellow's paranoia, but he decided not to run the risk.

The truth was that he didn't know what his own position was in the whisperer's 'design'. Enigma must certainly have foreseen that Mila would turn to me, Berish thought, so he will have considered the role I'd have to play.

He thought about this side of the situation for a while, as the rain pitter-pattered on the car roof. It was a pleasant sound. Berish felt it was necessary to fully take advantage of every quiet moment, since there was no knowing what lay in store for them. He was afraid the worst was yet to come. He couldn't admit it to Mila, but it was improbable that this business would end with Alice's rescue.

Nobody survived a whisperer – she'd said it.

Berish dismissed the sense of foreboding from his mind; it was no use letting himself be influenced. Then he started back on the road that led to Lea Mulach's old high school.

The building had been erected according to pre-1980s'

standards. You could tell by the subsequently added disabled ramp and emergency exits. It was composed of two separate parts with a central tower and a clock at the top. The area was circumscribed by a halo of lamp posts with orange lights.

Berish parked the saloon fifty metres away from the entrance, so it wouldn't be too obvious. Then he sat watching.

There was no custodian, but he couldn't rule out the possibility that the school might be under surveillance to avoid burglary or vandalism. He got out of the car and headed to the west wing because one of the lamp posts by the windows wasn't working. He wiped the rain from the pane with his sleeve, then framed his hands around his face and leaned against them to look inside.

It was a science lab.

He checked that there wasn't anyone around, then took off his coat, rolled it tightly around his arm and, with his elbow, struck the glass until it broke. The noise was muffled by the teeming rain. Berish made the opening wider and removed the sharpest shards. Then he heaved himself up onto the windowsill and landed inside.

No alarm went off.

He switched on the torch he'd brought with him and scanned the area for security cameras. Not finding any, he carried on searching down the corridor. There, too, just like in the science lab, was no sign of a security system. He walked on, pointing the beam of light down so he wouldn't be noticed from the outside. He was heading to the admin office, where he assumed the personnel files of the teaching staff were kept. Having reached the door to the management offices, however, he spotted a security camera. Crossing this boundary was impossible unless he could neutralise the electronic eye. Still, he didn't give up, because he thought of somewhere else he could look.

He headed to the library.

The large room was home to thousands of books. Berish had no time to search through the index, so he quickly swooped the torchlight over the shelves, certain that the year-books would occupy prime position. And so it was: there was actually a whole section devoted to the last sixty yearbooks. Berish was interested in the ones that dated back to the time when Lea Mulach attended the school. He carried them to one of the tables, propped the torchlight next to him so it would shine on the books, put on his glasses and began to leaf through them.

He found her amid the pages of a volume dedicated to her final year: in the photo, Lea had her hair up and wore a pair of glasses with golden frames. She was smiling. The caption described a model pupil, captain of the majorettes' team and editor of the school paper. Moreover, given her passion for the East, Lea had successfully managed a twinning with a high school in Beijing, which had resulted in a pupil exchange.

Berish looked for the files of her teachers, intending to draw up a list. The profile he was after was that of a male under thirty-six, because, according to criminology literature, serial killers had harboured an urge to kill since adolescence and were unable to restrain it past that age.

He immediately put on the list a handsome gym teacher, as well as a history and chemistry one. Then he added the vice principal because he thought it better to avoid possible surprises. Finally, he looked at the four names on the page.

One of these men had crossed paths with the whisperer. Enigma had detected in him the dark aura of evil, persuaded him to listen to the secret voice within him that had always told him killing was in his nature, so couldn't be wrong. He'd given him the motivating prod to satisfy a need harboured for who knows how long, as well as an unavowable desire: to possess the girl with the blonde hair and glasses, pick the forbidden fruit of her youth. Even if that meant annihilating her. Berish shuddered at the thought that the ordinary appearance of one of the men on his list concealed the UniC killer. Now, he and Mila would go knocking on the doors of these upright teachers, these family men above suspicion. They would have to ask difficult, ambiguous questions, then study their every reaction, notice the slightest change in their expression while seeking confirmation. It wouldn't be easy. Years spent playing a double role would certainly put them at an advantage in relation to their opponent.

Still, every mask has a crack in it, Berish told himself while leafing absent-mindedly through the pages of the yearbook: there were photos of the spring ball, when final-year pupils said goodbye to their teachers and their friends in the lower forms. He stopped, noticing Lea Mulach in the middle of a group of other girls: she looked radiant in a red silk dress embroidered with dragonflies and peach blossoms. Then, relying on a stroke of luck, he searched for an adult among those around her, hoping to catch a teacher giving her a glance, one of those creepy looks that sometimes unwittingly revealed the true intentions of a maniac. But he saw nothing of the kind.

He realised he'd been naive. How could he have believed it would be so easy? He shook his head, and was about to close the yearbook when he froze. His hand remained in mid-air, holding the other half of the book: in the gutter, just on the border between light and shadow, his eyes had glimpsed a familiar face.

Berish realised he'd got everything wrong until then. But it was Mila who had made the most serious error. He prayed that she had called the rescue services in time and left like she'd promised. If not, she was in serious danger.

In the grooved photo, there was a spotty young man, staring at the girl with a glass in his hand. The schoolmate who had developed an obsession for her, to the point of becoming a serial killer, was Timmy Jackson, also known as Fishbone.

Follow him.

What had the child in the red T-shirt tried to tell her? Whatever it was, by now it was too late. Fishbone was there with her, she could hear him moving in the room, only Mila was trapped in Elsewhere.

The veiled mother kept weeping. The baby's motionless little legs were starting to turn purple. Elvis had stopped singing. But the most worrying thing was the shadows outside that were heading towards the bar.

'You can't leave ...' Fishbone reminded her, whispering into her ear in the real world.

She wished she could congratulate him for the effective staging: pretending to be a prisoner of the UniC killer had been an excellent ploy to divert suspicion. And to think that she'd felt she'd been ruthless, leaving him chained in the cellar. But Fishbone could have freed himself at any time. Instead he had waited for her to be connected to Two.

What did he have in mind? She was scared she already knew the answer, having felt his hands gripping her neck in Elsewhere. She'd been stupid to trust him, but she'd been tricked by the red balaclava. Was Fishbone also Pascal? Impossible: their voices and build were too different.

Now, however, she wasn't interested in reconstructing the logic of the events. She was thinking about Berish, who wouldn't be able to save her. Because she'd lied to him, he'd be thinking that she was far from this house, certain that she had already called the rescue services for the wretched prisoner.

Mila was still suspended between the two worlds. Meanwhile, her daughter's father stopped carving the bone, went to the door of the bar and opened it for the guests who were coming to join the family celebration.

'I know you can hear me, Timmy,' she tried to say. 'I can even imagine how much fun you're finding all this, and I've no problem admitting that you're very clever . . . But my daughter needs me . . . I've never been a good mother. I've never told her I loved her, partly because it wouldn't have been true . . . I never wanted her inside me, or in my life. But I must ask you a favour . . . '

You didn't get away from a serial killer, she knew that. But she was angling for something else.

'I know I'm going to die, and that's fine. But can you take care of my little girl?'

She hated herself for saying that, but it was an act: for the likes of Timmy Jackson, there was nothing worse than a victim who accepted their own destiny, and Mila wanted to deprive the bastard from reaching orgasm while killing her.

'Shut up!' Fishbone indeed yelled. 'You have to shut up!'

'Alice needs you, Timmy,' Mila insisted vehemently, in order to provoke him. 'You can't refuse me this favour.'

In response, she felt his fingers positioning themselves on her throat. That was exactly his purpose, partly because, in the meantime, the shadows had entered the bar and were coming to take their places around her. She preferred to die in a few minutes, strangled by Fishbone, than go through a long agony in Elsewhere because of the hallucinogenic effects of the Angel Tear.

Hurry up, you son of a bitch.

All she wanted was to go quickly into the real world, because an irrational terror told her that if she died in Two, she would be trapped in the game for ever.

When the killer started to tighten his grip, she thought about Alice and everything she hadn't done for her. Mila didn't believe in an afterlife, even though she'd been to hell many times. With her death, Enigma had won. *His prize is my daughter. And it's no one's fault but my own.*

While the shadows around her were reaching out with tentacle-like hands to caress her, looking forward to the suffering they would inflict on her, Mila exhaled all the air from her lungs, to make Fishbone's task easier.

It all happened very quickly. First, she heard an explosion and thought that another piece of Elsewhere had come crashing down, but this time it was much closer. Then, Fishbone's grip loosened inexplicably. The monsters were practically upon her, but the thin skin between the two worlds suddenly snapped.

Mila found herself in the real one.

Someone had removed her visor, but she was still under the effect of the drug. Her head was spinning hard. The first thing her eyes were able to make out was Fishbone lying on the floor: he was spurting blood, like an absurd fountain, from a hole in the middle of his throat.

As the killer was dying in despair, the ropes that tied her to the chair by the PC were being untied. Mila searched for her pistol on the table, but it wasn't there, and neither was the red balaclava.

Behind her, Pascal appeared: his face was covered and the weapon was tucked into his belt.

'There's no time for thanks,' he said, speaking first.

Mila realised she didn't trust him. He noticed it.

'Why was your balaclava here?' she asked, indicating the keyboard.

'I wanted to let you know I was nearby, but clearly you didn't understand the signal.'

'That's not true,' she said accusingly, feeling increasingly unwell. 'You're involved . . . I don't know how, but you are.'

'When you and the other man came into the villa, I hid in the garden,' Pascal said, defending himself, although he was agitated. 'We have to rush. They're coming.'

'Who?' Mila asked, her voice drowsy with nausea.

'The ones you saw down there,' he replied, pointing at the computer. 'Except that these are real. Enigma is sending them.'

'I don't believe you,' she said, standing up abruptly then collapsing back into the chair from dizziness. 'And, besides, before this bastard bleeds to death, he has to tell me where my daughter is.'

'Don't you see he can't talk?'

She wasn't moving, however. So Pascal took the pistol from his belt and handed it to her. Mila hesitated, but then remembered what the ghost had told her.

Follow him.

She stared at the man in the balaclava the same colour as the child's T-shirt, thought for a few seconds, then grabbed the weapon from his latex-gloved hand.

Pascal put the black duster jacket over her shoulders, then his arm around her waist to help her up. Mila realised her legs were weak but did her best to keep her balance. He dragged her away with him, but Mila was aware of being a dead weight. They walked across the villa as fast as they could, heading for the exit. Meanwhile, they kept checking every window, afraid to see a presence, and her heart skipped a beat whenever they turned a corner.

For Mila, everything felt confused and rarefied. She could tell that Pascal was short of breath from the effort of holding her up; she could smell his pungent sweat. She couldn't help thinking about her own death and the men who were on their way.

They crossed the conservatory and the wholesome cold evening air slapped her in the face. Before they walked into the thunderstorm, Mila instinctively turned towards the bush of black roses, as though to say goodbye to it. She noticed something sticking out of the soil.

A matted, dirty lock of Lea Mulach's blonde hair.

JOSHUA

19

The car was an old wreck, but it darted down the city streets in the rain.

Pascal had got her to lie down in the back and hadn't even removed his balaclava, trusting that the night and the sheet of rain would prevent anyone from noticing that there was a hooded man behind the wheel.

In fleeing from the shadows sent by Enigma, every so often they would dodge a car coming in the opposite direction and were reproached with a honk.

Mila was still on her Angel Tear trip. She kept trying to sit up, but the weight of her head would push her back down. She was drenched, cold and huddled in her black duster jacket. She didn't know where they were going; all she could see in the dark were the headlights of the other cars.

'You have to try and remain conscious,' Pascal said as he drove.

Many addicts would fry their brains with synthetic drugs, but Mila didn't need Pascal to remind her of that. 'Why did you dump me in the burnt-out house?'

'Because I couldn't trust you yet.'

'You promised you'd help me find Alice.'

'You see? You don't listen, because you think only of yourself.'

Mila was shaking, unable to stop her teeth from chattering. 'Okay: what do you mean?'

The car took a right turn and the tyres skidded briefly on the wet asphalt. Pascal kept checking the rear-view mirror to see if they were being followed.

'The game you're playing doesn't just concern you and your daughter,' he said. 'There's something much more important at stake.'

'And that is?'

'We started monitoring the game many years ago.'

'We? Who are you talking about? You and who else?'

'I've already explained that Elsewhere was originally conceived as a great social experiment. After the "virtuoso players" dropped out, we thought it would be a good opportunity to observe how human behaviour evolved in an environment with no rules. We wondered: "What happens when an ordinary person is placed in a reality where absolute anarchy reigns and where you can be anybody and do anything you like without paying the consequences? And will this kind of society automatically veer towards good or evil?"'

Mila overlooked the meaning of the argument for a moment, because she realised that the jargon was familiar to her. 'Wait a minute . . . Are you a criminologist?'

Pascal did not reply. He suddenly swerved and drove up a deserted street on the wrong side.

Mila had thought he was a hacker because he'd chosen to be called after the computer programming language, but clearly she'd been mistaken. 'Who do you work for?' she asked insistently.

'For no one,' he replied. 'Anyway, in the beginning, the purpose of our research was a noble one, I assure you. Then, it all went to hell . . . '

'What the fuck are you trying to tell me? That it was you people who took those monsters into Two?'

'They weren't monsters before they joined the game,' he specified, confirming her suspicions. 'At least not all of them . . . But many were borderline: they did have in them those germs of violence and cruelty required for their behaviour to develop in a sadistic way.'

Mila thought of Fishbone and Karl Anderson, of how they'd been transformed: from a harmless teenager with acne and a family man, they'd become, respectively, a serial killer and the author of carnage.

'Two produces a paroxysmal effect on people's imagination,' she said.

All of us imagine killing, but it's one thing if that thought remains within the bounds of secrecy in our mind, monitored by shame and fear of consequences, and quite another if it's fuelled by the illusion of impunity, gratified by power and driven to the limits of possibility. Then that unavowable idea becomes desire, the worst poison of human nature.

'In the beginning, it was a controlled experiment,' Pascal said in his defence.

Mila was furious. 'What does "controlled" mean? How can you presume to control evil?'

'Trust me, I know what I'm talking about: I'm a monitor.'

'A monitor?'

'When the game was transformed, there were already a lot

of us. Our job was to monitor the anomalies of Elsewhere. Naturally, we expected something would spill over to this side ... Every now and then, someone made the *leap*; it was inevitable.'

The leap? What was he talking about?

'One fine day, a harmless bank clerk would go into Two and become a serial rapist. When we realised he was about to do the same in the real world, we would intervene and either dissuade him, or report him to the authorities.'

'Then why didn't the system work?'

'They wiped us out ... Something happened and they started hunting us down out here, that's why I erased my identity and now try to live without leaving any trace.'

Mila was sure that the 'something' Pascal was talking about – the cause that unleashed the chaos – was the whisperer.

'I don't know how many monitors are left; I lost touch with the others a long time ago and now I'm on my own.'

They drove up an iron bridge that led out of the city. The tyres, in contact with asphalt suspended in the void, were making a hollow sound.

'What's all this got to do with me?' Mila asked in despair. 'Why have they dragged me into this business?'

'I have no idea, but if you want to save yourself, you'll have to find out.'

All she wanted was to save Alice.

'Have you ever wondered why Enigma's body is covered in numbers?' Pascal asked.

'I gather it's a kind of map of Elsewhere.'

'Exactly. And have you worked out how your game works?'

'Since my very first trip into Two, I've been shown crime scenes ... In the case of Karl Anderson, I was immediately given the solution to the mystery, but only so I'd understand how things would play out. But later, in Chinatown, I had to conduct an investigation starting with a few elements I'd seen in Elsewhere, so I went back to Lea Mulach's murder.' As a matter of fact, she'd been thinking about this for a while. 'The question concealed in the setting I find myself in within Two is always linked to a real crime, and each time I solve it I'm allowed to move on to the next level of the game. Only I don't know how many are left.'

'Does the man you're with know everything?'

'Yes, he's a former colleague of mine.'

'You know you may have shafted him, don't you?'

Yes, she'd thought about it, but she'd had no alternative. A year earlier, she'd suddenly severed all relations with Simon Berish, but then she'd appeared in his life again without considering the danger to which she was exposing him.

You should be with the woman with the lily-of-the-valley and jasmine perfume right now but, instead, you're probably wondering what's happened to me and if I'm all right.

'Did you notice any changes during your last trip to Elsewhere?' Pascal asked. 'I mean in comparison with the other times . . . '

Mila thought for a moment. She remembered the roaring sounds and the scene with the skyscraper crashing down in the centre. 'Somebody's destroying the city.'

'That's right,' he said, then shook his head. 'Not good, not good at all . . . '

'Can you explain to me what it means?'

'When we arrive,' he replied, heading out of the residential area. 'Now you need to take the antidote to the LHFD and rest.'

'Where are we going?'

'To a safe place.'

The safe place was a ruin that had once been a country house. Pascal helped Mila get out of the car and she was able to study the building in the rain. Half of it had been burnt down some time ago. Once again, Pascal had picked a place that had survived the flames.

He took her indoors, even though it was still raining down on them over the threshold, since part of the roof had collapsed. After walking through a couple of devastated rooms with charred furniture and floors black with soot, they came into a third, which had been spared by the fire. It had a wardrobe, a bed and an armchair. Pascal got Mila to lie down then went back to shut the door. Then he took a small bottle of water from a shelf and handed it to her along with a 4 gram niacin tablet.

'I feel nauseous afterwards,' she said, pushing the latex-gloved hand away.

Then Pascal opened the wardrobe and started looking for something. He returned with a blanket. 'Dry yourself with this.'

Mila threw it over her jacket, hoping to put a stop to her shivering.

'Better?' he asked.

'Better, thanks.'

She had doubted him, and yet once again he'd come to her aid and saved her life. Why? Also, he was attentive, but Mila had learned to mistrust kindness. She mustn't let her guard down, because she knew nothing about him. Who was this stocky man with flat feet? Where did his faded brown suit come from? Why did he wear a tie? Who looked after him? He gave the impression of being alone.

Meanwhile, Pascal went to sit in the armchair. In the half-light and against the muffled sound of the rain falling on the house, Mila's thoughts began to drift. She then saw her mysterious friend removing his balaclava. From where she was, she couldn't make out his face, and he knew that.

'I'm sure you've sometimes thought of what you would do if you could go back in time . . . '

I wouldn't have Alice, Mila said to herself.

'I've been thinking about that a lot lately,' Pascal continued. There was weariness but also a sense of despondency in his voice. 'Human beings are capable of inventing extraordinary things; their genius has no limits. But often their most beautiful creations end up turning against us . . . I was thinking about Two: no matter what you'd done or experienced in real life, and no matter how irreversible, you had a chance to make amends in the game.'

'What do you mean?'

'If someone couldn't walk any more as a result of an accident, they could do it again in Elsewhere. Someone who had come out of a coma would learn to live and do essential things again. In the beginning, Two was used by rehabilitation centres to restore patients' hope.'

Sensing that something painful had happened in the stranger's past, Mila was sure he was carrying a heavy load inside him. 'What torments you, Pascal? Why don't you say it straight out?'

The man stroked his head. 'They told us the internet was an indispensable revolution. But nobody foresaw how much it would cost us . . . To begin with, it's not as free as they'd have us believe: why else would we all use the same search engine? They want us to have the same information, they've made our thinking uniform without our noticing ... And then the internet isn't even equitable: it's tyrannical. It's not true that it repairs social injustice: on the contrary, it doesn't forget and doesn't forgive. If I write something about you, nobody can delete it. Even if it's a lie, it'll stay there for ever. Anyone can use the web as a weapon, and, what's even worse, is that they'll remain unpunished ... People have poured their anger onto the net, and we let them do it; it was like sweeping dirt under the carpet. But, however vast it may seem to us, the internet is not able to contain what's worst about us. Sooner or later, this hatred will look for an outlet ... We live in the illusion that we can control everything just because we can do our shopping from the sofa with a fucking smartphone. But all it would take is a solar explosion that's more powerful than usual and within a few minutes the world's electronic devices would go berserk. It would take years to fix the damage and, in the meantime, we'd be plunged into the fucking Middle Ages ... '

There wasn't a single flaw in his analysis, Mila thought. But what was most disconcerting was that these truths were before everybody's eyes, and yet nobody seemed to realise the real danger.

'The skyscraper you saw crashing down and the roaring sounds you heard ... ' Pascal left the sentence hanging, as though he found it hard to continue with his story.

'Yes?' she said, urging him on.

'Somebody introduced a virus into the program. Elsewhere is self-destructing.'

'Aren't you glad?'

'You don't understand: Two isn't just a parallel world, it's how we really are ... If the game ends, evil will invade our streets – there'll be no escape for us.'

Mila wasn't sure she shared Pascal's apocalyptic vision.

'And one of the consequences would concern you directly,' he continued. 'If time runs out in Elsewhere, it'll also run out for your daughter.'

Mila hadn't considered the fact that the game could be halted by a cause independent of the will of the players. What would happen to Alice then? Where would she find the information necessary to free her? A new fear gripped her. 'How much time is left?'

'I don't know, but certainly not long. You have to get her out before it happens, or you'll never see her again.'

Mila was overwhelmed with sudden despair and was about to get up. The man quickly put his balaclava back on and went and stopped her.

'You're in no position to do anything in this condition,' he said sternly. 'Stop relying on your instinct alone and use your head, damn it.'

'I can't wait ... Alice can't ... ' she said as dizziness pulled her back on the bed.

'Yes, you can,' Pascal replied. 'You need to recover your strength, because this is a game of cunning.'

'I'd promised to take her Indian food for dinner and that we'd find her cat that had got lost ... '

'I'm allergic to cats,' Pascal said laconically.

'I know.' She could still remember their first car journey, when he kept sneezing because of Finz's hairs.

'Did you find any useful elements in the last scene?' he asked.

Mila thought about the inland harbour, the veiled

mother and her daughter's father. 'An emerald-coloured snake,' she said.

'Is that all?' he asked, surprised.

'It was painted on a tarot card, but all the others had the faces of missing persons.'

'Well, in the morning you'll have to search for the meaning of the snake and connect it to a crime to be solved,' Pascal replied, handing her the niacin once again.

This time, Mila took it without arguing and swallowed it.

'You'll be gone by the time I wake up, right?' she asked, even though she knew the answer.

'When I told you a little while ago that, if I could, I would go back in time, well, maybe I'd do it just to put an end to all this.'

'Do you mean you'd commit suicide?'

'I mean that there comes a moment when you lose everything, and then it makes no sense to keep going. You don't commit suicide out of grief, that's bearable in the long run. You do it because you no longer have a task in hand. Now I have one, but it shouldn't have been my task and, above all, I didn't choose it.'

Mila didn't understand what he was referring to exactly, but the tablet was beginning to take effect and she felt too exhausted to go into details. 'I saw a child in Elsewhere,' she said, her eyes closing. 'There shouldn't be children in hell, don't you think?'

She noticed that Pascal had taken a small step back. 'What child?'

'He was wearing a red T-shirt and tried to warn me. I've already told you about him, but the first few times it was just a voice . . . now he appeared before me.'

The ghost was a friendly figure among the shadows and his T-shirt was the same colour as Pascal's balaclava.

'Forget about that child,' he said. 'Leave him alone.'

Follow him.

'And yet he knew you'd come for me ... It's a sign,' she said, almost mumbling, her eyelids getting heavier.

Pascal knelt to look into her eyes. 'You will eat Indian food again and you'll find that damned cat ... But if you want to have your daughter back safe and sound, don't trust anybody.'

Mila felt she was about to yield to sleep. 'Not even you?' she barely managed to ask.

'We all have an avatar in the real world,' Pascal replied.

20

Her awakening was brusque and sudden.

Mila looked around the room: Pascal had vanished.

The orange glow of the sun was seeping from under the door and through the beams in the ceiling. Her first thought was that it was the second night Alice had spent away from her, a prisoner, God knows where.

The rain had stopped and she could hear birds singing. Pascal's last sentence was echoing in her head.

'We all have an avatar in the real world.'

What did he mean? It made no sense.

She sat up in bed. Her head was still spinning and the pain all over her body told her that sleep hadn't been restorative.

She slipped her duster jacket on, put the fleece hood over her head and left the burnt-down house.

At dawn, in the middle of the countryside, there wasn't a soul to be seen.

She ventured down the deserted road. After the copious rain, the air was permeated with fragrances. It would have been a pleasant stroll if not for the gloomy thoughts crowding her mind. She continued for another couple of kilometres, then saw a van coming. She flagged it down and asked the driver, who was on his way to town, to give her a lift.

During the entire journey, she kept thinking about the veiled mother, her daughter's father carving a bone and Alice dying in the cradle, and also about the words of her balaclava-wearing friend, his urging her not to trust anyone, and that strange reference to the time remaining. A virus was destroying Elsewhere, but Mila had got the impression that something equally devastating had happened in Pascal's life.

'I'm sure you've sometimes thought of what you would do if you could go back in time . . . '

Everybody thought about this, without exception. The errors of the past were the remedy of the present. Everybody looked back and attributed their problems to distant, one-time choices. But it was only an alibi for making more mistakes.

Once they were in town, Mila asked the driver to drop her off at a metro station. She then caught a train to the department, hoping that Simon Berish had already started work.

She walked into the building through a side entrance, taking advantage of the shift change of the cleaning staff. She pulled down her hood but, in the Monday morning chaos, no one noticed her, so she reached Limbo easily.

Stepping into the Waiting Room, she noticed Berish sleeping on a chair. He immediately straightened up.

'Are you all right?' he asked, going towards her, looking upset. 'I went back to the villa and saw Fishbone's body.'

'You were right,' was the only thing Mila managed to say, as she ran her fingers through her hair. 'I've been an idiot. But now I have a million things to tell you.'

And so she did over the next hour, after drinking a scalding coffee Berish made her with the office machine. She told him Timmy Jackson was the UniC killer, apologised once again for failing to heed his advice to leave that house straight away – even though, deep in her heart, she knew Fishbone would have found a way of attacking her anyway.

'I can't understand the rationale of all this,' Berish said. 'Why does Enigma involve you by tattooing your name on himself, but then his followers repeatedly try to kill you? And someone kidnapping Alice doesn't make any sense either. If you were the target, why not eliminate you immediately in the lake house?'

Actually, Berish wasn't wrong. There was an obvious contradiction between the various elements.

'It could be my game,' she said.

Finally, she told him about Pascal, her suggestion that he was a criminologist and his not denying it.

'We should try and discover Pascal's identity,' Berish suggested, even though he knew the man had erased all trace of himself. 'As you know all too well, it's impossible to disappear completely.'

That was true, and Mila had experienced it during her years at Limbo, hunting missing persons. You could alter your appearance, your habits, clean up your fingerprints and every organic trace that could reveal your DNA, but there was always something about you – maybe something you didn't suspect – that never changed. She recalled the case of a woman with a husband and children, who'd gone missing for twenty years. Mila had identified her only because she'd kept the unconscious gesture of pulling out her eyebrow hairs when she was worried.

'For the time being, we have no clue to start from,' Mila said, attentive to such details. 'He's very careful.'

Berish wasn't convinced but decided to defer to her. 'What have you brought back from your new trip to Elsewhere?'

'This time, my memento is an emerald-coloured snake.'

Mila deliberately left out the description of the grim family reunion and busied herself entering the keywords into the database of the Bureau of Missing Persons.

'In Two, I was shown some tarot cards,' she said to Berish. 'They had the photos of missing persons, like the ones here in the Waiting Room.'

'But if the snake is connected to a disappearance, why not simply show you the person's face?' he asked. 'Something tells me this isn't the right track.'

Despite Berish's scepticism, Mila was certain. However, searching under the keyword *snake* yielded no result.

'Maybe we should start with a different element from the scene,' he suggested.

Mila thought, but another option came to mind. 'We could go and check if the bar where I was, in the harbour, really exists.'

It was a nameless place at the end of the pier, outside the shipyards and surrounded by low buildings designated for boat storage. There wasn't a sign over it because people only went there in order to drink and whoever needed to know it, knew it.

'Alcoholics don't require any frills,' was Berish's immediate comment. 'All they need to know is that they'll find a bottle there.'

The inland harbour was located right at the mouth of the

243

river, which made the bar into a strange junction between river folk and sea folk. They were greeted by the gentle sound of wind chimes, which immediately reminded Mila of the ones she had heard in Elsewhere. It was all so identical that she felt uneasy.

The jukebox, by which her daughter's father had stood carving a bone in the nightmare, was in the corner, except that a sign was taped to it, saying OUT OF ORDER. There was no knowing how long it had been off. Berish was right, there was no need for music in this kind of place. As a matter of fact, at nine fifteen in the morning, the handful of silent patrons sitting at the long counter were mostly busy anaesthetising their demons. They didn't need to chat or socialise, everything they needed was being poured into their glasses by a young barmaid.

She had long brown hair and wore a checked flannel shirt over a pair of jeans. She might have been just over twenty years old, but since the skin on her face was damaged, she looked at least ten years older.

'Good morning,' Mila said, introducing herself. But she immediately felt that their visit had been expected because the young woman turned pale.

'Have you found her?' she asked, her voice trembling. Her question confirmed that they were in the right place.

'Can we talk for a moment?' Berish said, implying that it would perhaps be better to continue the conversation in a more private location.

'You're cops, aren't you?' she asked, suddenly wondering if she'd made a mistake.

'Yes,' he replied.

'Just tell me if she's alive,' she begged.

Mila intervened. 'Is it your sister?'

The young woman shook her head. 'No, it's my mother.'

Her name was Laura Ortis and in less than five minutes she turfed out her customers so she could be alone with her new guests. She then led them to a saloon bar with booths. Mila sat in the one where she'd met the veiled mother.

'We don't have any news,' Berish immediately made clear to avoid giving her false hopes. 'But perhaps you could help us understand what happened to her.'

The young woman sat down and put a packet of Marlboros and a rusty Zippo down in front of her. 'Rose has always been messed up,' she said, practically banging the lighter on the table. 'And it's usually up to me to pick up the pieces.'

It was evident from her gestures that the relationship between mother and daughter was tormented. The fact that she referred to her by her first name was also significant, Mila thought.

'Rose isn't capable of taking care of herself,' Laura said, sucking the Zippo flame through the tip of the cigarette. 'She likes to disappear then reappear in my life as she pleases. But she's never gone three months without being in touch.'

'Can you tell us about her?' Berish asked, taking his glasses and notepad out of his raincoat pocket.

The young woman exhaled a cloud of smoke. 'Rose is fifty-six, even though she tells everyone she's thirty-six and acts like she's sixteen. This place used to be hers, she left it to me and basically comes back to me only when she needs money. She's never been married and claims she brought me up on her own, even though I'm the one who's always taken care of her.'

Not a flattering portrait, Mila thought. But, aside from that, Laura seemed genuinely concerned about her mother.

'In the past year, she discovered a new way of ruining her life and got obsessed with social media.'

The net, once again, Mila thought. But she didn't believe Rose had ended up in the claws of Two: a single, middle-aged woman wasn't the video-game type. 'What was your mother looking for on these sites?'

'If you think about it, it's the perfect place for a self-centred exhibitionist. She was constantly posting stuff, including photos and personal details: her whole fucking life ended up there. I tried to tell her in every possible way that it wasn't right. Rose thinks everybody fancies her, but she couldn't tell the difference between a compliment and a wind-up. And other people have always taken advantage of that.'

'If I told you about an emerald-coloured snake,' Berish asked, 'would you somehow connect it to your mother?'

Laura didn't hesitate for a second. She unbuttoned her shirt and took out a pendant hanging on a necklace. A green enamelled iguana. 'Like this one?'

Berish looked at Mila, who nodded. It was very similar to the snake she'd seen in Elsewhere.

'She's been making jewellery for a while and selling it online, no need to tell you she barely made back her expenses. The snake you mentioned is her very first piece: a ring she never parts with.'

Mila remembered the snake's vice-like grip in Two, but dismissed the image straight away. 'You think Rose has gone missing, don't you?'

'Yes.'

'Then why didn't you report it to the police?'

'I did!' Laura was indignant. 'But no one's contacted me until today.'

Mila exchanged glances with Berish. 'How is it possible that there's no sign of the report at Limbo?' she said.

Berish shook his head; he had no answer.

'Maybe it's because of the email,' Laura said.

'What email?'

'It came before I reported her missing. It basically said that Rose had met a man, that she was in love and that they'd decided to go and live in Guadeloupe.'

Mila realised what had happened: because of this email, the police officer who'd received the report must have thought she'd left of her own free will, and that it wasn't worth passing the information on to Limbo.

'Are you sure the email is from your mother?' Mila asked.

'It's typical of her to decide to go and live abroad with a total stranger. And it's her email address. But if you're asking if the words were written by Rose, then I'd say no.'

'What do you mean?' Berish asked.

'My mother was an airhead, but she had a phenomenal memory. There are things that don't add up in that email.'

The young woman left for a couple of minutes and returned with the printed-out email she'd had for heaven knows how long. It was dated December of the previous year.

'**Dear Laura, sunshine,**' she began to read.

Something extraordinary has happened to me: I've met a wonderful man, his name's Tom and I fell in love with him straight away. I know what you're thinking, that it's your kooky mum's usual rash behaviour. But this time you're wrong, because he also loves me to distraction and I trust him. Don't be angry, but we've decided to go and live together in Guadeloupe. You know how much I love

the sun and that I've always wanted to spend my old age on a Caribbean island, so my dream's coming true. As soon as I'm settled on the island, I'll write to you again (I'm not phoning because I know you'd insult me and I don't want you to spoil this for me). I've spoken to Tom and he thinks it would be lovely if you came to visit us for your next birthday, on 26 June. He can't wait to meet his stepdaughter. I hope you'll be happy for me, I love you.

Rose

Laura put the sheet of paper on the table and looked at them. 'So, what do you think?'

'What doesn't add up?' Berish asked.

'Rose has never mentioned her "old age", not even when drunk. It's true she was obsessed with the Caribbean, but she was scared of flying and, even though she ran a bar in the harbour, just seeing a ship would make her seasick.'

'It does seem a tenuous reason to rule out a voluntary departure,' Berish said.

'But that's not the only thing, because the oddest thing is my birthday.'

'You weren't born on the twenty-sixth of June?'

'That's what it says in the documents, because Rose forgot to register my birth for a week. But she actually gave birth to me on the nineteenth of June and since I was a child we've always celebrated on that day.'

Mila realised what Laura was attempting to tell her. 'You think your mother was in danger and that she was trying to send a message only you would understand.'

'Somebody forced her to write the email so I wouldn't worry

248

or try to tell the police, but Rose found a way of inserting details only I would know about. This email is a call for help.'

After trying in vain for three months to find someone to listen to her theory, Laura Ortis was happy to work with them and had even given them the key to her mother's apartment. She had already looked through it, but the trained eyes of two police officers would certainly be better at spotting any possible anomalies.

'What do you think?' Berish asked, while driving to the old Dutch district where the missing woman lived.

Mila thought for a moment. 'I'd like to tell you that there are elements in favour of the daughter's story. But if I hadn't received the snake clue in the game, I wouldn't see anything to justify an investigation.'

In her years working at Limbo, she'd seen it happen a few times. Disappearances that turned out to be elopements, abductions that occurred with the consent of the alleged victim. Some even went as far as staging their own death to avoid revealing to their loved ones an inconvenient truth – bankruptcy, betrayal or never taking any university exams.

According to her daughter, Rose was an eccentric woman. However, her decision to suddenly move abroad with a man she'd only just met wasn't as absurd as it seemed. On the contrary, it happened quite frequently.

Rose lived in a block of flats from the Sixties, a three-storey complex with a swimming pool in the middle. The building seemed to have been built around it, but now it was empty and was being used by skateboarders.

Mila and Berish arrived at around eleven o'clock, after dropping by Limbo to pick up a blood-print kit. For budgetary reasons, the department would only send Forensics in cases of confirmed crimes. So, over time, they'd learned to make do.

The missing woman lived in a small flat on the second floor. Mila and Berish found it thanks to the number on the door. When they opened it, they found at their feet a heap of advertising brochures and old bills.

'This is absurd,' Berish said, giving Mila a pair of gloves. 'Her daughter keeps paying the rent even though she doesn't live here. Maybe she thinks her mother might come back at any moment.'

'Or maybe she was waiting for someone to finally take her seriously,' Mila replied, putting on the latex gloves.

They looked around to decide where to start. It was a modest apartment: a living room with an open-plan kitchen, a bedroom with a small wardrobe and a windowless bathroom. The furniture was a mishmash of styles that resulted in kitsch. A sofa and an armchair covered in hippy scarves, Oriental rugs, a bed with a canopy, incense burners, different-sized Buddhas and a whole series of chinoiseries.

There was a PC on the dining room table.

'Focus on the computer while I take a look around,' Berish suggested.

Fortunately, the electricity hadn't been cut off, so Mila was able to access Rose's world. Apparently, she had profiles on all the social media sites. There were no passwords or special protections to log on, so it was easy to explore the woman's virtual life.

The first thing that caught Mila's eye was the fact that the personal pages had last been updated three months earlier, in other words, shortly before the woman's disappearance. For someone obsessed with social media, this was surely unusual. Laura Ortis was right: her mother shared every detail of her day online. It occurred to Mila that many people didn't have fulfilling lives, so sought validation with likes and followers. But, aside from the illusory aspect of that kind of approval and the dangers of making yourself vulnerable to other people's curiosity, one wondered how long particularly dependent people could live without the internet.

Mila paused on one of Rose's many photos. She was smiling, standing against the backdrop of a natural panorama – a plain surrounded by mountains, where a herd of horses was grazing. She had bleached hair and flashy make-up, especially around her eyes. On her finger, she was wearing an emerald-coloured snake that, Laura had said, she never parted with.

Meanwhile, Berish was opening doors and drawers. 'Found anything interesting?' he asked from the bedroom.

'There's a lot of stuff on her profiles, but I haven't found any trace of the mysterious Tom who allegedly persuaded Rose to move to Guadeloupe.'

'Some clothes are missing,' Berish said.

There were empty hangers swaying in the wardrobe. Everything suggested the woman had, indeed, packed her bags and left.

The internet search was proving fruitless. In any case, Mila thought, if someone had devised a plan to make Rose's disappearance look like a voluntary departure, they would have had no trouble deleting the signs of their presence on her social media page. It might be better to rely on material evidence, so she joined Berish.

The first thing she did was go to a dressing table with a mirror, like the one Pascal always had with him. But when it came to make-up, cosmetics and beauty creams, there was no one like Rose Ortis. Everything was there, from fake eye-lashes to contact lenses, to lipsticks of a thousand different shades, and even contraptions she'd never seen before.

She was especially struck by a display of blue crystal bottles aligned on a shelf. They were empty but at one time must have contained Rose's perfume. Mila realised that once it had finished, instead of throwing away the bottle, she added it to her collection.

'There's nothing suspicious here,' Berish said from the kitchen.

The fridge was usually a tell-tale element. People who staged a deliberate escape of a house's residents to conceal a crime – like murderers and kidnappers – were good at packing bags but would forget to throw out left-over food. You could tell by the state of decay that something had happened and even when.

Mila went to the small, windowless bathroom. She turned on the tap, checked the drains to see if anyone had thrown anything into them in an attempt to get rid of it. She examined the taps and the ceramic fixtures. The toothbrush was missing, and that supported the theory of a departure, but then a little white towel caught her eye.

There was a tiny brown stain on one of the corners.

'Come and see,' she told Berish. 'It could be blood.'

Simon examined the find. Of course, it wasn't uncommon to find bloodstains on an ordinary towel. And, to an untrained eye, the quantity wouldn't have suggested anything of concern. But Berish and Mila were right to be alarmed.

'I don't like the shape,' Berish immediately said.

According to the BPA – Bloodstain Pattern Analysis – you could discover many things by analysing one or more bloodstains. There were different classifications, depending on their shape. This one was oblong, which suggested that the fluid hadn't dripped but had been splashed. Various factors might have accounted for that: the distance from the starting point, the speed of impact with the towel, the force of impact of the object that had caused the injury.

It was evident to anyone that bloodstains left around by someone who'd cut himself shaving were very different from those generated by a gunshot.

The one they had before them suggested a violent trauma.

'It's worth checking,' Berish said.

They took out what they needed from the blood-print kit they'd brought with them.

'Maybe we should find out if Rose had any guests before she disappeared,' Mila said. 'Coat everything with luminol, while I go hunting for fingerprints.'

They divided the equipment as well as the tasks.

Berish took the vaporiser and the camera, then shut himself in the bathroom in search of more blood. Even if it had been washed away, the use of detergents didn't prevent the subsequent finding of blood traces, because the chemical substance called 3-aminoftalidrazide was able to highlight them in 1 to 5,000,000 dilutions. However, the fluorescent effect of this technique was temporary, so to secure the evidence, you had to photograph the result before it disappeared.

Mila's task was less complex but definitely more productive on the result front. Everybody leaves fingerprints, she'd been taught at the academy. Sometimes without even noticing. And it was possible to make them emerge from the surface of an object even after a long time. Naturally, the outcome depended on the shape of the material on which you were working, but, in Mila's case, she was spoilt for choice, since she had at her disposal a house filled with knick-knacks.

Mila had forgotten how exciting this kind of hunt could be. A hidden print was the first clue to a stranger's identity. Often, in the spiral left by the caress of a finger pad, you could sense something about the person who'd left it. For example, if there had been strength, urgency or fear. It was like when some geneticists manage to glimpse someone's appearance simply by looking at their DNA.

Like Berish, Mila did not have access to sophisticated means to conduct this preliminary investigation. She had to make do with traditional methods, which would only allow a superficial examination. But they might be sufficient for what they were hoping to find.

To start with, Mila used the so-called 'highlighting powders' – aluminium, magnetic and fluorescent – spread with a little brush: they would be absorbed by a watery or lipidic substance, and so reveal the papillary pattern.

She went through the smooth surfaces, but no prints appeared. That meant someone had taken care to erase them, and, if so, they had something to hide. But when she did the same with other underlying surfaces, she obtained the same result.

Strange, she thought. It would have been preferable to use cyanoacrylate, only she did not have access to a lab with a pressurised room.

The strangest thing was that she couldn't find, not only the fingerprints of an intruder, but also Rose's. Mila decided to look among the little blue perfume bottles she'd noticed earlier, but there again she was disappointed.

Berish came out of the bathroom, disconsolate: he hadn't found anything either.

'No prints,' Mila said.

'If someone cleaned the apartment, then something happened,' he replied, reaching his earlier conclusions.

'There's more,' Mila said, having gone even further. 'It's as though nobody's ever lived here. It's like being on Mars and we're the first humans to set foot there.'

Police called it 'the devil's paw'. A definition that matched this kind of inconsistency, which risked compromising the logic of an investigation.

'It's possible,' Simon replied.

A little brown stain and no hidden prints – that was all they had.

Mila immediately thought this was a far more careful staging than the one her colleagues had faced at the Andersons' farm, when they'd found the victims' blood but not their bodies.

Another of Enigma's tricks.

'I have a bad feeling,' Mila said. 'Not only did Rose Ortis never go to Guadeloupe, but she also never left here.'

'So what do you suggest?'

'Maybe you'd better go and get Hitch.'

Hovawarts were not cadaver dogs, but had an especially fine sense of smell, and were often used for locating people missing in natural disasters. In any case, Hitch was their only resource.

While Berish went home and back, Mila thought about

the implications of the case. She had no idea what role Rose Ortis played in Enigma's game, nor who'd want to hurt an apparently harmless woman. Her only certainty was that things hadn't ended well for Rose. Her instinct told her so, but so did the email her daughter had shown them: Laura was convinced that her mother was in danger, but she was thinking of an abduction, while Mila knew that handling a hostage was complicated and only professionals would embark on such a risky crime, and then usually only when there was a financial benefit, otherwise it wasn't worth taking the chance. But Rose Ortis wasn't rich. The likelihood, therefore, was that she was dead.

A lonely, promiscuous woman was the perfect prey for a sadist. Unfortunately, the few elements at their disposal weren't sufficient for reconstructing a modus operandi or discovering the murderer's signature. However, all killers, even the most well-organised, committed *conscious* errors. It was part of their nature.

In relation to that, she remembered what Alice's father always used to say, quoting the paradox of 'Buridan's ass'.

Jean Buridan was a fourteenth-century philosopher who'd told the story of an ass that stood before two stacks of hay: unable to make up its mind about which it was best to eat, the animal died of starvation. Criminologists – and also some economists – used this example to explain *economic behaviour in the rational human*, who, unlike an animal, is always able to choose, and whose decision is always determined by usefulness. Even so, the only individuals incapable of fully applying opportunistic calculations were sadists. They were often driven by an irrational need. Mila remembered that, after killing, many felt the need to remove an item from the victim – 'a fetish', as they said in the jargon. Even though this exposed them to the risk of being connected to the crime, it was an irrepressible urge. It allowed them to relive the feat in secret, as a fantasy.

Mila remembered the case of a murderer who'd taken off the shirt from a woman whose throat he'd just slit and, after washing off the blood, had given it to his girlfriend. The woman, unaware of anything, wore this hunting trophy before the unsuspecting eyes of relatives and friends, and that increased the killer's self-esteem.

Looking at Rose Ortis's apartment, one couldn't exclude that whoever had taken her away had also taken away a memento. But the fact that items had been removed to stage an escape made the search practically impossible.

At that moment, Berish knocked on the door of the apartment and Mila went to open it. Hitch came in and started walking lazily around the room.

'Let him get used to his surroundings,' Berish said. 'He hasn't done this sort of thing for some time.'

As they watched the dog grow familiar with the objects, Mila wondered if she'd put too much hope in this attempt. Maybe Hitch was too old for this kind of task.

'We should give him a clue to sniff,' Berish suggested.

'How about Rose's perfume? There's bound to be some left in one of the blue crystal bottles.'

Berish murmured something in disapproval, which immediately dampened her enthusiasm. 'We have the blood, don't we? Why not take advantage?'

'You think such a tiny stain will be enough?'

Berish looked at her. 'Trust him.'

They called Hitch and let him sniff the towel from the

257

bathroom. The dog moved his muzzle over it, then walked away only to come back for another sniff. He did this four times, then headed to the front door and began to scratch at it with his paw.

'He wants us to go out,' Mila said, hopeful.

Berish said nothing and just opened the door.

His muzzle on the ground, Hitch led them to the inner staircase of the building. He wasn't sure of the direction and changed route a couple of times.

'I think he's leading us off the track,' Berish said sceptically.

'What makes you think that?'

'I know him. Anyway, even if he is following a trail, it'll be contaminated after such a long time.'

Mila wondered why Berish had agreed to involve the dog if he was that distrustful.

They went to the ground floor and reached an iron door that probably led to the boiler room. Berish made sure there was nobody around and forced it open. Hitch immediately dived in, as if he'd found what he was looking for.

They followed him. It wasn't a boiler room but one containing the purification system for the swimming pool that hadn't been used for years.

'Yes, he's smelt something,' Berish said, noticing the dog's sudden agitation.

Mila hoped he wasn't mistaken.

Meanwhile, Hitch headed to a wooden door with a large gap underneath it. Berish realised where he was aiming and tried to stop him, but, despite his size, Hitch quickly slid through the gap and vanished from sight.

'Damn it,' Berish said. Then he launched a kick at the handle.

The door flew open before them, revealing a storage room with pipes running across the ceiling and electric wires sticking out from the brick walls.

The dog was moving anxiously in the empty space. Berish approached and, to calm him down, gave him something to eat. 'Good boy,' he murmured. Then he turned to Mila. 'There's nothing here.'

But she hadn't moved from the doorway and was looking at the wall on her right.

'What's the matter?' Berish asked.

Mila stretched out her arm. There were three numbers engraved on the bricks. 'This time we have only the latitude,' she said. Where was the other piece of the coordinates? 'I think we need to see what's behind the writing.'

Berish didn't seem very convinced, but he walked out of the storeroom anyway. Shortly afterwards, he returned holding a metal bar. 'Hold him,' he said, referring to the dog.

She grabbed him by the lead while his owner started hitting the wall with the bar. With each blow of the iron against the surface, there was a deafening noise that echoed in the basement. Increasingly large chunks of wall broke off until, finally, something started showing through the barrier.

It was a very large black trolley suitcase, secured with a padlock.

Once the hole was large enough, Berish stopped hitting the wall and grabbed the suitcase by the handle to pull it out. It fell on the ground with a hollow thud.

He looked at Mila as if waiting for her agreement. When she nodded, Berish gave another blow of the iron bar, making the padlock snap open.

He lifted the lid and they prepared for the worst.

Inside, however, were Rose Ortis's clothes and personal effects. They were crammed in tidily.

She'd been the one to pack it, Mila thought. Someone cheated her. Someone led her to believe that the story about the trip was true, but only to keep her calm.

Rummaging through the clothes and other items, Berish found the ring with the emerald-coloured snake, but also a hammer stained with dried blood and fragments that looked like cerebral cortex. Bleached blonde hairs stuck to the tip of the hammer.

Hitch began to bark and Mila struggled to restrain him. They had the evidence they'd been looking for, but the pursuit of the culprit had only just begun.

The last thing they found was the most disturbing.

A porn magazine that most probably had nothing to do with the wretched victim. In the middle pages, somebody had enjoyed cutting out part of the women's faces in the photos. Eyes, nose, lips and ears had been removed with surgical precision. And perversion.

21

It was just after four o'clock in the afternoon and they had decided to split up again.

Berish had taken the metro with Hitch to go to the department and search the database for any matches regarding the porn magazine cut up by the killer, and if this behaviour had recurred in any other crime.

It was typical of sadists to fuel their own fantasies with that kind of pastime, Mila thought. It was usually a prelude to the attitude they would then take towards their victims. She wondered what tortures Rose Ortis had suffered before she'd died.

Mila had borrowed the duty car from Berish to drive to the harbour and see Laura again. Her mother's trolley suitcase was on the back seat.

When Mila walked into the bar, she found her wiping the counter with a cloth. Laura recognised the suitcase at a single glance.

Once again, they sat in the booth. As well as her cigarettes,

Laura brought a bottle and immediately poured herself a drink.

'I should have guessed it,' she said after taking a sip. 'Rose was too stupid not to get into trouble.'

'We don't have anything definite yet,' Mila replied, although she didn't harbour any hopes.

But the woman was already disillusioned. 'Do you seriously believe Rose is still alive after three months?' she asked, looking at her.

No, she didn't believe it. But Mila wasn't there to comfort her. 'The mysterious Tom in the email is almost certainly not called that but is equally certainly a very cunning individual. If he made her write that email in order to throw the police off the track, he also knew full well that, thanks to that trick, any possible report would never be passed on to the Bureau of Missing Persons.'

'Seems that for once Rose managed to find herself a man with a brain,' Laura said with contempt.

'He convinced her to pack the suitcase.'

'But why?'

To remain in control of the situation, Mila thought. If victims panicked, they became impossible to manage. Many killer-rapists made their victims put their clothes back on only to give them the illusion they'd be let go. The lie had a calming effect on them.

But she replied, 'I don't know. Now I'd like to show you something, but I need your attention.'

'All right.'

Mila stood up and heaved the suitcase onto the table. Then she opened it, revealing its contents. Berish had removed the hammer, which was most probably the murder weapon, and put it into an evidence bag he'd brought with him. All there was inside, therefore, were clothes and personal effects.

'Could you please look through these things and tell me if you think something's missing?' she said.

'What do you mean?'

'I imagine you knew Rose's habits well, so you'd be able to tell me if there's a dress or an item your mother would have never forgotten to put in the suitcase.'

Mila still trusted in the Buridan's ass theory and therefore in the possibility that the killer may have taken a 'memento' so that he could relive the murder in private, even at the risk of being discovered.

The young woman started to rummage gingerly through the suitcase. It was obvious this was painful for her, but Mila could not forego her assistance. Laura started to take clothes and objects out and lay them on the table, compiling a sort of inventory. When she'd finished, she actually had an answer.

'Her perfume isn't here,' she said. 'Rose used it her entire life.'

Mila thought of the collection of empty blue crystal bottles on the shelf in her apartment. 'Are you sure?'

'Absolutely. It was essential for her. She always said, "When I walk in the street or step into a room, everybody must know it".' Then she thought about this. 'She always carried a bottle in her handbag; she even left one in the private bathroom – I'll go and get it for you.'

'There's no need,' Mila tried to say, but Laura was already on her way.

She returned, holding the crystal bottle and crying. 'I can't, I can't cope,' she said, sobbing.

Mila wanted to tell her how sorry she was, that she sympathised, but it wouldn't have been the truth. The only thing she was able to say was, 'Nobody's forcing you to cope, Laura. We all have the right to feel grief.'

She wished it could be true, especially for her.

There was nothing else for her to do there, so she began putting everything back into the suitcase, intending to leave. Moreover, doing this allowed her to ignore the young woman's crying.

Just then, a loud noise made her jump. Mila turned and saw that, in a sudden act of hysteria, Laura had hurled the crystal bottle to the floor.

'I apologise,' the young woman said. 'I didn't mean to . . . '

Tiny blue fragments were scattered everywhere. Mila was about to say something, but, as soon as she smelt the fragrance exuding from the shards of glass, she froze.

Lily-of-the-valley and jasmine.

Yes, somebody had taken a memento and was now flaunting it like a trophy over his new conquest. Someone who knew every trick to make someone disappear without arousing suspicion. Someone whose job should have been finding those who went missing.

22

We all have an avatar in the real world. Pascal wasn't wrong about that.

As Mila drove to the department at full speed, she was beginning to understand the meaning of Pascal's words. There was no need for an alter ego in the damned virtual world. We lead a dual existence even without the internet. Because there's a part of us – the deepest and most unreachable – that lives its own life. In it, we hate in secret, covertly envy others and wish them every misfortune, we manipulate, we lie. We use it to overpower the weak. We feed it the worst perversions and allow it to do whatever it wants inside us. And, finally, we blame who we are on it.

Simon Berish was a disciple of Enigma. Simon Berish was a murderer.

Was it possible? Yes, it was.

The whisperer has the power to change people. He turns harmless individuals into sadistic killers.

Berish had forced Rose Ortis to write an email in order to

jeopardise any possible missing-persons report. She was the perfect victim – so ingenuous, so naive. Was that why he had chosen her as his victim? Mila couldn't get the photo she'd seen on social media out of her mind – Rose posing on a plain in front of the mountains, a herd of horses in the background.

Actually, she had let herself be tricked by Berish. Thinking back to the last hours, she remembered every time he'd thrown her off the track. Like when she had suggested they get Hitch to sniff Rose's perfume.

'We have the blood, don't we? Why not take advantage?' he'd objected, and she hadn't insisted. The blood. Berish had examined the bathroom only after she'd found the stain on the towel. Mila was convinced that in actual fact he'd used the luminol to locate other bloodstains he might have missed when he'd cleaned everywhere after the murder.

And then he'd taken away the hammer they'd found in the suitcase concealed in the wall. He'd probably got rid of it by now. The same fate must have befallen the porn magazine, she was sure of it.

If it hadn't been for Laura's angry gesture, Mila wouldn't have suspected anything. She had to thank a random event, just as she had accidentally detected the same scent in Berish's car and on his shirt.

We all have an avatar in the real world. Perhaps Simon Berish had learned to be another person in Elsewhere.

Had he left the numbers on the bricks, or had it been some other acolyte? That was what she had to discover.

After running a few red lights, Mila reached her destination. She drove the department saloon straight down into the underground garage, hoping no one would ask her to explain. She used the side entrance again and went into the remotest, and so least monitored, part of the building. She had the gun on her, and if she was caught with an unlicensed weapon in a government building, she'd be thrown in jail without a trial. But she had to chance it.

As she walked towards Limbo, she thought about what she'd say to the man with whom she'd shared work and friendship for years. The only person she'd allowed near her.

Berish was in the Waiting Room, at his desk computer. Hitch was curled up at his feet. 'No match for the hammer or the porn magazine,' he said when he saw her. 'But I managed to get the same issue and I want to compare the missing parts.'

The findings were still on the table. Maybe Mila had truly arrived in time, or perhaps Berish was so sure of his act that he'd delayed destroying them.

Comparing the missing parts of the porn magazine; what a good liar he was, she thought.

'Something else I thought of,' he added. 'The "devil's paw": nobody can erase all the prints in an apartment. It's almost impossible to do.'

Apparently you know how, Mila thought.

'We must have missed something, and I reckon the answer is in the magazine,' he insisted. 'How did it go with Laura?'

Mila was trying to appear calm while studying him. 'It went well,' she said. She approached him, ready to pull out the pistol.

'Are you going to tell me about it, or shall I start guessing?'

When she was a couple of metres away from him, she stared at him. 'Simon, what happened to you during this year we haven't seen each other?'

He shifted on his chair, looking puzzled. 'Why? What's supposed to have happened?'

'Something's changed. You've changed.'

'Mila, what's wrong?'

'Simon, where's Alice? You can tell me now.'

Berish was looking at her as though genuinely wondering where this accusation was coming from – what a hypocrite. He slowly removed his reading glasses and put them down on the desk. 'Mila, I don't know what you're talking about. Can you just explain it to me, please?'

She took the pistol from her duster jacket, but didn't aim it at him, holding her arm at her side to communicate to him that she was in earnest.

'Did something happen in the bar? Why don't we talk about it? Perhaps I can explain.'

'Tell me where my daughter is. Or else put me in touch with them.'

'Who's "them"?'

'Enigma's disciples, the other players, call them what you like, but tell me who they are.'

'You're clearly not yourself,' he said, shaking his head and looking away from her.

'Look at me,' Mila said in a loud voice.

Berish turned to her again, disbelief in his eyes. 'Who do you think I am?'

'I don't know any more,' Mila replied, lifting the weapon and pointing it at him.

He put a hand to his mouth, not knowing what to say, his eyes moist.

'The missing coordinates,' Mila said, referring to the partial sequence they'd found on the brick wall in the basement of Rose Ortis's building. 'I want the longitude . . . This time, you'll come into the game with me and take me to Alice.'

She had to return to Elsewhere before the virtual world could self-destruct because of the virus. She sensed there wasn't much time left.

Still aiming at him, she approached what had once been her desk, opened the top drawer, took out a pair of handcuffs and threw them at him to put on.

'You're making a mistake: I have no longitude.'

'And I have no desire to listen to this bullshit.'

Berish put the first cuff on his left wrist and clicked it shut. He was about to do the same with the other one, but, instead, lunged at her. Mila should have fired, but she still saw her old friend in him, the person who loved her. Her brief hesitation cost her dearly, however. Berish managed to knock her to the floor, then grab the gun.

Hitch's bark echoed through the Waiting Room and thousands of eyes focused on the scene and on Mila. Thousands of smiling eyes and faces.

'Bastard,' she said from the floor.

Berish didn't move a muscle. He just stood there, holding the pistol, an unfathomable expression on his face. Just as Mila thought he was going to aim the weapon at her, she heard a voice behind her.

'Freeze,' Delacroix said by the door, holding a semi-automatic. 'Drop the gun.'

They took her to a room with no windows. Bauer, as well as Delacroix, were there. They were waiting for Shutton, but she still hadn't arrived.

'What'll happen to Berish?' Mila asked.

'For now he's being held for conducting an unauthorised investigation,' Delacroix replied.

'Then so am I,' Mila said.

No one answered her.

'Let me talk to him.' She wanted to make him admit what he knew about Alice's abduction.

'Do you think it'll be easy to make an interrogation expert confess?' Delacroix shook his head. 'You're so naive, Vasquez.'

'Are you going to charge him with Rose Ortis's murder?' she asked in an attempt to work out if they knew what she knew.

'That depends on you,' Bauer replied.

Mila had the impression he was bluffing and that he actually needed no admission on her part, because they were already aware of everything. 'How long have you been onto us?'

Bauer let out an amused laugh. 'We lost sight of you a couple of times, but we've been following you since you left the department to go back to the lake.'

'So you know what happened to my daughter. Who took her? And why didn't you intervene to stop them?' She was beside herself with anger.

'We were watching you from a distance,' Delacroix said. 'We could never have expected what would happen, nor could we have stopped it.'

'And what did you want from me? What were you expecting me to do?'

'We're not interested in you,' Shutton said, making an entrance, followed by Corradini. 'It's another subject we're interested in.'

As usual, she looked elegant in a cream-coloured skirt, white blouse, a pair of leopard-print Louboutins and a string of pearls around her neck. Mila noticed that Corradini was carrying a black briefcase. He put it down on the table and opened it, but the lid was preventing her from seeing what was inside.

Shutton took a photograph out of the briefcase and slid it towards Mila.

Pascal.

The picture had been taken with a zoom lens while she'd been with him at the panoramic viewpoint by the lake, when they'd first met and the man in the red balaclava had been holding up his arms as she'd aimed her pistol at him.

'What do you want me to say?' Mila asked, realising she had power over them.

'Everything,' Shutton replied. 'We came across him at the same time you did. But the man was too crafty, and we lost him that day and then once again while you were escaping from Norman Luth's villa after killing Timmy Jackson, alias Fishbone.'

It seemed that her hooded friend was better at shaking off a tail than she was.

'Who is he?' Bauer started. 'What's your relationship with him? Have you ever seen his face?'

'I don't know who he is,' she replied without hesitation, looking at them with defiance. 'He only helped me. I've never seen his face. Why are you so interested in this man?'

'Because as well as going around masked,' Shutton replied. 'He wears latex gloves so that he doesn't leave any fingerprints and only drives cars that are at least twenty years old. But above all because, despite this, nobody's ever noticed him and he doesn't appear in any security footage in the city.'

'Does he remind you of anyone, Vasquez?' Bauer asked sarcastically.

'Enigma,' she said. If they'd seen Pascal's dressing table

with the make-up and the wigs and his collection of disguises, maybe they'd realise that the answer to their question was rather elementary.

Cosmetic skill and discipline.

Corradini leaned on the table. 'That morning at the lake, you were intercepted at a distance with a directional microphone, so we heard everything you said to each other.'

Mila tried to remember her first conversation with Pascal, but recalled that on that occasion Pascal had only made a vague allusion to the game, and left the rest for when they were in a safe place.

'You'd better tell us everything,' Shutton said menacingly. 'Then we'll decide whether your version more or less matches our information.'

It dawned on Mila that Shutton and the others knew a lot less than they would have her believe. After all, they certainly couldn't have followed her on her journeys to Elsewhere. 'And what if I don't cooperate?'

Corradini took another photograph from the briefcase and placed it on top of Pascal's. It was an old ID snapshot of Father Roy, the fake priest. 'His name was Marcel Turquoise, he was a hacker who specialised in paedophile forum sites. He spent most of his life in and out of jail. We know you killed him and that Berish hid the body. We can charge you with homicide.'

'Then why don't you?' she said.

'Because of the phone call,' Shutton promptly replied. Then she exchanged glances with Bauer and Delacroix so that they'd continue on her behalf.

'As you no doubt remember, Enigma was found following an anonymous tip-off,' Delacroix began.

Someone had told the police that the car they were looking for, a green station wagon, was near the old abattoir, parked inside a disused warehouse. The officers sent to the spot had found blood in the vehicle. Then the dogs had sniffed a presence in the building. Finally, a raid had led to the arrest of the tattooed man, who was in possession of the murder weapon from the Andersons' farm.

Mila understood where they were leading. 'You compared the voice of the anonymous caller with the one you intercepted with the directional microphone by the lake, and it turns out it was the man in the balaclava who called you.'

'Exactly,' Delacroix said.

'And what's that got to do with me? Why should this information force me to cooperate?'

Shutton nodded at Corradini, who took out of the briefcase the pièce de résistance they'd prepared for her.

A small tape recorder.

Corradini switched it on and, after a brief rustling and a couple of rings, came the operator's voice.

'Police – what's your emergency?'

'I'm calling about the man you're searching for,' Pascal's voice said. *'I know where he is.'*

'Give me the address, please, and we'll see if we can send someone to check.'

'Look in the old abattoir, in one of the abandoned warehouses. You'll find a green Passat and also the man. Have you noted everything down?'

'Yes, sir, I've got it all down … Sir, can you give me your name?'

'No. Be careful, that man is a whisperer.'

The recording stopped. Mila was still in shock. 'You

273

knew it,' she said, incredulous. 'You knew he was a damned whisperer . . .'

'Yes,' Shutton replied without batting an eyelid.

Mila stared at her. 'So when you came to the lake, you were lying. The photo you showed me was a fake: Enigma never had my name tattooed on him.'

She should have been relieved, because this detail had made her anxious from the start. But all she could think of now was that the Judge had lied to her in order to draw her into the investigation, because Mila was the only one who'd had dealings with a whisperer in the past.

'Otherwise, you would never have agreed to work with us,' Shutton replied without any qualms.

She couldn't believe it. And yet it all made sense. Enigma hadn't chosen her. On the contrary, he hadn't even known who she was when she'd gone to see him in the Grave. The fact that he'd provided her with the initial coordinates to access Two meant nothing; it made no difference if it was her or another police officer. The whisperer wanted to fight the battle in Elsewhere, on *his* territory. The followers who were after her, trying to kill her, were simply playing the game.

Still, one question remained unanswered: why had Alice been abducted?

In any case, it was Shutton's fault.

Mila lunged angrily at Shutton and Delacroix restrained her just in time, holding her with an arm around her waist.

'You bitch!' she yelled.

Shutton wasn't in the least perturbed. 'Your daughter is in danger and we're going to help you find her. But you have to tell us everything.'

Mila kept kicking and hurling insults at her. Corradini's phone rang. He answered and immediately handed the device to his boss. The Judge listened to what the interlocutor had to say, and Mila saw her expression alter.

Joanna Shutton was suddenly worried.

Trying not to show anything else, she hung up and turned to Bauer and Delacroix. 'Make sure she decides to cooperate,' she commanded before hurrying out of the room.

After a while, they took her back to Limbo. Mila didn't ask why, but as they walked through the offices, she noticed much agitation. The phones were ringing without pause and officers were coming and going, many wearing bullet-proof vests, about to go into action.

'What's going on?' she asked.

'Nothing that concerns you,' Bauer replied with his usual contempt.

And yet something was certainly happening, even though she had no idea what the emergency was.

Once they were back in the Waiting Room, she saw Hitch. He was lying under Berish's desk, looking sad. He lifted his muzzle and looked at her as if hoping for news of his owner. Mila felt absurdly guilty towards the wretched animal.

'Stay here,' Delacroix told her. 'We'll come back for you shortly.'

They left and closed the door behind them. Once she was alone, Mila's only thought was to go to the bathroom and splash some water on her face.

She looked at her reflection in the mirror above the sink. It was Monday evening and this affair had begun just ninety-six hours earlier, when Shutton had come to her house by the lake. And yet her face looked as though months had gone by. She suddenly felt an irrational fear of having forgotten Alice. As though a virus were affecting her memory, capable of destroying everything the same way as it was happening in Elsewhere. She forced herself to think of her voice.

'There's a squirrel's den in the tree,' the girl had announced, chilled, after returning from looking for Finz in the garden, shortly before their lives were capsized by the arrival of the Judge.

Mila couldn't have imagined that, instead of a cat, she would have to search for her daughter.

She brought a bowl of water back for Hitch. Then she opened the drawers of Berish's desk, looking for dried meat, because she knew he always kept a stash for the dog. She found some and gave it to him, patting him on the head.

'Don't be angry with me, okay?' But maybe the animal was also feeling guilty. After all, he'd contributed to his owner getting caught by finding Rose Ortis's suitcase behind a brick wall.

No, we're all responsible. So am I, Mila thought. For getting tricked.

She recalled what Berish had said about the internet and the senseless online violence without anyone intervening. She wondered when his own descent into the abyss had begun. Had he met Enigma in Two?

Had the whisperer really manipulated him and persuaded him to kill an innocent person?

Her eyes wandered to the desk.

Either Delacroix or Bauer had taken away the bag of findings containing the hammer soiled with blood and brain matter, with which Rose had most probably been murdered.

But they had left the porn magazine behind. Maybe they didn't know it was linked to the case.

Mila sat down and started leafing through it, looking for the photos in which the women's faces had been partly cut out. Eyes, nose, mouth, ears . . . What kind of perversion was this? Was this how Berish tortured the women in his sick imagination? Had he done the same with Rose?

She pictured again the innocent smile of the fifty-six-year-old in the photo of the excursion to the valley with the horses. Where was her body? Someday, perhaps a thousand years from now, somebody would dig in a secluded area and find the remains of a nameless victim who'd been murdered with blows of a hammer, then barbarically disfigured. Or maybe that would never happen.

Mila felt the need for a coffee. She closed the magazine because she didn't want to think about it any more. Underneath it, however, she noticed an identical copy and remembered that Berish wanted to compare the missing parts.

Another trick to throw her off the track?

She opened the unmutilated magazine and saw a woman in an obscene pose, the same whose eyes had been removed in the sister copy.

Those eyes seemed suddenly familiar.

She went looking for a pair of scissors and found them in a pen holder. Before using them, she asked herself if what she was about to do made any sense.

Yes, it does, she decided.

So she set about cutting out the picture, then moved on to the nose of another porn star, then the ears of a third. In the end, she had gathered at least ten parts.

She didn't know what she was doing, or perhaps she did but

was afraid to admit it. She moved the magazine aside, took out a blank sheet of paper, laid the fragments on it, and started putting them together like the pieces of a jigsaw. Once she'd finished, a face emerged.

Mila had a pang in her stomach when she saw it.

The result resembled a smiling fifty-six-year-old in a photograph that, in actual fact, had never been taken.

Someone had created Rose Ortis's face from nothing, then superimposed it against the natural landscape. It wasn't hard. All you needed was good computer software.

Rose's social media profiles were elaborate *fakes*.

That was why there were no prints in her home, Mila thought, remembering the devil's paw.

The magazine was the solution to the mystery, and it had been left brazenly before her very eyes.

That woman had never existed.

This implied two things. That Berish was innocent and that the young woman who'd introduced herself as Rose's daughter was a disciple of Enigma.

23

Pascal's prophecy was coming true.

Even though the door to Limbo was locked from the outside, Mila kept a spare key in a colourful cup on her old desk. She used it to escape. Hitch looked at her with big sad eyes and she realised she couldn't leave him alone, so she took him with her.

As soon as they stepped out of the door, they found themselves in the midst of the chaos into which the department had fallen.

The officers were in a crisis because they were unable to be in various parts of the city at once. From what they were saying, it sounded like criminals had suddenly emerged from the shadows in which they'd sheltered for the past few years, to ravage the city.

Mila realised she was witnessing the dramatic end of the 'Shutton Method'. Pascal was right: sooner or later evil would come out of Elsewhere and invade the real world.

She walked through the bustle with the dog, without

anybody noticing them. She wanted to know in which room Berish was being kept under arrest, but she didn't have time to free him and, besides, it was too risky. She would think about how to get her friend exonerated later. Moreover, once again she owed him an apology.

They took a lift down to the second basement floor. She had decided they would leave the department through the shooting range. Usually, there were many officers there, practising, but now, given the situation, it was empty.

Once they were outside, Mila immediately looked for a car. It took her a while to find an old model she could steal: this time, she chose a reddish-purple Volvo from the 1980s, practically an antique. It must have belonged to an engineer or an architect, because inside there were rolls with plans and building trade samples.

As she drove, with Hitch lying on the back seat, she noticed there wasn't a soul around. She could hear the sirens of police cars whizzing through the city streets. Stopping at a junction, she counted at least six driving past at full speed.

Mila turned on the radio. The news reported that a bomb had exploded in an all-night supermarket, that a shootout in a city centre bar and a robbery at a jeweller's in a large hotel were still in progress.

A realisation suddenly came over her: these simultaneous events weren't random, but everything had started as soon as she'd been arrested at the department. Something told her that Enigma's disciples wanted her out of there so they could start hunting her down again.

They wouldn't have to wait long, because she was heading to the very place where they were waiting for her.

*

In the inland harbour district, a strong wind was pushing orange clouds across the sky, like legions of souls escaped from hell.

Mila parked outside a driveway where the piers began. She told Hitch she'd be back soon, but also left a note under the windscreen wipers: when they came to tow the car and the dog away, they'd also find Officer Simon Berish's contact details.

She walked along the boat jetty. There was nobody there. This may have been normal at 2 a.m., but not that night, she thought. She had therefore better be cautious and reach Laura Ortis's bar from a different direction.

The young woman had played the part of the daughter anxious about her irresponsible mother skilfully. The scene in which she hurled the blue crystal bottle on the floor in a hysterical gesture had proved to be a perfect coup de théâtre. Berish had been well and truly framed. The plan had relied not on cunning but on affection: it exploited the intimacy between Mila and Berish. Enigma's acolytes knew she wouldn't fail to notice a detail that revealed the presence of a woman in her friend's life. But if they'd managed to discover in such a short time a detail as intimate as that of Simon's girlfriend, then Mila had to expect any surprise.

Still, for a reason she was unable to explain to herself, she was convinced they wouldn't kill her in the real world. As she'd already had occasion to experience, her death would occur in Elsewhere.

She reached the bar and, as expected, all the lights were off inside. She forced the lock on the back door and entered. She was immediately overwhelmed by a strong smell of alcohol. She ventured into the darkness of a drinks storeroom. As she walked, she sensed the crunching of broken glass under her feet: whoever had preceded her had smashed the bottles on the shelves. The same fate had befallen those on the main room's counter. Mila looked around: the bar furniture had also been wrecked.

Near the booths, on the only table that was still standing where it had been, there was a white envelope. From a distance, she noticed an Angel Tear pill on top of it.

She figured the contents of the message must contain her prize for solving the Rose Ortis trick.

The longitude she needed to go back to Two.

Though gripped with the fear of an ambush, she took a couple of steps towards the table. The stench of cheap spirits was unbearable and should have put her on her guard. But she noticed the danger only when she knocked against something thin with her knee. She also heard a click, looked down and saw the nylon thread winding quickly around the reel of a fishing rod attached to the wall on her left, while on her right the line was attached to Laura Ortis's rusty Zippo, secured to the leg of a chair, which lit a wick soaked in alcohol.

Mila realised she'd inadvertently triggered an incendiary trap.

She tried to halt the mechanism by kicking the chair but wasn't in time to stop the sparks from falling onto the floor, wet with flammable liquids, and start spreading.

A wall of fire rose before her. She could have found an easy way out behind her, but in order to reach the table with the letter, she had to throw herself into that inferno.

She swore and cursed Enigma. But there wasn't much time left to decide. She took a deep breath, then lunged into the fire. She was immediately assaulted by incandescent tongues that wrapped around her from the bottom, eating away at the fabric of her trousers and part of her jacket. Mila held her arms in front of her face to shield herself from the gusts of heat, but had to stop after barely a couple of metres. She caught her breath and tried again, but advanced very little.

She looked ahead: beyond the mocking dance of the flames, the letter had been reached by the fire before her and was beginning to curl. The rational part of her was telling her that it was too late, but an unsuspected maternal instinct was pushing her forward. Until then, she'd mistaken it for a sense of guilt towards Alice because she didn't love her, but now she knew it was something different: you don't take the risk of burning alive for someone you don't love, she said to herself.

Even so, she was forced to give up because the letter quickly turned to ashes.

She turned back through a blanket of smoke that was blinding and suffocating her. She kicked the door jamb to get out and the tragi-comical sound of the wind chimes heralded safety.

Once outdoors, she fell to her knees and leaned with both her hands on the cobblestones. She coughed hard and retched and was suddenly scared she'd faint. Then, slowly, she began to breathe again.

As soon as she was able to, she looked behind her. Everything was lost, everything was over. *Game over*. There was no way of going back to Elsewhere.

24

She drove around aimlessly until four o'clock in the morning, with Hitch asleep on the back seat. Mila envied him. Half an hour ago, an idea had sneaked into her mind and would not leave her. In the end, she decided to yield to it.

The envelope in the bar had reminded her of another letter. The one that arrived every year, asking her to make a decision.

Mila arrived outside the private hospital, stopped the car and sat watching the illuminated windows of the building surrounded by a large garden. The place was comparable to a citadel where the rules of the outside world were of little or no consequence. A kind of Elsewhere, only more peaceful. There, time was calculated differently: there was no difference between day and night, and life and death were equivalent to each other.

Within those walls, in the bed of a room on the fourth floor, her daughter's father had been living and dying for the past ten years.

Mila had been there on other occasions, even at odd times

of day, like now, so she only needed the reception staff to recognise her to be let in. And precisely because they knew who she was, the nurses on duty decided to overlook her appearance and the fact that her clothes smelt strongly of smoke. Mila would have liked to explain that she had nowhere else to go. She took the lift to the ward for coma patients.

The ward was immersed in a faint bluish light, as if to signal that permanent rest was not to be disturbed. The walls and linoleum floors were green. The night shift operated in a blanket silence, tactfully.

The room Mila wanted was the last one at the end of the corridor, the one with the worst view: an inner courtyard where the sun never shone. After all, it would make no difference to the man who was lying there, attached to life-support machines.

She'd been the one who'd had him admitted there, and who, month after month, paid a considerable sum to keep him alive. Every year, she rejected the doctors' appeal when they wanted to put an end to the patient's suffering. But, since Alice was his only relative and Mila was legally responsible for her until she'd be of age, it was only up to her to decide whether to pull the plug on him or not. She didn't want to do it because she did not believe in the death penalty. What that bastard deserved was a life sentence.

'I'm sure you've sometimes thought of what you would do if you could go back in time,' Pascal had said. And, if she'd had that opportunity, Mila wouldn't have given birth to Alice. Because whenever she looked at her daughter, she also saw her father – the man who'd lied to her, used her, betrayed her.

'On the morning Alice disappeared, there was a large stag in my kitchen,' she said, not knowing why.

At that moment, she wished she could tell him that another

whisperer had come into her life, like the one through whom they'd met a long time ago. The man on that bed would be the only person, besides her, to comprehend the gravity of the situation. Because the fact that Enigma was held in a maximum-security prison didn't change anything. He still constituted a threat.

If only Mila could show him the Photoshopped picture without his tattoos – it was in her pocket – perhaps he'd be able to solve the mystery behind *the face of an ordinary man*.

Because he, too, had once taken on the deceptive appearance of a kind person.

Mila wanted to describe to him the scene in the Elsewhere bar, when she'd seen him conscious but altered and busy silently carving a human bone. She wanted to confide in him that their daughter was always asking about her father, and that even though she'd told Alice that he would never wake up again, she was still waiting for him. Maybe I'll really have to pull the plug on him, she thought. At least then this farce will end once and for all.

But she wasn't there, like the other times, to talk to him or to delude herself that, wherever he might be, he could still hear her. She had come because of Pascal. She remembered once again their exchange on that last night in the burnt-down house. 'If someone couldn't walk any more as a result of an accident, they could do it again in Elsewhere. Someone who had come out of a coma would learn to live and do essential things again. In the beginning, Two was used by rehabilitation centres to restore patients' hope.'

At the time, Mila had been distracted by the thought that Pascal may have had a terrible, irreparable experience in his own past, and that he was still carrying its load. The implications of what he'd said crossed her mind only when she was driving the Volvo, not knowing how to return to Elsewhere without the new coordinates. Every now and then, someone on the brink would wake up from a coma. It was therefore essential to re-educate them in order to restore to them, even if only in part, a normal existence.

Mila put an end to her brief visit, turned her back on the only man in her life and walked away. She took the staff lift down to the hospital basement.

As she had imagined, there was a storeroom down there crammed with old computers and rehabilitation equipment. There were visors and joysticks, and this looked hopeful. She picked up a monitor and a central unit, and assembled a PC inside the storage closet.

She switched on the computer and waited with trepidation to see if she'd see the circular Two icon on the desktop. It was there. She couldn't yet be too overjoyed, however, because she'd only achieved a part of the endeavour. She started the program and the screen with the by now familiar globe and box appeared. Using the game's options feature, she managed to create herself an avatar that looked very much like her. She didn't know if it would work, but the plan in her mind had a purpose.

Now came the complicated bit. Typing in the latitude and longitude. Without specific indications, she had to pick at random. So she inserted the coordinates of the place where anyone looking for her would certainly have found her.

Limbo.

She searched her pocket and took out another Angel Tear pill. She placed it on her tongue, knowing that if another danger presented itself, like a strangling shadow or an immobilising snake, this time there would be no Pascal to save her. She would have to save herself. Or else succumb, just as she was sure Enigma expected with those who entered his realm of shadows illicitly.

Once again, she repeated to herself, 'I'm ready.' Then she put on the visor and plunged into the oblivion of Elsewhere.

She was greeted by a series of roaring noises that reminded her that the apocalyptic world was dissolving.

In the Waiting Room, the smiles in the photos on the wall seemed eerie. The eyes of the missing persons were full of hatred and resentment. Women, men and children appeared to be asking her, silently, why she'd stopped searching for them and fled to the lake with Alice.

She wished she could set them free from these deceptive images and restore them to the shadows that, on a random day in their lives, had snatched them away for ever.

There was Beatrice, who'd vanished into thin air at the age of thirty-seven, six months pregnant with her second child. Michael, the family man who, on a day like any other, had gone to work at the office and had been spotted for the last time, wearing a jacket and tie, by two ramblers on a mountain path. Larissa, twelve, whose mother still received strange calls at night, where she could only hear someone breathing.

Mila had never met them, but they were like family to her. Every time the photo of someone new arrived at Limbo, she would unwrap a razor blade and make a small mark on her skin. The pain served to formalise a pact, create a bond, impress a memory.

While formulating these thoughts, Mila heard a rustling sound: something was moving in the room. She tried to look, but the shape kept escaping her. 'Who are you?' she then asked.

'I can't tell you my name,' a child's voice replied.

Pascal had told her to keep away from this ghost, but Mila had nothing else to resort to. And she was glad he'd found her. 'Why can't you tell me your name?'

'I'm not allowed to talk to strangers.'

'But you've already talked to me and you're doing it again now,' she replied, pointing out the inconsistency. 'So maybe I'm not a stranger ... Maybe you know who I am.'

'You're her mother,' the little boy said.

She was startled. Did the ghost know Alice? 'Where is she? Is she here, in Elsewhere? Can you take me to her?'

He did not answer. Mila didn't insist and changed her question. 'Is she all right?'

'She's safe.'

At that moment, the shape began to assume a more definite consistency. The ten-year-old boy in the red T-shirt appeared before her. He had short, tidy blonde hair. And pale-coloured eyes.

Mila immediately realised something about him. 'You're not an avatar, are you?'

'How did you work that out?'

'Because every time I've been in the game, you've always been here.'

'I live here,' the boy said.

A clang followed by a tremor made everything around them shake. Mila was frightened but the child remained impassive.

'Why are you helping me?' she asked, remembering all the times he'd intervened to warn her of the dangers she'd faced.

'Because you're not like the others, you're different.' Then he added, 'They mustn't know I'm here. That's why I always have to hide.'

Another roar, another earthquake.

'What's happening to the game?' Mila asked.

'Soon it'll all be over.'

'Are you the one doing all this?'

'They don't know it, though.'

It was as she thought: the ghost was the virus Pascal had mentioned. 'You must stop.'

The boy gave her a puzzled look. 'Why should I? You don't like this place either.'

'If you don't stop, I won't be able to find Alice.'

The boy shrugged his shoulders, as though to say there was nothing he could do about it.

'At least tell me how much time is left . . .'

'There's still time,' he assured her. 'But you have to hurry.'

'What do I have to do to finish my game?'

Once again, the ghost did not reply and turned away. 'I have to go now.'

'No, wait,' she said, trying to stop him. 'I still have things to ask you.'

'It was nice talking to you,' he said, drifting away.

'Just a moment, please . . .'

'She loves you and she's nearby.'

He said it while distancing himself. Mila was sure he was referring to Alice. 'What do you mean by nearby? How near?'

The ghost had nearly vanished. 'The mind sees what the mind wants to see,' were his last words.

25

Four grams of niacin to come out of the trip.

Mila stole the supplement from the hospital pharmacy, but some of the Angel Tear effects persisted. For instance, the cold, tremors and dizziness were preventing her from walking straight. So, before leaving, she had to recover fully. It was just before six and soon the place would be filled with people, but, in the meantime, she went back to the PC closet with a couple of bottles of water to rehydrate herself. As she drank, she remembered the last sentence uttered by the ghost – the same one she'd heard Pascal say.

The mind sees what the mind wants to see.

This couldn't be a meaningless coincidence. Mila was convinced that these words had been extrapolated from a context: perhaps a book, an article, or some other publication. She was close: it was the motto of the 'Red Forest Neuroscience Institute'.

Its website hadn't been updated for years. At first glance, it looked more like some old public organisation than a modern private enterprise. The homepage had just the logo: a stylised human eye with, inside it, two red trees and a building dating from the last century. There were just a few sections, consisting mainly of photographs. Some were of the actual building in the middle of a majestic beech forest. Others had been taken inside the building and were a mixture of medical clinics and computer workshops, with people wearing white lab coats.

Aside from the few captions, there was a page with a general description of the business.

The Foundation deals with research and innovation in the field of neuroscience. Its aim in the community is to implement a fruitful synergy between the human mind and artificial intelligence, disseminating discoveries in this field and sharing the progress achieved for the well-being of humanity.

Mila jotted down the address and decided to take a look in person.

She went back to Hitch and rewarded him with a few snacks she'd got from the vending machine in the lobby for having waited for her. Berish never spoilt him like this, but the dog had earned it. She let him out of the car to run around a little while she drank yet another bottle of water, leaning against the Volvo.

Dawn was lighting up the horizon. Mila felt very close to discovering something important. She got back into the car; she would need to drive many kilometres to reach her destination. It wasn't easy to find. She had to leave the motorway and drive up the winding roads of a mountain, through a couple of villages, and take a narrow path that climbed among beech forests.

At last, after a couple of hours, from behind a hill, the pock-marked brownstone façade of the building Mila had seen in the photos online appeared.

She parked not far from the entrance and headed to the main lobby. She expected a futuristic centre, but got the impression of a decommissioned building. Faded posters adorned the lobby, representing IT technicians working in a team with doctors. But from their clothes and the technology they were using, they looked like figures from a distant, super-seded past. It was also strangely desolate. Shortly afterwards, she stopped an attendant and asked where she could find the manager of the institute.

'Dr Stormark is in his office,' he said, pointing the way.

She walked down a corridor with a high ceiling that made her footsteps echo. She reached Stormark's door and knocked. A cavernous voice asked her to come in. Mila opened the door and found herself in an oddly dark room. She could barely make out a desk and a man behind it, smoking.

'Is it on or off?' he asked, but Mila didn't understand. 'The light,' he explained.

'It's off.'

'Then I apologise, you can switch it on if you like.'

When she did, she realised the reason for that strange exchange. Dr Stormark was blind. The office was very messy, but stacks of books in braille and old electronic devices were arranged on the floor in such a way as to allow the man to walk through. The air was permeated with a strong smell of cigar.

'My name is Mila Vasquez,' she said, introducing herself, sitting opposite him while Hitch lay down under her chair.

Stormark was wearing a yellow jumper soiled with ash. He was obese and the chair on which he sat barely contained him. His face and hands were streaked with capillaries and he had strange, frizzy hair. Unlike many blind people, he didn't wear dark glasses and his darting glance leapt around the room.

'Have you come to sell me a guide dog?' he asked, laughing at his own joke. 'If, on the other hand, you're looking for a job, you've come to the wrong place: it's still only February, but we've already exhausted this year's funds.'

'No,' she answered gently. 'I'm here to ask you a few questions, if you don't mind.'

'Concerning what?'

'I'm conducting a private investigation.'

The scientist grumbled something. 'If it's because of last week, the youngsters went too far, but the insurance should cover everything.'

'That has nothing to do with what I have to say to you,' she said, trying to reassure him.

'In that case, I'm all ears,' he replied, taking a puff on his cigar.

'I'm looking for someone. A man, to be precise. I think he may have had a connection with this place in the past. I think he may have been a criminologist.'

'We've had many, it's because of our research.'

'Actually, I'm not quite sure what it is you do . . . '

'You won't believe it, but the Red Forest Institute was in the vanguard of the internet,' he said, scratching his bristly cheek. 'Many innovations we now have online were born within these walls. Until a few years ago, we were planning the future here.'

Mila still didn't understand. 'Could you be more specific, please?'

Stormark smiled. 'Yes, sorry, of course. The centre was created to teach artificial intelligence and distinguish good from evil.'

Mila was stunned. 'And can that be done?'

'It's the challenge of this century, trust me ... Before entrusting our safety to a machine, we have to be certain that it can interpret the data correctly: it goes without saying that a child with a water pistol is quite different from a robber with an automatic, but computers can't yet tell them apart. Just as right now I'm not able to tell if your face is expressing astonishment or fear.'

'Both,' Mila replied. 'So, one day, the internet will be intelligent?'

'Only if we can teach it the meaning of a sunset,' he said. 'But for as long as a computer isn't moved by the sight of the sun descending below the horizon, that won't be possible.'

Mila thought about her alexithymia: perhaps she, too, was a machine made of flesh. 'Human beings sometimes see sunsets where there aren't any,' she objected. 'The mind sees what the mind wants to see.'

The man corrected her. 'The *heart* sees what it wants to see.'

These words struck her.

'Sometimes, we cheat our intelligence with emotions because we don't want to accept reality,' he continued. 'The mother of a self-confessed murderer will never be totally convinced that her son is guilty, because in order for that to happen, she'd have to admit she was a bad parent. It's a self-preservation mechanism.'

Mila realised she had established some trust with the man,

so decided to push her luck. 'A while back, I came across a virtual reality called Two.'

Stormark's expression clouded over.

'I was wondering if you'd ever heard of it . . . '

'The game,' was all he said.

'Since coming here and listening to you, I figured this could be the best place to create something like that. Am I wrong?'

'Two wasn't created here, but in the past we've done some research on it.'

From the dismissive tone of his answer, Mila sensed that Stormark didn't much feel like talking about it. But she had to know. 'I imagine you must know its story.'

'The utopian world that turned into hell? Yes, I know it. But given my condition I've never been able to put on a visor and visit it.'

'I met a kind of artificial intelligence down there: a little boy. He wouldn't tell me his name, but he told me he lives there . . . '

'Oh, my God,' Stormark exclaimed. 'Blonde, with blue eyes?'

'Yes.'

'Joshua,' he said softly. There was something compassionate about the way he'd uttered that name.

'Did you people create him?'

'No, Miss Vasquez . . . He really existed.'

'You mean . . . '

'I mean he's dead.' He paused. 'You can leave the dog here. Come with me, there's something I want to show you.'

The discovery that the boy in the red T-shirt was a real ghost was disturbing.

Stormark took a stick for the blind, with a white marble on

296

the tip so he could sense his route better. With its help, he led Mila down the institute's corridors to a laboratory.

In the middle of the dark room, there was a platform surrounded by projectors, even on the ceiling.

'The quality may not be the best,' he said, apologising in advance. 'The effect would be different with modern microprocessors, but we can't afford that kind of technology.'

'What's going to happen?' asked Mila, who had no idea where they were.

'Trust me, it'll soon become clear,' he replied. Then he went up to give instructions to a technician.

The latter went behind a control panel, activated some commands and, shortly afterwards, the platform started turning and the projectors came on and generated laser beams, giving life to a hologram.

A one-year-old boy was sitting on the ground, playing with his shoelaces. He had blonde hair and blue eyes, and he was smiling. And he was wearing a red T-shirt.

'Joshua,' Stormark said, introducing him.

'The little boy I saw must have been at least ten, but he does look like him.'

Stormark shook his head, visibly annoyed. 'It shouldn't have happened . . . But it's my fault.'

'What's your fault?' Mila had had enough of mysteries and wanted to know the truth.

'Joshua's father used to work here.'

Mila realised he was talking about Pascal. 'Was he a criminologist?'

'A criminal anthropologist,' he said. 'His name is Raul Morgan.'

So that was the name of the man in the red balaclava.

'Raul was head of research on the game.'

Pascal had mentioned an attempt to draw borderline subjects into the by then depopulated virtual world. The aim was to see if the seeds of violence and cruelty they had in them would evolve in a sadistic way. Only, the experiment had degenerated and led to the present version of Elsewhere.

'We lost control of the situation,' Stormark admitted. 'But by the time I realised that, it was already too late. I should have stopped everything, so the responsibility is mine.'

Pascal had described himself as a 'monitor'. He'd said that there were many like him: their duty was to monitor anomalies in Elsewhere, because every now and then a player would take the *leap* and take his violent fantasies into reality. Then the man in the balaclava had been left to carry out that task alone, without knowing what had happened to the others.

But before that, something must have happened in his life.

'What happened to Raul Morgan?'

'He was too involved, he was becoming paranoid: he saw enemies everywhere and didn't trust anyone.'

The description corresponded to Pascal.

'He claimed he'd met someone in the game, "a dangerous presence", were the exact words he used.'

Mila immediately thought of Enigma, the whisperer.

'I underestimated the problem until the accident . . .'

'What accident?'

Stormark grew sad. 'Raul Morgan was a good man; he had a family: a wife and a beautiful, one-and-a-half-year-old son . . . It shouldn't have ended that way.'

'What accident?' Mila insisted.

'By then, Raul was living in the parallel world: he wasn't

just absent-minded but totally dissociated from reality ...
Every day, before coming to work, he would take Joshua to the
nursery and his mother would pick him up in the afternoon.
One September morning, Raul came in at 9 a.m. as usual and
promptly went to his lab. Eight hours later, his wife called to
ask why he hadn't dropped their son off at the nursery. Only
then did Raul realise what had happened. He rushed to the
car park and found him right where he'd left him: in the baby
seat at the back of the car.'

Mila was dumbfounded.

'The child had probably fallen asleep on the drive from
home and Raul didn't notice that he'd skipped the nursery
stop of the journey. But even looking at the little body, he kept
repeating that he'd left him at the nursery, that there had to be
another explanation. He kept dismissing the evidence, even if
it was staring him in the face.'

The heart sees what the heart wants to see, Mila thought,
remembering Stormark's earlier words. She couldn't begin to
understand that kind of grief for a parent. But, this time, it
wasn't because of a lack of empathy. There is suffering that's
impossible to even imagine.

'Three months later, Raul resigned. I haven't heard from
him since.'

Mila looked at the hologram of the child in the red T-shirt,
playing without a care. 'Why this?' she asked, referring to
the ghost.

'After he left, by chance we found the program on his computer. We never found out what drove him to create it, but we
could easily guess.'

Stormark lifted the stick that helped him navigate the shadows of his blindness, removed the white marble from the tip

and threw it in front of him, guessing the trajectory towards the child.

Joshua raised his arm as though he wanted to catch it on the fly. It wasn't just a hologram, Mila thought.

'Joshua interacts,' Stormark confirmed. 'But, above all, he learns.'

'If he's ten years old now, it means Raul took him into Two so that he'd grow in the game like an ordinary child.'

'*I live here,*' the ghost had said.

'As you've seen, Miss Vasquez, Joshua was able to respond to external stimuli even as a young child, albeit in an elementary way. If you've spoken to him, it means he's evolved a lot over the past years. I'm not surprised, Raul Morgan was really good at his job.'

'But you said he was a criminal anthropologist, not a programmer.'

'True: he taught machines what evil is.'

26

'I was thinking about Two: no matter what you'd done or experienced in real life, and no matter how irreversible, you had a chance to make amends in the game.'

Raul Morgan, alias Pascal, had uttered those very words the last time they'd met. That was why he'd created a digital clone of his son. But it was no more than a lie, a dangerous illusion.

After leaving the institute, Mila set off in the Volvo again. She had a new clue.

The connection between Pascal and the ghost was now a fact, even though the man in the balaclava had advised her to keep away from the child. During their last meeting, Joshua had told Mila that Alice was safe, which meant that he knew where she was. And if she knew, then so must Raul Morgan.

The only way to check was to find Pascal.

Stormark had been very helpful and had given instructions that Mila be given the information she required. He hadn't even asked her what she needed it for. He must have sensed that her visit was in connection with the tragic event of all those years earlier. And precisely because he felt responsible for what had happened, he had dismissed all hesitation. Even so, Mila hadn't found much in Raul Morgan's personal file. For one thing, there was no photograph. Even the one on his lab ID had disappeared. She figured this was Pascal's doing, because of his obsession with erasing all traces of himself.

The only piece of information she was able to gather was his wife's name: Mary.

It was pouring with rain on her drive back and it was difficult to find her bearings in the mountains. Mila managed to spot a takeaway restaurant with a payphone.

She went in with Hitch. Given the bad weather, there was no one there except for the staff. A cosy fire was lit in the stone hearth, old skis adorned the walls and there were also a couple of stuffed stag heads. Except for this macabre detail, there was a welcoming atmosphere and Mila needed rest. She ordered a sandwich she would share with the dog and a bowl of cool water. She asked the cashier to give her the change in coins, which she took with her to the payphone booth.

She made a series of calls to former department colleagues who owed her for past investigations and whom she could therefore ask for favours. Meanwhile, the waitress brought over her order, but it took nearly an hour to find Mary Morgan's last known address. Still, after several phone calls, Mila managed to reconstruct the last ten years of the woman's life.

Following her son's death, Mary had been admitted to a private hospital where she'd stayed for a long time because of severe depression. Meanwhile, she'd divorced her husband. Over the years, she'd tried to start her life again. She'd lived in various places, done different jobs, but hadn't adapted to any of these changes. In the last three years, however, she'd acquired some sort of stability by retiring to a Buddhist community in the hills, in a remote area many kilometres away.

Mila figured the trip would take too many hours – time that Alice and Elsewhere did not have.

She had to speak to this woman.

The community didn't have a telephone, so she found the number of the police station in the nearest town.

'Even if I go all the way up there,' the local policeman said when Mila asked if he could put her in contact with Mary by taking a mobile phone to her, 'I don't think she'll want to talk to you. Those people are odd: they're vegetarians,' he added, as though that were truly incredible.

'It's an emergency,' she insisted, without supplying further details. 'Please, I'm a former fellow police officer: my name is Maria Eléna Vasquez. You can check if you like.' She was appealing to the solidarity among police officers, hoping it would be sufficient.

The man thought for a moment. 'Okay, but I warn you: it'll take at least forty minutes to get there and it's by no means certain that there'll be a phone signal in the middle of nowhere.'

Mila thanked him and dictated the restaurant number. Then she waited. Time seemed to stand still and the forty minutes went by with no news. Anything could have happened and she wouldn't have known about it. The mobile phone might have no signal or Mary Morgan might refuse to talk to her, or else the police officer had lied and possibly already forgotten their conversation and at that moment was doing something unrelated.

A quarter of an hour later, the restaurant phone rang and Mila rushed to answer. The connection was poor. 'This is Mary,' a voice said, in a tone of annoyance. 'Who's speaking?'

'My name is Mila Vasquez; thank you for calling me back.'

'What do you want from me? The officer says it's an emergency, but I'm telling you now, whatever it is, I'm not interested.'

'I understand, Mrs Morgan, and I apologise for invading your privacy, but I have no choice: my daughter went missing three nights ago.'

'And why should that concern me?' Mary replied brusquely.

'I think you can help me find her.'

'I don't see how, since I've been living outside the world for so long.'

'I know you can understand me,' Mila then said. By alluding to the fact that Mary, too, had been a mother, she was taking a big risk: the woman might decide to cooperate or else erect a wall and refuse to continue talking on the phone. But Mila was hoping that her frankness would pay off.

Mary Morgan said nothing, perhaps that was a good sign: she was finally wavering.

'I imagine it must be hard to keep going,' Mila said, suggesting she knew her story. 'Some wounds don't heal, I know. It's like living with a hole in your belly: it suppurates and starts bleeding again when you least expect it . . . That's why I don't want to end up like you, Mrs Morgan.'

These last words were hard to take, but Mila couldn't feign compassion.

'When you lose a child,' Mary Morgan said, agreeing with her, 'you spend the rest of your life living like a leper. Everybody avoids you because they think that your misfortune can happen to them, too. They say they feel sorry for you, but they're just relieved they're not in your shoes.'

Mila took advantage of her willingness, afraid she might change her mind. 'I'd like to talk about your husband Raul.'

'What do you want to know?'

'Do you know where I can find him?'

'I've not heard from him since our divorce,' she replied.

'But I think he's in some way still connected to the past. I have a feeling he hasn't been able to leave his memories behind in these past few years, even though they're sad memories.'

'It wasn't like that at the beginning: he seemed determined to delete everything. He was the one who insisted we got divorced.'

Mila was struck by this revelation. She thought his wife had wanted the divorce. After all, Pascal was responsible for the accident in which their only son had died.

'I tried to forgive him,' Mary said. 'God knows I tried! But he wouldn't allow me to go near him any more.'

'He didn't allow anyone near him,' Mila said. 'I think he's been living secluded from the world ever since.'

'We fell in love very young and marriage was a decision we both took for granted. We bought the house and he was enthusiastic about his work at the institute; he said it was the first time he'd carried out research that involved him so much. When our son was born, Raul would devote all his free time to us: he actually built him a cot shaped like a spaceship.'

'Then what happened?' Mila asked, even though she already partly knew it.

'I should have noticed that something was wrong ...' Mary said. 'There were small signals, but that wasn't the reason I underestimated them. The fact is, Raul had always been a very reliable man, so I never would have imagined he was about to have a breakdown.'

'Are you referring to the paranoia?'

'Yes, but not only that: he'd say that somebody was trying to get into his head.'

'And *suggest* thoughts to him,' Mila said, realising what she was talking about.

'Exactly,' Mary confirmed. 'Now, maybe you'll think I'm crazy, but he mentioned a tattooed man who harassed him on the internet . . .'

Mila didn't think she was crazy at all, but she couldn't tell her that there and then.

'Raul described him as a man with numbers tattooed from top to toe.'

The portrait matched and filled her with unbearable anxiety. 'And you never suspected that your husband might be losing his mind?'

'There was an episode, a couple of months before the accident. I'd gone to my parents' house with our son, and when we got back our house had burnt down.'

Mila thought of the fact that Pascal had taken her to two houses that had caught fire.

'The firefighters and the insurance company said it had been a short circuit, but I discovered the truth after our son died, when Raul confessed that he'd set the house alight to escape from the tattooed man.'

Mila felt a chill go through her. But the time had come to say goodbye to the woman. 'Thank you, Mrs Morgan, you've told me more than I needed.'

'I hope you manage to find your daughter,' Mary Morgan

said with great sadness in her voice. 'You know? Joshua would have become a wonderful man.'

Mila noticed that it was the first time she'd uttered her son's name. 'I know,' she said, unable to tell her that in some way she'd met him and owed him a debt of gratitude for having protected her in Elsewhere.

'I'll never forget that morning,' Mary continued, now apparently not wanting to stop talking. 'I dressed him in his little bedroom. Put the fleece trousers on him, the socks with coloured polka dots he liked so much, his first pair of white All Stars and a cardigan because it was September and it was beginning to feel chilly. He was wearing a red T-shirt underneath . . . How could I have imagined that those were the last minutes we were spending together?'

Mila heard her starting to cry on the other end of the line. She inevitably made the comparison with the last moments she'd spent with Alice. If she'd let her sleep in her schoolfriend's house instead of taking her back to the lake with her, perhaps nothing would have happened. But while driving to Jane's house, after being pursued by Enigma's men, she selfishly thought she'd take refuge in her daughter's hug. Even though there never had been that hug, since, as usual, she'd been too much of a coward and had entrenched herself in her alexithymia – the perfect excuse for not feeling anything.

'If you asked me to make an impossible wish, I'd ask to see Joshua again – even just for a little while. I'd like to say goodbye to him at least.'

Mila didn't know if she'd ever be able to experience this woman's distress and didn't want to find out. That was why she had to do everything to get Alice back. Because time is a trick and while it passes it forgets to warn us that it's passing.

'Thanks again,' she said, about to hang up.

Mary Morgan stopped her. 'Wait. If things don't turn out as you'd like them to, don't blame yourself: trust me, it's pointless ... Raul tried to offload part of his grief onto me, and made me believe that I was a bad mother because I didn't give sufficient credence to his persecution theories. I actually discovered that he wanted to abduct Joshua and take him far away, and when I asked him why, he said he wanted to save him from the tattooed man.'

Mary Morgan's final words had the effect of an epiphany. At last, Mila knew who had taken Alice.

ALICE

27

He taught machines what evil is.

The words Dr Stormark had used to describe Raul Morgan's work were clear: perhaps Raul was unable to resist an obsession with the evil he had the illusion of knowing so well.

'I'm a monitor ... When the game was transformed, there were already a lot of us. Our job was to monitor the anomalies of Elsewhere. Naturally, we expected something would spill over to this side ... Every now and then, someone made the leap; it was inevitable.'

Once Mila was back in the city, she went into the library to consult the internet. She searched the local newspaper websites for articles about house fires in recent months. She drew up a shortlist, leaving out the addresses of the two where she'd already been with Pascal. She got back into the car and went to see them.

A biblical downpour was beating down on the city. In the late afternoon, Mila reached a small detached house in a working-class area. The fire had devoured exactly half of it. One part was untouched, with curtains at the windows and plants on the small balcony. The other part was black from the smoke and there was an eerie hole instead of the façade. The house, she thought, was the perfect emblem of good and evil.

This was her third attempt after a couple of unsuccessful ones. But maybe this was the right place because, at the end of the path, she saw an oil-green Škoda from the nineties.

She didn't have a weapon on her but was sure that Pascal wouldn't be intimidated anyway. She decided to take Hitch along.

'You'll have to help me, okay,' she said, patting him. 'Look for her.'

They got out of the car and walked through the blanket of teeming rain towards the courtyard of the house. Mila intended to find Pascal before he noticed their presence and, while she distracted him, she was hoping Hitch would find Alice.

Mila looked through the ground-floor windows to check if there was anybody inside. It was all dark except for one light that was on. Mila saw a figure in the kitchen, but couldn't tell if it was Raul Morgan. But she realised that, because of the devastation caused by the fire, the front door was the only way into the house.

She moved under the portico. Covered by the noise of the rain, she picked the lock and went in, followed by Hitch.

She immediately smelt burnt plastic. She looked around: deformed monsters were staring at her in the semi-darkness, but they were just pieces of furniture that had melted in the heat of the flames.

She motioned to the dog to stay at her side as she walked towards the kitchen light. In fact, there were sounds coming from there – an open tap, the clatter of pots – so there had to be someone there. When she saw a man with his back to her, doing the washing up, she set the dog free to explore the rooms.

As she stepped into the dining room, she was able to confirm that the man was Pascal. He wasn't wearing the red balaclava, and all she could see for the time being was the back of his neck and his jet-black hair. He was still wearing his brown suit but had removed his jacket. Instead of the customary latex gloves, he was wearing a yellow rubber pair, the kind you use for household chores.

'Where is she?' Mila asked.

The man was not startled, nor did he turn around. 'She's sleeping upstairs,' he said. 'Don't worry, Alice is fine.'

'I want to see your face,' she said.

Pascal finished rinsing the last plate, then put it to drip in the drainer with the others and slowly closed the tap. Only then did he turn towards her.

He had a side parting and a moustache, green eyes and a pale complexion, ruddy cheeks and thin lips.

Now Mila knew what his face looked like.

'Your daughter is an interesting girl,' Raul Morgan said. 'We've had long chats over the past few days, and I've had occasion to see what an excellent job you've done with her – congratulations.'

She didn't want to hear that from this man, it sounded fake, almost a tease. 'You made the anonymous call to frame Enigma, but you knew that by saying he's a whisperer, they'd involve me.'

'You mean the police?' he said provokingly. 'Yes, I knew that.'

'On my way here, I wondered for ages why you took Alice. And don't go telling me it was just to protect her from Enigma, as you wanted to do with your son. I'm not stupid.'

'You're right, perhaps that wasn't the only reason ... I decided that it was essential to take Alice away from you, because otherwise you wouldn't have learned the lesson.'

Learn, this verb chilled her. He taught machines what evil is ...

'You see, Mila, it was important that you understand what enemy we're dealing with ... But only the suffering of deprivation, the feeling of imminent danger and the pressing necessity to find a solution to the worst possible scenario could have motivated you.' Pascal cocked his head and gave her a look of compassion. 'Tell me, my dear friend: in the past few days, has your heart continued to keep its feelings silent from you, or has it started to free you from the curse that's pursued you since childhood?'

'Sorry, Pascal, my alexithymia is irreversible.'

'Bullshit,' he said harshly. 'You felt something inside you, I'm certain of it. And it's that something that has led you here.' He paused. 'The mind sees what the mind wants to see, but so does the heart ... So stop being blind and look at what it's trying to show you.'

She wished the man was wrong, but only because she hated the idea of agreeing with him. And yet he was right. In a different time, another Mila would have tried to make up with a razor blade the absence of angst at her daughter's disappearance. If she hadn't done it, it was because the emotions she had felt had proved to be sufficient.

'Did you think that by retreating to the lake the darkness wouldn't be able to track you down? Did you really think that would be enough?' He began to laugh. 'We're not like others, Mila Vasquez. We carry on us the rotten odour of the shadows we've visited ... The darkness can smell it even miles away. Escaping from it is preposterous.'

I come from the darkness ...

'You and Enigma were at war with each other and I ended up caught in the middle. It was you who created my game, wasn't it?'

'You got your training,' was Pascal's only comment.

'I've wondered why the whisperer had taken Alice and at the same time was trying to kill me: you were both playing with me ...'

'But with different aims,' he insisted on making clear.

'There is no other monitor, is there? The story about your being all decimated is false: you've always been on your own, you damned paranoid madman.'

'You don't understand: this war will go on for as long as the internet exists. The solitary man can only hurt himself. Only when they're together can human beings become evil. So I wonder: what else could we expect from history's largest interconnection?'

'The same is true about good,' Mila replied.

'If that were true, the net would be the happiest place on earth,' Raul said sarcastically.

Mila wanted to answer that it wasn't so, that this was only the vision of a disillusioned man who lived like a hermit and who, when not wearing a balaclava, was constantly altering his appearance with make-up and wigs so he wouldn't look human. Instead, she said, 'And what am I supposed to do now?'

'You'll be an excellent monitor . . . I've showed you the way, now you know where to look.'

'Except that Elsewhere is dying.'

'That was also to hurry you . . . But I'll stop Joshua; I know how.'

Mila thought about the little boy, about his sadness. 'You should set him free instead. Let him go . . . '

At that moment, Hitch emerged behind her from the darkness: Alice also appeared in the doorway. She yawned and rubbed her eyes. 'What's going on?' she asked calmly. 'Why is Hitch trying to take me outside?'

She was wearing the clothes from the day she'd gone missing. She still looked the same and Mila thought it was a kind of miracle, because she knew what effect the darkness had on those who went missing, even if it was only for a few hours.

She went to her daughter and hugged her.

At first, the girl shifted away, surprised by such a welcome on the part of her mother.

'How are you?' Mila asked, brushing her daughter's hair away from her forehead. She was unconcerned by her cold reaction, what mattered was that she was well.

'Okay,' was all Alice replied, using a teenager's practical jargon.

Mila looked at Pascal again, to work out his intentions now.

He saw the question in her eyes. 'I have no more reason to keep you both here,' he assured her.

Then Mila took Alice by the hand. She was about to head down the corridor to the door, but, instead, turned towards him again. 'You haven't answered my question: what do you expect me to do now? Because you might as well know that I'm not going to end up like this,' she said, indicating him in a

316

tone of blame. 'I'm not going to spend my life erasing all trace of me, living with fear and paranoia.'

Pascal smiled at her. 'The heart sees what the heart wants to see,' he reminded her. 'Now take your daughter and go home, Mila Vasquez. You can run away from the darkness. But you can't stop the darkness from looking for you.'

28

The blossoming lime trees outside the house were giving off a sweet fragrance that married perfectly with the crisp June air. The effect wasn't constant, however, or it would have been sickly, Mila thought. It was pleasant to be caught in some part of the house by a sudden gust through one of the open windows and follow the smell before the wind took it away.

It was one of the first summer mornings. The lake was calm and there was a jubilation of colours all around it, handed out by nature with impartial harmony. Ever since school had finished, Alice had been sleeping in late. Instead, Mila had got up early and was putting in the oven the cakes for that afternoon's small refreshments.

A few of her daughter's friends were coming over, but the invitation had also been extended to their mothers.

Mila felt odd; she'd never done anything like this. The other mothers also looked at her with suspicion when they saw her at teacher-parent meetings at school, at class councils or at Christmas and end-of-year shows. She didn't mind at first: to them, she was 'the former city policewoman', a good topic to break the great boredom of wives and at-home mums, so she'd let them. But for some time now she'd realised that maybe Alice didn't like to be the daughter of a standoffish mother proud of her bad temper. In time, she would pay for it by being shunned by her schoolmates.

Dr Lorn had immediately approved the idea of a little party. The psychologist had recommended introducing small changes into the daily routine. Alice went to see her twice a week. Strangely, the girl had displayed no trauma from her albeit brief abduction. Mila should thank the heavens, but, instead, she was concerned about this apathy and wanted Dr Lorn to sound her daughter for motives. But she was equally anxious to know where Alice had got her obsession about a father she'd never really known.

It's not easy being the daughter of a monster, she thought. Sooner or later, Alice would wonder if and what part of him had ended up as a part of her. Mila, too, was afraid of discovering that, but perhaps it wouldn't be a problem.

She wondered why, whenever she thought of Alice's father, she remembered Raul Morgan. He, too, was responsible for something terrible and irreversible. The only difference was that in his case, it had been an error caused by an unforgivable distraction that had cost his only son's, his child's, life. Mila couldn't even feel contempt for him any more for what he had done to her because, in any case, that man would always serve a heavy sentence decreed by the worst possible judge: his own conscience.

After the events in February, Mila wanted to say that everything had quickly returned to normal. But that was not how it had turned out. Her nights were being claimed by insomnia and terrible migraines always awaited her in the morning.

'It's practically impossible to find a newspaper around here,' Berish complained as he walked into the kitchen and slammed a daily on the table. 'I had to drive around for an hour before I found a newsagent.'

He was wearing khaki Bermuda shorts, loafers and a pale blue shirt: he managed to look impeccable even when dressed casually. Mila always felt inadequate next to him, with her acetate tracksuits and trainers.

'There's not many of you left who appreciate paper,' she said, making fun of him and pouring him freshly made coffee.

'People think that's how we'll save trees, because that's what the IT industry has inculcated into them. But somebody should tell them that trees are being planted precisely for that reason. Without books and newspapers, we'll see forests only on computer screensavers.'

Mila shook her head and couldn't help a smile.

'Go on, laugh: as soon as Alice wakes up, I'll take her fishing.'

'You really don't want to accept that we're vegetarians, do you?'

'Are you aware of how many insects have been ground with the grain of the flour in your cakes?' he said, pointing at the oven. 'Bon appétit, vegetarian.'

'Has it ever occurred to you it might be an ethical choice?'

'Those who don't want to break down other people's opinions with dictatorship sterilise them with political correctness.' And, having said that, Berish put an end to any counter-argument and went out to sit under one of the lime trees and enjoy his coffee and his paper in peace.

Berish had come to stay with them for a few days and Mila was glad to have him there. He had been suspended from service until further notice. Together, they'd conducted an illegal investigation, with suspected homicide, concealing a body and obstruction of justice. But, although almost four months had gone by, he hadn't been formally charged by the disciplinary committee yet.

The only consequence of their actions was that Limbo would be closed down and its responsibilities shared among the other investigation units. The photos of the missing persons would be taken off the walls of the Waiting Room, so that it would be easier to forget about them. After all, there was no glory in hunting for shadows.

It was the Judge's revenge.

The sudden, inexplicable rise in crime had marked the end of the 'Shutton Method'. Mila and Berish were convinced that was why she had avoided lashing out at them. It would have risked compromising the outcome of the only case that still allowed her to keep her job as chief of police: Enigma.

The only charge against the whisperer was that he had incited Karl Anderson to carry out a massacre. Rather tenuous to justify a life sentence in the Grave. A disciplinary investigation of the events would have brought out the truth, but also all the department's shortcomings.

On the rare occasions Mila managed to fall asleep, she would also go back to Elsewhere in her dreams. To the city apartment of the Andersons before they'd moved to the farm, to be exact. There, she had witnessed the slaughter of Frida and of little Eugenia and Carla. She couldn't forget that Karl would go to Two to make his fantasy of exterminating his family come true. Nor could she forget the reflection she'd seen in the dressing-table mirror in the twins' room when, following the advice of the ghost, she turned to see the face of her own avatar and discovered that the person responsible was the father.

Look at yourself . . .

Mila had asked herself so many times if Frida had noticed that something was wrong in her husband. She must have, since she had supported his decision to give up technology and relocate to a remote wasteland in the country. But, deep down, she didn't feel like blaming the woman: she, too, ten years earlier, had ignored the signals from her daughter's father.

The heart sees what the heart wants to see.

For this reason, Mila dismissed these toxic thoughts and resumed watching Simon Berish through the window. Hitch ran up to her for a pat. She felt a sense of gratitude for having both of them in their lives. Alice was very fond of the dog and appeared to have completely forgotten her cat, Finz, who'd run away a few months earlier.

So much the better, Mila thought. In this her daughter was better than her. We must always leave behind us whoever gets our care then abandons us, she said to herself.

The picnic at the lake began under the best auspices. Mila had set a long table under the lime trees. There were sweet and savoury cakes, pastries and colourful canapés with vegetables and cream cheese. Ice cubes glistened in pitchers of lemonade and iced tea, and the tablecloth fluttered in the breeze blowing down from the mountains.

Hitch was guarding the food, secretly hoping that something might fall off the table.

Mila had succeeded in persuading Alice to wear a skirt. She'd recently gained a couple of kilos and got hung up about being fat. Maybe these diatribes between them heralded what was to come from imminent adolescence. Her daughter's insecurity might have been caused by something else, though: Mila had discovered that Alice's schoolmates called her 'the oddball' and thought this was due to the fact that the girl was never surprised by anything and viewed the world with a curiosity other people found frightening.

The girls arrived at around four, without exception. This was a great relief for Alice, who feared she wasn't popular. She received many presents and unwrapped them, her eyes sparkling with satisfaction. Meanwhile, her friends' mothers competed in socialising with 'the former city policewoman', hoping that Mila would upset them with a horrifying detail of her past work.

The party was proving to be a success. They ate with Elvis Presley songs playing in the background and time passed amid harmless chatter and laughter.

Berish had organised group games to entertain the girls and had unexpectedly turned out to be an excellent entertainer. The afternoon was flowing peacefully. Until the moment for the treasure hunt came.

It all happened very quickly, but in the years to come Mila would often think about the dynamic of the events. The girls were searching for the third clue Berish had concealed. The riddle they had to solve clearly alluded to a hiding place by the water. One of the girls broke away from the group and, without anybody noticing, headed for the lake shore where there was an old, abandoned boathouse. Her mother was talking to her friends, so it took a few moments before she realised her daughter was missing. Mila was preparing more lemonade, but saw the woman's worried look through the window and felt a tickling sensation at the base of her neck. She immediately rushed out.

Not finding the girl, the mother started calling her by name. As her level of anxiety grew, her voice became more and more piercing. The party atmosphere vanished in an instant. Everybody suddenly fell silent.

Berish exchanged a quick glance with Mila and let Hitch off the lead. Within a short time, all those present started searching, calling out the girl's name.

Until a sharp cry – distant and drawn out – brought down silence again. It was coming from the boathouse and everybody ran towards it.

Berish was the first to cross the threshold with the dog, with Mila right behind them. They immediately saw that the girl was all right: nothing terrible had happened to her, she was just shaken. But this was no relief to them, because what was behind them made them freeze. Unfortunately, those who came in after them saw it, too, especially the mothers of the other girls, and that would weigh heavily on Alice's future relationship with her friends. For a few seconds, they all stood dumbfounded before the unfathomable scene. But although they might not have been able to express it in words, deep down they understood the implications.

A large, red heart was painted on the timber wall, surrounded by a swarm of flies. From the dirty knife on the floor, you could tell that it was made with congealed blood.

While everyone stared at the macabre mural, Mila was looking around. That was when she noticed Alice, and what she saw scared her to death.

Her daughter was the only one with an unperturbed expression.

The knife had come from the house. Mila hadn't even noticed that it was missing from the kitchen drawer.

'You can run away from the darkness. But you can't stop the darkness from looking for you,' the madman with the moustache and the jet-black hair who hid under a red balaclava and called himself Pascal had said. But until that moment, Mila had never considered the possibility that Raul Morgan might be right.

In the silence of the night, after the guests had left and Alice and Berish were asleep, Mila sat on her bed, staring at the wardrobe in front of her, wondering what to do. For the first time, she had no answer, no theory from her daughter's father to come to her rescue. She was devoured by uncertainty and the urge for a razor blade was very strong. Her anguish was only trying to find a way out of her. A painful injury would have provided release.

After torturing herself with pointless thoughts for a few seconds, she finally went to the wardrobe and opened it to look for the box with her old clothes. She found the jacket she'd worn during the Enigma case. There was still something that concerned her in the pocket, and Mila hadn't forgotten it. She could have got rid of it, but, deep down, she feared a moment like this one.

The photo of the whisperer with the computer-doctored face clean of tattoos. *The face of an ordinary man.* She looked at it in the darkness, wondering for the umpteenth time who that man was. Sometimes, we forget that monsters aren't actually monstrous, she said to herself. That was why she wanted to see that picture again.

The heart sees what the heart wants to see. And perhaps Mila had let herself be cheated, too. But the time had come to put things right.

She went downstairs and found Hitch lying on the sofa, next to the extinguished fire. She called him and they went out through the back door. Mila switched on the torch she'd brought with her. She also had the knife with the dry bloodstains. She gave it to the dog to sniff.

'Search,' she said.

Hitch smelt the ground, then she saw him heading to the wood. She followed him but he soon disappeared among the trees. She couldn't see him in the tangle of the forest. In vain, she called him. Then she heard a sound of leaves and soil being turned over about ten metres to her right. She let herself be guided by it until she found the dog.

Hitch had squeezed himself into a bush and was digging a hole. Mila pointed the torchlight at him and saw something sticking out of the ground.

It wasn't hard to recognise Finz's coat. The body had deep knife wounds.

The heart *does not* see what the heart does not want to see. And now she had confirmation of that.

Taking it for granted that it had been her daughter, a terrible thought sneaked into Mila's mind. How long had the cat been there? Had it happened before or after Alice's abduction? Because that would make a huge difference. In the former case, the origin of the violence could be genetic – the evil inheritance of the man in the coma. In the latter, something would have surely happened to her daughter while she'd been away.

Mila didn't know which theory she preferred. Both were

hard to accept. But she *had* to know. She couldn't spend the rest of her life with that question.

And there was someone who could give her an answer and deliver her from that deathly spell.

29

The Hyundai trundled up the hills while sunset coloured the horizon.

She'd travelled a long way, but she was nearing her destination. As she drove, Mila was thinking about what she'd say once she arrived. Everything she needed was in a black bag lying on the back seat.

The local policeman who, months earlier, had gone all the way up there to speak to Mary Morgan was right: the place was in the middle of nowhere.

Luxuriant greenery and woods were besieging the strip of asphalt, as though they would soon conquer back the space that had been snatched away from them by force. The sun vanished and the Buddhist community appeared in the windscreen like a cathedral of candles in the middle of the darkness.

When she reached the wooden gate that delimited the property, Mila was welcomed by a few members who kindly escorted her to a bar. They gave her a drink and some fruit.

Shortly afterwards, a slight woman appeared, wearing a yellow linen tunic, with grey hair in a long plait and eyes as blue as her son's.

'I thought I'd never meet you in person, Mila,' Mary said, on first-name terms.

Mila realised that what she meant wasn't that she wanted to be left alone, but that she expected everything to have been resolved by now. 'On the phone, you told me that if you were asked to wish for something impossible, you'd want to see Joshua again, even if just for a short time. At least to say goodbye to him.'

Mary's expression suggested turmoil: perhaps she feared her wish might come true. 'We say many things to lighten our hearts, but it doesn't mean we really want them.'

'It won't be real, but as though it was,' Mila said, indicating the black bag she'd brought. 'Raul poured his own memories of Joshua into a digital clone. He took advantage of a virtual reality game to make your son live again.'

Fear flashed across Mary's eyes. 'You can't live in the same form again after death,' she stammered, tapping into the philosophy she had embraced. 'Joshua's soul has left to reincarnate into other appearances and certainly not to remain a prisoner of computer circuits.'

She was repeating these words, but evidently also wanted not to believe in them. That was why Mila decided to be frank and gave her a further motivation. 'I must ask Joshua a question, but I fear he wouldn't tell me anything. I'm sure he'll answer his mother though . . . '

Mary thought for a while, then saw that Mila hadn't come to use her or to take advantage of her grief. 'What do I have to do?'

In answer, Mila took an old laptop from the bag, as well as two visors and joysticks. Before coming here, she'd stopped off at a drug dealer's.

'What are they?' Mary Morgan asked, looking at the blue pills in Mila's hand.

'Angel Tear. One for you and one for me. Trust me.'

Mary swallowed the drug, but then grabbed Mila by the arm, staring at her with anxiety. 'And what if I then don't have the courage to leave him? What if I want to take him away with me?'

Mila had no answer to her questions. She just handed her the joystick and the visor. The Two icon appeared on the screen and she created two avatars that were good likenesses. She connected to the internet with a portable modem, then typed in the coordinates of Joshua's childhood home, because she was sure she'd find him there.

They walked down a psychedelic corridor and reached a child's bedroom. There were games and a cot shaped like a spaceship. Pascal had built an identical one for his son in real life, as Mary had told her. Mila noticed that Mary was startled: she had already been there, they were in the right place.

'That's impossible,' she said. 'It's all so . . . so real.'

Outside the window, the chilly darkness of Elsewhere lay in ambush, but there was a sense of warmth and safety within these walls.

They heard a sound: the melody of a music box that had come on by itself. A merry-go-round with horses. At the same time, the boy in the red T-shirt appeared out of nowhere before them.

Mary recognised him immediately, even though the clone was ten years older than the child she had lost.

Joshua had the same inexpressive eyes, but there was a change in his face. Curiosity. 'Mummy?' he asked, showing no emotion.

Mary started to cry. 'Yes, my darling . . . '

The little boy was bewildered, as though suddenly unable to process this presence.

'You shouldn't be here,' he said, chiding her good-naturedly.

'I've wanted to see you for such a long time,' she confessed, sniffing. Then she tried to reach for him with her arms.

At first, Joshua stepped back, but then let her stroke his blonde hair. Mila couldn't believe this was truly happening.

'How are you?' Mary asked, a question all mothers always ask their children. Her enquiry allowed for countless possible replies, but a mother could always glimpse the truth in a lie.

'Dad never asks me,' he answered in earnest. 'Maybe he's scared to find out.'

'He should never have brought you here,' Mary finally managed to say with disappointment and anger. 'He shouldn't have done it.'

'I tried to destroy this world, but I didn't manage it. But I'm still good, aren't I?' Joshua expected her approval. 'I'm a good boy.'

'Of course, you are, my love.'

The child looked around. 'I'm tired of being here, I don't want to be alone any more,' he admitted, looking unhappy.

Mary looked at Mila, not knowing how to help him.

'I want to die, Mummy,' Joshua said, surprising them both. 'Can you help me die, Mummy?'

It was a distressing request to one who had given him

life. But, Mila thought, after all, only a mother would have the compassion to kill a child who was asking her to. Mary didn't have the technological knowledge, however, to do that for him.

'I can't do it, my love.'

'Please.'

'I'm sorry . . . ' she said, bursting into subdued weeping.

Mila hated Pascal for condemning the child to a prison of fear and violence only so that he would have the illusion that the fatal distraction that had led to his death had never happened.

But Joshua was not perturbed by his mother's answer: he simply registered it. 'So then you've just come to say goodbye to me . . . '

'No, I wanted you to know that I love you. I always have and always will.'

'For ever?' he asked, almost surprised.

'For ever,' she assured him.

'Now that I know that, I feel much better, thank you.'

'Only I also need a favour . . . I'd like you to help this woman.'

The boy in the red T-shirt focused his attention on Mila. 'All right, but first you must take her away: I don't want Mummy to see.'

Mila turned to Mary and explained how she must leave the game. 'Remove the visor and immediately go and lie down to stop the effect of the drug, then take the niacin.'

'I'd like to kiss him . . . Can I?'

Even though Mila wasn't sure she would feel anything, she didn't feel like advising her against it. Mary approached her son, reached out to his forehead with her lips and closed her eyes. Joshua did the same, and when he opened his eyes again, his mother had gone.

A few seconds of total silence went by. Then the boy in the red T-shirt looked at Mila again.

'I need to know what happened to Alice,' she said.

'He has the power to change people,' Joshua said, referring to the whisperer.

'Are you sure?'

But, by now, she could no longer pull away.

The setting changed in an instant.

Mila lost control of her joystick and found herself impersonating another avatar. She could only see what it was seeing but was unable to direct it.

It was a late summer's day and it was sunny, She was behind the wheel of an economy car, a Ford. There was a road lined with red beeches ahead. The car radio was playing some cheerful music: an old-fashioned swing tune – the musicians sounded like they were having great fun playing it.

The car drove over a speed bump and ended up outside a building dating from the last century. The pockmarked brown stone façade was that of the Red Forest Neuroscience Institute.

Mila suddenly realised whom she was impersonating: at that moment, she was Raul Morgan, driving his car on the morning he left his son in the child seat in the back.

She didn't want to be him. She didn't want to witness the scene for anything in the world. She just saw her eyes – Pascal's eyes – in the rear-view mirror of the Ford – and tried to shift the joystick so that they would frame the one-and-a-half-year-old child in the back seat. She harboured the illusion that this way the father would notice him. Perhaps she could still reverse destiny.

The Ford stopped in the car park. Pascal's avatar cut the engine and the music stopped at the same time. In the silence inside the vehicle, nothing else could be heard. If only he had been aware of the sleeping child's breathing . . . Instead, he opened the door and got out. He raised his arm, holding the remote control, and, after a brief bleeping tone, the four centralised locks clicked shut.

Mila heard her steps sizzling on the asphalt as she walked away from the vehicle, but something happened that she didn't expect. Instead of heading towards the main entrance of the institute, Pascal circumvented the car. Why? Where was he going?

The avatar halted right by the back window. On the other side of the glass pane, Mila could clearly see Joshua in the red T-shirt. He was blissfully asleep. And, just as she saw him, so had Raul Morgan, his father, seen him, ten years earlier.

When the man walked away, Mila received confirmation of what had really happened. It hadn't been an accident, he hadn't been distracted. He'd left him there to die, on purpose.

She was convulsed by a retch, she'd seen enough and was upset. She wanted to tear off the visor, but froze. As she walked towards the building, she saw her avatar reflected in the windows of the other parked cars.

That was how Mila was able to see the face of the man she was impersonating. It wasn't Pascal, though she had already seen him before. To be precise, in the computer-doctored image, without the tattoos that covered him.

The face of an ordinary man.

But if Raul Morgan was Enigma, who was the man she'd known as Pascal?

The prisoner in the Grave, whom everybody called Enigma, was Raul Morgan. But he wasn't the whisperer. Pascal was the whisperer and he was still out there.

The tattooed individual Mila had met in the maximum-security prison was actually his disciple. Why else would he have agreed to get caught in his place?

Raul Morgan – the man with the ordinary face – had frequented Elsewhere as a criminal anthropologist, but had never rebelled against the will of the subliminal serial killer. On the contrary, he had yielded to his seduction. Like Karl Anderson, in the name of that evil pact, he had extinguished the blood of his own blood.

After the carnage at the farm, Pascal had reported Morgan with an anonymous call to prevent the police getting to him.

Mila was driving the Hyundai at night, desperately hoping to find the sense in all this. He lied to us. He lied to me.

It was raining heavily and the drug was enveloping her senses, but, once again, she *had* to understand.

A stag came out of the forest, crossed the road, and everything suddenly slowed down. Mila lost control of the car and exchanged a brief glance with the noble animal: it was the same as the one who'd stood in her kitchen the day Alice had disappeared, or was it a hallucination triggered by the Angel Tear?

She didn't have time to find the answer because the Hyundai overturned and ended up off the road, crossed a ditch, and crashed into a tree.

The roar was deafening, but then all that was left was the ticking of the engine, drowned out by the rain.

Mila was head down, trapped between the metal sheets, and was struggling to keep conscious. She'd hit her face against something hard. A slimy substance was sliding down her forehead, along with the raindrops that were coming in through the shattered windscreen. She must have a gash on her head. She could also feel something throbbing just below the sternum. She lifted her head to try and see, but didn't have enough breath. The steering column from the wheel was stuck in her belly and a black liquid was gushing out of the hole – blood mixed with bile. She tried to plug the wound with her trembling hands, but it was useless.

Mila was in the middle of nowhere and didn't know how to call for help. Overwhelmed with panic, she began to cry because she realised she'd be dead soon. Her tears began to blend with the blood, the mucus and the rain. Over the years, she'd had so many brushes with death, but only now was she certain that she was about to go into the darkness that had always secretly called her towards it.

She thought about Alice, about the fact that she would be left alone. She was also crying for her. She had never known how to take care of the only gift life had bestowed on her. She cursed herself for being the way she was.

She wouldn't see her grow up, she wouldn't be at her side in sad or happy moments. She couldn't protect her or teach her to do it herself. She had lost everything now. Now that she had to say goodbye to her, she realised that the emotions she'd held inside her all her life were suddenly gushing out all together.

Grief wasn't the same thing as what she was good at inflicting on herself with a razor blade. It came from the soul.

How wonderful it was to be human again.

She was about to accept her fate when she saw headlights in the distance. A car was coming in her direction. Mila couldn't believe it; it was a sign. She hoped that the blanket of rain wouldn't prevent the car occupants from noticing the Hyundai in the ditch; it would have been a real joke if they drove past her.

Luckily, the car slowed down. It was an old, black Audi 80. Mila saw the driver's door open. She squinted and forced her eyes to focus on the driver. A shadow slowly walked to her car. All she noticed was that it was wearing black leather gloves. A detail that frightened her. It was an irrational fear, she knew that, since she was already dying. Still, she was unable to shake it off.

The figure walked into the beam of the headlights and stood motionless. Even though she was upside down, Mila could see it well. It was a man. A brown, threadbare suit, flat feet.

Pascal appeared as he was under the balaclava, when Mila had seen his face. But this image only lasted a few seconds. The jet-black hair and the moustache began to fall under the effect of the rain – strands of his hair scattered in the puddles under him. At the same time, the skin on his cheeks began to melt, running down the collar of his shirt and his tie. Mila remembered the dressing table with the cosmetics and wigs. As the make-up progressively vanished, washed away by the pounding rain, patterns emerged on the skin.

Numbers.

The man then also slipped off his gloves. Mila had never seen his hands, but she thought it was a way not to leave prints. But they were also covered in tattoos. Now the genuine, unique Enigma was standing before her.

Using the last breath in her lungs, Mila wanted to ask him what he'd done to Alice while he'd kept her with him after kidnapping her. What evil spell had he whispered into her daughter's ear? What would become of her daughter in time?

But Mila was unable to utter a word.

The man stood watching her for a long time, perhaps waiting for her to give up the ghost anytime now.

'Enjoy this gift,' he said in a persuasive voice.

As her senses abandoned her, Mila saw him turn away and return to his car. She watched him get in and start the engine. She saw him drive away in the thunderstorm, into the night.

Alone again, Mila Vasquez closed her eyes and her memory summoned Alice. She could finally say goodbye to her.

Her lungs were running out of breath and she was letting herself slip into the oblivion she had skirted a thousand times without ever falling into it.

'The mind sees what the mind wants to see.'

Who had spoken? She hadn't imagined it; it was really the voice of the ghost. What was he doing in the wood? How had Joshua got out of the game?

She was blinded by a liquid flash of lightning. It was as though both her eyes had been torn out, when only her visor had been removed.

Mila looked around.

There were figures bending over her. And voices chasing one another in the room. 'Check her pressure ... Give her more oxygen ... Four grams of niacin into the vein: is the syringe ready? ...'

Mila managed to focus on them and realised they were paramedics. She hadn't had any accident – at least not in the real world. The blood and her injury were a hallucination. But, as well she knew, it could be fatal. Once again, Joshua had saved her by reminding her of the most basic rule of Elsewhere.

She couldn't believe it. A sudden euphoria took hold of her. She had another occasion to be different from what she was. To finally be a mother. Maybe she had definitely been cured of the secret illness that prevented her from being like others.

But, in the midst of this jumble of new feelings, a dark thought crept in.

The aim of a whisperer was not to kill and, paradoxically, not even to harm. The latter was a totally secondary consequence of what truly animated him.

The power to change people, to turn harmless individuals into sadistic killers.

That was what gave them absolute gratification, maximum pleasure.

Mila had been wondering since the beginning why she'd been chosen for the game and what was the aim of her match. Now she felt emotions which, because of her alexithymia, she didn't think she would ever feel again. That was enlightening. She realised that the whisperer had acted on her, too. But while in the case of others, he exercised his power to make them evil, with her it had been used in the opposite sense.

Enjoy this gift.

She should have been grateful to him for this new version of herself, for what he had transformed her into. Instead, she felt sudden disgust and contempt because she realised that, in the end, he'd won.

But that didn't mean she would resign herself.

Mila now knew that somewhere a shadow awaited her. A new whisperer was out there.

I come from the darkness, she said to herself. And if I don't look for the darkness, the darkness will come looking for me.

Acknowledgements

Stefano Mauri, publisher – friend. And, together with him, all the publishers around the world who publish my books.

Fabrizio Cocco, Giuseppe Strazzeri, Raffaella Roncato, Elena Pavanetto, Giuseppe Somenzi, Graziella Cerutti, Alessia Ugolotti, Tommaso Gobbi, Diana Volonté and the never-failing Cristina Foschini.

You are my team.

Andrew Nurnberg, Sarah Nundy, Barbara Barbieri, and the extraordinary members of staff at the London agency.

Tiffany Gassouk, Anais Bakobza, Ailah Ahmed. Vito, Ottavio, Michele. Achille.

Gianni Antonangeli.

Alessandro Usai and Maurizio Totti.

Antonio and Fiettina, my parents. Chiara, my sister.

Sara, my 'present eternity'.